ROAD TO
NOWHERE

A novel by Evan Shapiro

© Evan Shapiro 2014

Evan Shapiro asserts the moral right to be identified as the author of 'Road To Nowhere'.

Cover design and typeset by Green Avenue Design.

Original cover photo © Hector Marcel

Published by Cilento Publishing, Sydney Australia.

ISBN: 978-0-6482398-5-7

This novel is entirely a work of fiction. Any resemblance to actual persons, living or dead, is entirely coincidental.

If you are a human being, however, this book is about you.

To Lili and Joel, for all that being your dad has taught me, and to Leone Sperling, my Mum, for coming on the journey. I hope I'm as brave when my children fill my head with crazy ideas.

The first draft of this novel was written in Hania, Crete. 5 September to 6 December 1996.

PRELUDE

One hundred and fifty million kilometres away from the Earth a big ball of fire busily burns away, converting four hundred million tons of hydrogen into helium every second in a seemingly endless nuclear fusion.

As our world orbits the Sun, we revolve our lives around our own daily concerns, forgetting that the big bright light in the sky, by its very nature, creates our day and feeds our existence. Eight minutes after its atomic birth the light that reaches Earth helps plants photosynthesise, taking in carbon dioxide and releasing oxygen.

Buried by our needs, our hopes, our dreams, our petty dislikes, our great loves and our monstrous hates, is a forgotten truth. It is so intrinsically human that we are capable of pushing this thought to the dark reaches of our primitive brains, that we know the words but don't truly appreciate the concept. We can tell ourselves what we like but there's no getting away from it. You can't hide from the truth forever, and this is true, so listen up.

Our lives are just a by-product of a cosmic breath!

Patrick closed his notebook, content with another great thought committed to paper. As he reclined into the comfort of his manager's plush office chair the feeling of self-satisfaction gave way to a pervasive self-doubt: how likely was it that a set of human eyes other than his own would ever read his words? His thoughts would remain just that, his own. To ensure that fate, he hastily removed the notebook from sight and shoved it into his bag. He shifted focus from the sense of his own mediocrity to that of his manager's. Leaning back further into the leather-padded chair he surveyed the room with contempt. Except for his position of authority, Patrick's manager was an inferior in every respect. The man's gruff manner, his constant barking of orders, ensured his control but alienated him from his subordinates. To Patrick he was a man to be managed. There were ways of dealing with him to get what you wanted: picking times when he was most distracted to ask for personal leave, never presenting him with an unsolved problem, always offering a solution no matter how stupid it may seem. Like a dog gnawing into a bone your offering would be viciously snatched and ripped into pieces, devoured before your eyes and the remnants spat back at your feet. But he would be secretly grateful you threw him something to sink his teeth into. Yes, he was to be managed and by no means trusted. A company man through and through, a company man who had access to information being withheld from Patrick. He looked around the room again, attempting to intuit where his superior would hide things he didn't want his subordinates to find.

The office was dark other than the light emanating from the desk lamp and a few beams of orange glow that crept in around the edges of the block-out blind covering the large window on one side of the office. A glint of light reflecting on the stainless steel filing cabinet in the corner of the room pulled Patrick to his feet and drew him towards it.

The vivid orange light from outside was easing rapidly, receding as the day drew to a close. Another twilight gone, another twilight spent alone, the most precious part of the day nearly over and nothing but a long lonely night ahead. With the sun setting fast Patrick had to increase his pace if he didn't want his break and enter to be discovered, if he didn't want to waste having braved the intense heat of the sun to be in the office a few hours early. His colleagues would soon filter in, once the cover of night gave them safe passage. He stood at the locked cabinet and tugged ineffectually at the top drawer. Yes there was definitely something in here that was not meant for Patrick, making him all the more determined to gain access.

Back at the desk he pulled open drawers, turned over papers, lifted up objects. No key to be found, nothing. He spotted the coffee cup next to the keyboard. 'Let me drop everything and fix your problem' branded on it in large type. His manager would often sit behind his desk holding the cup at eye level while subordinates talked to him, not answering, just waiting for them to read the message, get the point and get out of his office. If they took too long to register he'd soon throw them out, barking at them as they retreated. In all the time Patrick had worked with the man he'd never actually seen him drink from it. The cup was just a prop, another object littering a cluttered desk. Patrick picked it up, raised it to his eye in the manner of his superior, fleshing out what it felt like to be such a dickhead, before tipping it over and pouring the key into his palm.

Patrick rummaged around the now unlocked filing cabinet drawer. A bottle of vodka, some retro porn magazines, there must be more the man was hiding. Then bingo, official looking documents – 'Project Helios' – it smelled clandestine. His eager fingers took hold of the report and he could feel its suppression itching to be released.

With the document in hand he quickly covered his tracks – easy enough given it was a mess when he'd arrived. Lock the cabinet, key back in the cup, papers back in their stacks. He scooped up his bag and hit a button on his manager's desk. The large block-out blinds rose allowing the last vibrant orange rays of the sunset to fill the room, removing all shapes and objects with its intense glare. Then as the sun dropped behind the horizon and the room crept into darkness, Patrick closed the office door behind him and moved quietly to his workstation.

Compared to his supervisor's office, Patrick's desk was uncluttered and sparse. He'd never given the space much thought, other than to avoid it. What was the point in decorating? It annoyed him the way his co-workers littered their spaces with photos of families and friends, displaying them as some measure of achievement. 'This is what I have outside of this place, what do you have?' Why should he offer a window into his life to be assessed and ranked amongst the workforce? Worse still were postings of platitudes and self-motivating mantras, stuck to people's cubicles to help them through the day. At least Patrick wrote his own and kept them in his notebook. He didn't force them into his co-workers' field of vision the way they foisted their banalities on him.

His standard-issue ergonomic chair took his weight but creaked and squeaked as he shifted to find a comfortable position. He placed the document on the desk and pulled the chair in closer, ready, a little excited even, to discover what form of administrative ineptitude middle management had planned: a restructure, job losses, productivity gains? What idiocy would they be imposing on the workforce next?

As he began to read he was overcome with an acute awareness of the moment. As the words worked their way through his cerebral cortex he became filled with the horror of their reality. This was no minor administrative report. Patrick was discovering a truth that put his own concept of 'Cosmic Breath' into the realm of the pathetic. This was not a moment to be treasured, not a moment to be loved, but as clear a moment as any in his life, a milestone, a point of reference that couldn't be erased now that it had made its mark and he realised that from this point on his life wouldn't be the same.

Patrick sat with his hands frozen on the document and watched as workers began to arrive, safe now under the cover of night. Safe from the very sun in the sky that burned their lives into being but a sun now too strong for them to be exposed to.

He didn't move, didn't respond to his co-workers' 'good evenings', didn't react when the phone rang, didn't even realise he was continuing to breathe. There was only himself, the document before him and what was happening to his mind now that the information had transferred from paper to grey matter, nothing else registered, nothing else could.

Without fully knowing why, he stood, took the document in one hand, his car keys in the other and began to move. As he made his way steadily towards the exit he passed the early starters - some of them he knew, others he didn't, some he liked, others annoyed him, but they all looked like ghosts to him now. This pounding idea forced into his head by that wretched document made them all look dead, their activities meaningless, anything they might have to say useless. The information was infecting him – a vile fast moving virus corrupting and consuming his system.

The night air gave little relief, the ground still hot from the day's saturation of sunlight, the heat rising and filling his lungs. Every breath made him light-headed. He reached his car – the auto cooling made the interior a welcome relief from the outside air, but it didn't bring him back, didn't stop the pounding urge to keep moving. He started the car, capitulating to the unknown force propelling him forward. With no sense of destination, only a need to move away from that moment, that ground zero moment, he drove onto the open road. His lone vehicle travelled in the opposite direction to the stream of headlights making their way to work, collectively illuminating one side of the road as his sole set of headlights moved freely, seemingly unencumbered.

PART ONE

ONE

Linda and Richard had considered many names during the pregnancy. They knew their child would be a girl. That's what they'd requested and paid for from the IVF clinic. Accordingly, a female embryo had been implanted into Linda's womb, an embryo made of its mother's egg and a sperm donor hand-picked from various candidates around the globe. Though neither Richard nor Linda's hands were involved in the actual harvesting of the semen. If Richard couldn't be the biological father then the very least they could do was to choose someone from a scientific background. Richard wanted some chance that he might be able to communicate with his child on an intellectual level. If he was going to suffer the crying, the screaming, the nappy changing, the supermarket tantrums, the moody adolescence, then he wanted some intelligent conversation at some future point as a reward.

As the months of the pregnancy progressed, many names crossed the happy couple's minds but none they could agree on. Naturally there was some trepidation when Linda went into labour with still no name selected. Richard feared he would have a nameless child for weeks on end, while he and Linda paced around the house trying desperately to come to some agreement, but those fears were disbanded the moment the child arrived.

She came out barely crying, though it was hard to measure, as any noise from the infant was deafened by Linda's intense cries of pain. Richard found this to be a complex moment. He watched with amazement as the child emerged from his favourite orifice, stretching the aperture wider than he imagined it could ever be opened, yet the moment was stressful. Seeing the woman he loved writhing in agony in the hours leading up to the actual delivery had left him strained and teary. His uncharacteristic display of emotion was something he was glad his wife had been too delirious to register. He immediately noticed the child's bright piercing eyes and whispered her name inside his mind. "Angel".

The cord was cut and the baby was in Linda's arms before she could catch her breath. "She's got angel eyes, sweet little angel eyes," Linda said.

"Angel!" Richard said. "Let's call her Angel."

The baby rarely left Linda's arms. She would hold her daughter close, gently caressing her smooth pale skin. From the first touch of that iridescent baby skin Linda was hooked. She had no choice but to touch and caress whenever her child was near.

Apart from its irresistible texture that magnetised any carer's fingers, Angel's skin had other peculiar attributes.

"She has asbestos skin," Linda's mother would say, referring to its heat retardant nature.

Angel was 18 months old when chance first exposed these rare properties. Angel was not unlike other children, prone to running around excitedly without much reason or prompting, well adept at catching her parents off guard while they were engaged in other tasks.

Linda was boiling water to make pasta when Angel tore into the kitchen and tugged at her dress. She turned quickly to see what her daughter wanted and knocked the saucepan off the stove. Linda watched in horror as the boiling water showered over Angel, completely covering her tiny naked body. Linda screamed and immediately put the child into the sink and ran cold water over her. But Angel did not understand what all the fuss was about. To her it was the same as having a bath, only in the kitchen sink rather than the tub with her usual bath toys at hand. Still she made the most of it grabbing for the dishcloth and sponge to play with and eyeing off a scouring pad that remained out of reach.

Linda examined Angel's skin closely. She saw no burns, no marks, no change whatsoever. Its smooth creamy surface was entirely unblemished. Nevertheless, not wishing to take any chances, she raced her child to hospital. After a thorough examination the doctors proclaimed her normal. Richard had suggested that perhaps the water had not been boiling hot at all, that it was most likely only warm. The tiny burn marks scattering Linda's legs confirmed otherwise.

TWO

How many days? How many nights? The arid brittle air evaporated any moisture in Patrick's thoughts, leaving dry wrinkles of incomplete memory. Heat from the sun pounded down, increasing its intensity by the second. Patrick's head throbbed and his fingers moved under the arms of his sunglasses and rubbed his temples. He winced with the shooting pain that ran behind his eyes and into his brain, but he kept his eyes on the barren road and one hand on the wheel. He spotted a road sign ahead, the first one he'd seen in ages and was momentarily pleased. Perhaps it would be a sign from God or Nature, something to tell him where he should go and what he should do, something to help him forget about the 'truth' he now knew.

'Neverville' the sign read. It was not a sign from God, it was a sign from the Department of Main Roads. "Neverville, Great!" Patrick said to himself. "Where the fuck is Neverville?"

He lifted his sunglasses and rubbed his burning eyes. Again he tried to remember when he'd started this journey but the heat wouldn't allow it. All he could conjure were thoughts of movement, of feeling unable to stop for fear his mind would recall what he'd left behind. Refuelling was all he could manage, a bite for himself, a full tank of PetroSynth for the car, then back on the road.

He remembered at some point trying to sleep somewhere. He'd pulled into a motel, knowing he needed sleep; it was dangerous to drive exhausted and then there was the extended exposure to daylight. It was not the danger to himself that he was worried about, only a passing concern for other human beings that made him consider getting off the road. Once in the motel room he let himself drop heavily onto the bed, hoping the extreme fatigue would wrench him from the pool of desolation he had been drowning in, but the moment his head hit the pillow it started coming back. First the images: just a face, a face that he had looked at for so many years, a face so familiar he knew every nuance. Then the feelings moved in. As soon as he closed his eyes the harsh terrible truths came crawling out of the cracks in the wall and the floor and the ceiling, a spawn of venomous spiders moving towards him.

When Patrick felt their hairy articulated legs touch his skin he jumped from the bed, their fangs poised to strike, ready to flood his veins with poisonous emotions, a vile toxic truth flowing beneath his skin.

A bump in the road brought him back. He looked in the rear-vision mirror and saw the crackling cooking remains of a flattened wombat, frying in the unfiltered rays of the sun. He returned his eyes to the open barren road ahead and his mind to thoughts of his journey. He calculated that over the past few days and nights of driving he'd managed to get about 30 seconds of uninterrupted unconsciousness. Was that enough? It was certainly better than the pain he would feel if he gave in to the emotional spiders that lurked in the space between wake and sleep.

Patrick looked down at his dashboard. The car was running on empty. "Neverville it is!" he said to himself and put his foot down on the accelerator. Just as he was speeding up and burning the last few drops of PetroSynth in the tank, a kangaroo leapt from the side of the road. Patrick swerved to miss it but it was a big one and there was no avoiding it. The animal hit the car and was splattered onto the road. Patrick slammed on the brakes and the car skidded over the remains and into a gully off the side of the road. It lurched to a stop, coughed, spluttered and then fell silent.

Patrick sat quietly for a moment, listening to the sound of sizzling roo meat on his radiator. He lifted his hands from the wheel and put them behind his head. He closed his eyes and clenched his teeth. The vast openness of the dry landscape seemed to close in as the frustration in his body began to swell. A small whimpering squeal emerged from his throat as the pressure moved from his gut to his head. His temples pounded with blood as the squeal became a cry, his hands suddenly and viciously began pounding the steering wheel with all his force and his cry became a roar.

Just as suddenly as his outburst had started, it stopped. He tried to regain some calm as he filled his lungs slowly with air and exhaled. Realising his outburst had done little but hurt his hands and unnecessarily strained his larynx he decided on a different course of action and got out of the car. He contemplated kicking the crap out of the tyres but discarded the notion with the realisation that if anything needed to be kicked for this predicament it was his own head.

He leant back into the car to retrieve his solar hat. The damage at the front of the car evidence it was not particularly kangaroo-proof. He pulled a few chunks of frying meat from the radiator grill and watched it sizzle on the blistering hot bitumen, and became acutely aware of the sun's heat frying his own skin. He quickly got back into the car.

He turned the key and the car jerked and jolted but wouldn't turn over. He pounded the accelerator, with no success.

"Great. Fucking great." The car wasn't going anywhere, not even to Neverville.

He hit the emergency sunscreen dispenser built into the dashboard and applied the cream to his exposed skin, returned the solar hat to his head and adjusted his sunglasses in the mirror. It might be devastatingly hot out there, but he could not look anything less than cool. A few shakes revealed the bottle sitting in the cup-holder still had some water so he placed it in his bag. Slamming the car door on exit and throwing the bag on his back, he walked off towards Neverville.

It was the middle of the day. No one else would be outdoors except other idiots like himself. The rest of the country would be safely tucked away in bed, sleeping the day away. Not since before the climate crisis had people gone out in the midday sun. Certainly not in coastal communities like the city where Patrick had spent his childhood. It was even hotter inland where Patrick now found himself. It was too far back for him to remember but Patrick liked to contemplate what life must have been like for people 70 years before, in a world where daylight was the time for work and night the time for rest. He'd often wondered whether society could go back to 'normal' once carbon emissions were neutralised and PetroSynth had reversed climate change.

His parents had often talked about the transition from day to night, how the whole world had felt jet-lagged for years. Tired and cranky, the many who fought the change only found daylight existence unbearably hot and ultimately hazardous. Then PetroSynth Corporation came along uniting global governments in their resolution to switch human activity from day to night. But that was just history to Patrick, his thirty-three years on the planet had been a nocturnal existence and it was all he knew. His average day started with a twilight breakfast at 7pm, lunch any time from midnight to 2am, and dinner at

7 or 8am. He had naturally been out all day a few times but never without serious solar protection and only at approved all-day venues that provided full environmental control and protected transport services. Now he was walking right under one of the biggest hotspots. Despite all the good PetroSynth's genetically engineered shrub had done, even its ability to consume carbon could not undo the many years of damage. It would be decades before things returned, atmospherically, to the way they were before the industrial revolution. Regardless temperatures were still rising, something not even the mighty PetroSynth Corporation, the largest global conglomerate in history, could seem to provide an answer for.

Patrick found walking more soothing than driving, even though it wasn't getting him as far away from where he'd started as fast as he'd like. All he had to concentrate on was moving one foot in front of the other. He could even close his eyes without the dreaded truth advancing on him. As long as he just kept moving he would be okay. He placed one foot heavily in front of the other and the words, 'When in doubt, keep moving', repeated with every step, giving him the rhythm to keep moving. It was a little saying he used when waiting for a PetroSynth powered bus or train. Standing at a bus stop or on a platform always felt like wasting time. So he'd walk between stops hoping to catch the transport he would have caught if he'd just been a little more patient. This often extended his journeys, but kept him fit and meant he knew more about local geography than the average commuter. 'When in doubt, keep moving.' If ever Patrick had been in doubt it was now. He kept moving.

The heat became too much and he sat for a moment by the side of the road. He knew it was too hot to keep walking safely and with no shade in sight it was just as dangerous to stay still. He took a sip from his bottle of water and looked at his watch. 1:15. He pressed a button, 52°C. He pressed another button. UV = Max flashed up on his watch. Another press of the button would give him the date and Patrick was not sure if he wanted to look. He quite liked not knowing how long he'd been moving. There was a certain pleasure in being lost in place and time, free from his reality and the concerns he'd left behind. But his intrinsic desire to know the truth, that feeling that has both advanced and plagued man from the beginning of human existence, took over. Patrick could not resist the need know the truth, even if the truth was all consuming, even if the truth made living intolerable. But this was a small truth, only regarding the date, so he pressed the button on his watch. 1 April.

Patrick forced himself back on his feet and kept walking, knowing now that he had lost four days to the open road, four days to the truth. Four days since he'd read that cursed document so unconvincingly hidden by his hapless manager. Why couldn't the stupid bastard be more efficient, especially with mind-altering secret documents? Patrick could have been spared his present torment, have lived on blindly like the rest of the sheep on the planet, blissfully unaware of their fate, well perhaps not so blissful, but certainly unaware.

All that seemed of little consequence now, as he suspected he was going to die from the heat before someone came past. The back of his hands had started to blister and he imagined himself lying on the side of the road, a victim to the heat, fading in and out of consciousness. The thought that he would not have to exist any more, not have to think or feel or accept the truth, was increasingly desirable. The blistering grew worse by the moment, as did the desire for nothingness.

Delirium was setting in. That's all it could be, Patrick thought, when a beat up old utility pulled up next to him. Not only should there not be anyone around at this time of day but the vehicle next to him was an antique, manufactured in the last millennium. A petroleum-guzzling, environmental nightmare that should be in a museum or squashed into a cube and dumped in landfill or best-case recycled for its base elements.

An old man looked at Patrick from behind the wheel. They took each other in as Patrick stood shakily, trying to hold himself as still as possible to cover the extreme fatigue engulfing his mind and body.

The old man looked about to speak but then paused, elongating the moment as if to help Patrick complete his façade of not being helpless. Once Patrick became still the old man leant his head further out of the car window into the bright rays of the day.

"That your car in the roo guts back there?"

"The roo guts aren't mine. They were uninvited."

"You're from the city?" the old man asked.

"Yes."

"Well then, what do you think? Do people make cities or do cities make people?"

"What?" Patrick blinked and steadied himself

"Do cities make people or do people make cities?"

"You switched it round."

"Doesn't matter. What's your answer?"

Patrick wasn't surprised by the old man's question. His 'What?' had been more an involuntary reflex than bafflement nor was it a failure to hear what the old man had asked. He accepted the old man's question as part of the semi-delusional state that had taken him over from the moment he was compelled to drive off into the unknown, into the heat and the nothingness, into the wide-open emptiness. The road he'd driven down at times appeared only as a way for his mind to navigate an otherwise unfamiliar environment. The road was the only thing he understood about the environment he was traversing. Nature worked on its own agenda and didn't care about love or hate, social status, human suffering or bliss. Human lives, decisions, concerns were all rendered meaningless by nature's complete and total lack of interest. No wonder that Patrick had been drawn to this great nothingness to lose what he couldn't forget. Everything meant nothing and was dissolved in this space where man was not only not master, but irrelevant.

He ended the hesitation and gave over his answer.

"It's the chicken and the egg!" he replied.

"That's what I thought," the old man said, pleased with Patrick's answer. "You know you shouldn't be walking at this time of day. I'll give you a lift into town and we'll get you fixed up when the day cools down."

Patrick shuffled around to the front of the vehicle and climbed in.

"Thanks," Patrick said as his body folded into the retro vinyl upholstery.

"Air con? I hate the shit, but you look like you need it," the old man said. Patrick gave his new companion a look that required no speech. His aged but strong hand quickly wound up the car window, a sight Patrick found amusing, having only ever seen it done with a button, then he flicked a switch on the dash. The car's engine shifted in tone, there were a few rattles and then cool jets of air hit Patrick's welcoming skin, his exhaling breath revealing more than his relief at the change of temperature. The old man's foot hit the floor and the ute screeched off down the highway.

"I didn't think antiques like this were legal? Doesn't it run on lead petrol?" Patrick asked as his hand searched for something to hold. He found the handle for winding the window and discovered he liked the feel of its ribbed circular knob.

"This little beauty is a relic from the 1980s. I did some engine work and weaned her off the leaded stuff. She'll run forever now."

Patrick wasn't so interested but was happy to listen to whatever the old man said. Talk was good, talk stopped any other thoughts from entering his mind, talk held the truth back where it could do no harm.

"There's a first aid kit in the glove box. You can fix the skin on your hands."

Patrick retrieved the first aid kit from the glove compartment and applied the skin regenerator to the back of his hands. The raw blisters disappeared almost immediately and the pain was replaced with a cool tingling.

"You here to see the lights?" the old man asked.

"Lights?"

"Min Min lights. It's the only reason strangers ever come this way. Naturally they come at night, the people and the lights. Who drives in the middle of the bloody day?"

"Me. I was just driving. No place in mind. When in doubt keep moving."

"People spend years trying to see the Min Min lights. Some say they are solar flare reflections, others think they are aliens."

"What do you think?" Patrick asked.

"That's a good question. I'll tell you when I know you better. For now I'll say I hope they are what I think they are. If not I'll be very disappointed."

"Really," Patrick replied and he stared out the window, wondering if conversation was such a good idea after all. Perhaps he was right about idiots and the demented being the only ones out at this time of day? Even mad dogs and Englishmen were staying indoors. What did this old guy think was going to happen apart from Patrick getting his car back on the road and swiftly making a departure? It was not the start of a long and beautiful friendship. Patrick was not feeling ungrateful, on the contrary, despite his fatigue wearing his social conventions down to their bare minimum, he could acknowledge how fucked up he would be if the old man had not stopped and rendered assistance. Regardless, the sooner Patrick got out of Neverville, wherever the fuck that was, the better.

The ute moved along the highway with uncharacteristic speed and silence. There was a grace to the movement and Patrick's unfamiliarity with the vehicle's original specifications meant he failed to appreciate how quiet it was. The rhythm of the road was hypnotising, the bumps and grooves orchestrated into a calming melody and with the responsibility for controlling the vehicle out of his hands, Patrick struggled to keep his eyes open.

THREE

Kirby sat alone in the laboratory staring at a digital representation of the man she had spent a considerable part of her life with. His face stared back from the laptop screen, frozen in a contorted agitated pose. She hit a button on her computer and the screen split in two, her face on one side and his on the other. She tapped the keyboard again and the two faces came to life.

"Kirby, I can't believe you are a party to this!" he said.

"A party to what?" Kirby watched her recorded-self reply.

"I know the truth, Kirby. There's no way anyone up there doesn't know what's going on."

"What are you talking about? What truth?"

"Look if that's how you want to be, fine. I really didn't expect this from you!"

"I want you to join me up here," she said "We have a chance to be part of something unprecedented, can't you see that?"

"No, I can't see that and I can't believe you, Kirby. It's not enough that you sell your soul to PetroSynth but you want me to sell mine too? Enjoy your life!"

An 'End Transmission' sign appeared on the screen.

"Bastard," she said, slamming the laptop closed and turning her back on the machine. She took a few deep breaths and focused her eyes on the big blue ball on the other side of the reinforced glass. The Earth in all its fragility, sitting alone in the dark, held in place by invisible forces, patient, calm, present. Even now it was difficult to conceive that glowing blue ball was her home, that through the cleverness of human engineering she was orbiting the globe every 30 minutes at a ridiculous speed. And he was down there somewhere, failing to make contact, leaving her hanging for days without a word, the selfish prick.

How could he just disappear like that? How could he not contact her again after such an abrupt transmission? Perhaps he was dead? Perhaps he had walked off into the midday sun without his solar hat or sunglasses. She was powerless to help him or herself. She couldn't jump on a plane, she couldn't hail a taxi, all she could do was orbit the Earth; relentlessly reminded of the vast distance between them.

Feeling cornered and frustrated, all that remained was to de-construct what was going through his mind. If she could understand what he was thinking his actions might make some sense. It was not beyond her skill set to evaluate the available data and come to an informed opinion. Firstly, he'd never liked the idea of living away from Earth, a human being belonged on the surface of this miraculous planet, safely cocooned in that thin bubble of atmosphere teeming with life.

She could appreciate his perspective. Why would you leave a home of beauty, warmth and light – depending on your longitude and latitude – for a chunk of human engineered metal with environmental controls. Secondly, he was simply scared of getting on a spacecraft, plain and simple he'd never liked flying, never wanted his body taken from the surface of the earth. He'd constructed some mystically weighted argument about human beings and their connection to the Earth simply because he was scared of being in an air disaster. Thirdly, he was insecure; he was probably questioning their relationship. A life commitment seems pretty big sometimes, but at least on Earth there is always an out, there is always an exit strategy, separation, divorce, perhaps even a fresh start in a new city. What was he going to do if they broke up while they were off discovering the universe together in the confines of a space ship? Where was the potential to move on when everyone is partnered up and locked in for eternity? Sure they wanted to be together, but this was taking commitment to a new level. She was starting to scare herself a little now. If his fear of flying and commitment were going to cause him to shut down like this, to disappear, to be so wholly inconsiderate of her feelings, was he the person she wanted to spend her life with, confined in a sardine can floating in space or otherwise?

It was all this rubbish about the 'truth' that left her in the dark. What the hell was that about, some kind of bizarre fantasy to avoid joining her? Of course he wanted her to come home. She loved him and wanted to be with him, but she did not want to give up her place in history either. She wanted both, she wanted everything, why shouldn't she have everything? And now, instead, as she floated helplessly around the Earth, the black coldness of space seemed to creep in through the impenetrable glass and it chilled her to the bone. She shivered at the thought that she had already lost him.

Kirby took a deep breath and calmed her mind, returning to where she was and observing how her mind had replaced fact with conjecture. Another breath and her composure told her to simply wait. That only a conversation with the man could actually clarify what was happening for him. Then before the salt water drops could fully form and free themselves from her tear ducts, a hand rested on her cold shoulder and for a foolish moment she thought she recognised its warmth.

"Mind in the stars?"

Kirby recoiled from the touch as she recognised the voice, and rotated herself quickly on her swivel chair, grateful she'd kept her tears at bay. She looked into the professor's leering glare and she recoiled from the smell of his stale breath. How transparent he was; she could practically hear his lecherous thoughts. Her firm naked body pressed against his sagging middle-aged form. How deluded he was to ever think she would allow him such liberties, and the hapless way he covered up his flirting was simply ridiculous.

Sometimes Kirby felt like catching him out, saying, "Can I suck your cock Professor," or "Fuck me Professor, please fuck me, right here on the desk. I long to have you deep inside me as we spin around the Earth." His thin pretences would vanish as he pounced on her, all his wet dreams coming true in one glorious moment of employer/employee relations. But before he could touch her she would lift her hand and say, "Just kidding, Professor, a little joke your wife and I came up with."

But Kirby couldn't do it. It was enough to think it and know she was right. Her instincts didn't need validation.

"Just thinking of something I've lost," Kirby replied.

"Oh well, I'm sure you'll find it, whatever it is."

"No, I think it's pretty well gone."

"That's a shame. How are our subjects doing?" the professor asked.

Kirby hit a button on her keyboard.

"Everything is stable. The system is perfect."

"Excellent. I think I'll just go down and take a look anyway."

"Sure, Professor." Kirby replied and she lent over and pressed a button on her desk. The lift door opened and the professor walked inside. He put his hand in front of the door to keep it from closing.

"Will you be here when I get back?" he asked.

"I don't think so. My shift finishes soon."

"Oh, I thought we might get a bite to eat."

'Thought I might just bite the buttons off your blouse' is what he wants to say, Kirby thought.

"Professor, what about you wife?"

"Oh, she hasn't arrived yet. I just wanted to discuss a few work things." 'I just want to put my head between your legs and taste you'.

"Can it wait until tomorrow, during business hours?" Kirby replied.

"Certainly, of course it can. Have a pleasant day." Professor Gardener removed his hand from the door and it closed.

Kirby hit a few keys on her laptop and a picture of herself and Patrick came up on the screen. She traced his face with her slender index finger, questioning in her mind where he might be. She heard a door open and close and checked the monitors. It was the day shift technician coming to relieve her. How strange it was, she thought, that they retained night and day shifts when they didn't actually have a night and day. There had to be some order, some structure that resembled an Earth day so they continued to act like human beings. Was being a human being so closely tied to patterns created by the Earth and its rotation around the sun? Had she become less of a person now that she moved about the Earth like an orbiting moon instead of on its surface? For a glimmer of a second she realised why Patrick felt such attachment to the ground, how it defined him as a human, as a person. The thought faded, giving way to anger and frustration at his absence.

Kirby turned off her computer and tidied her desk.

"Everything all right?" the young man asked as he plugged in his laptop.

"Yeah. The old man's a bit horny this rotation."

"Thanks for the tip, I'll watch my back," the young man replied.

"Well I don't think he'll bother you. I suspect he's had another garlic sandwich for lunch though."

"Great."

"He's gone down to the freezer. I don't think he'll be there long. Just wants to marvel at his expertise. Why does the world's leading digital DNA specialist have be to be a smelly, annoying twat?'

The young man raised his eyebrows in agreement.

"I'd better go. They hate paying overtime!" Kirby grabbed her things and left, hoping that when she got back to her quarters there would be a message from Patrick. Wrapped up in that packet of hope was her wish that by now he would have come to terms with everything and an unequivocal apology would naturally follow. Once he had apologised they could put this behind them as a minor misunderstanding and move forward together. It was not an unrealistic expectation, as long as he wasn't dead, frizzled up by the side of the road like a crispy piece of bacon or worse still, in the arms of another woman trying to purge his connection to her. No he wouldn't do that. Nothing had ever given her cause to suspect that. His absence was cutting a deep and hurtful wound, as she imagined the effects of an infidelity would. In some ways another woman would have been easier to understand, unlike this 'Truth' non-sense, this hurtling of unqualified accusations followed by a disappearing act. How was she meant to process that? Didn't he realise how very far away from him she already felt.

FOUR

Wilfred looked around the large expanse of his office with an ever-increasing expression of melancholy. The lines on his brow deepened and his lips soured and pulled as though gravity were working harder on his face than on anything else on the planet. His success, his trillionaire businessman status, his immaculate office, his stunning view; all at contrast with the emptiness he felt growing beneath the surface. The papers in his hands demanded his attention. The words 'Helios' printed on the front cover evoked a deep sigh from his body that became even deeper once he had flipped the document open. He could only bear to keep it open for a moment, a split second before he needed to push the pages back together. So great was the fear and loathing evoked on Wilfred's face by those pages, he might as well have opened Pandora's box, as though in that moment of opening, the poisonous information could seep out and infect the world with all manner of malady. But he'd read these pages before, he was familiar with their contents and if they'd not yet managed to disease the world they'd certainly already poisoned Wilfred's. He shoved the file in his brief case, took a few deep calming breaths and regained his composure. He tapped the phone icon on the computer screen, and spoke softly. "Home," he said, and waited a few moments for the attractive olive features of his wife's face to fill the screen.

"Hi," she said.

"I'll be home for lunch tonight."

"Great, about twenty minutes?"

"See you soon." He reached forward and disconnected the call.

Wilfred's eye caught the digital photo frame on his desk. Funny, he thought, he'd had pictures from his life rotating on that thing for years but it was only every now and then that they registered, his eyes seeing the pictures, sending the signal to his brain, and then not doing anything with the information. His mother and father were in front of him now and he made a conscious effort to think of them and what this image told him. It was from a time in their history when they were young and healthy, just after they'd left Hong Kong and somehow ended up in Athens. Wilfred's face relaxed and a smile crept in as he recalled his father's sing-song voice, the melodic tones of Mandarin, describing their journey first from mainland China to Hong Kong and finally as part of the diplomatic service to Athens. No longer his father's story, this part he remembered, growing up and living in this ancient city, so completely different from any experience his ancestors had ever had, becoming as Athenian as anyone born there. As a young man he'd ridden his Vespa around the streets of the Plaka, taken his girlfriends to watch the sunrise on Likavitos Hill, naturally behind the solar safe viewing glass. He'd eaten so much moussaka, souvlaki and stuffed capsicum that Mediterranean cuisine had become more to his liking than any home cooked Chinese delicacies his mother had often encouraged him to eat.

Now it was his mother in the photo frame, back in her home village in China. She wore a smile more relaxed and natural than any he could remember seeing on her face in his living memory. Her whole face happy in a way he'd never noticed before. What would his life have been like, he wondered, had he returned to China with his parents? Would he too have discovered that smile, that look of knowing that you are where you belong? Or would he have been at odds with a simple life he couldn't begin to understand?

A photo of his early days with Virginia soon brought him back from that alternative reality. He'd stayed and created a successful life, with a beautiful wife, a major role with the most important company in the world, many corporate secrets in his keeping and one or two personal ones. There was no point contemplating how things might have been: perhaps there was no point even thinking how they had been as neither could be changed by his thoughts. He was where he was.

Wilfred pulled the power cable from the back of the photo frame feeling no further need to look at moments gone by. It was disturbing to think they'd sat on his desk for 15 years, infecting his thoughts and actions but not registering in his conscious mind. It was as though his past was always with him and who needed a digital photo frame as a constant reminder when the human brain could do the job far more relentlessly. He felt a little lighter now, one less burden on his mind. He got to his feet, took a lingering look around the office as if he wouldn't be seeing it again and walked from the room.

Holding his briefcase close to him, Wilfred walked through the mid-evening air toward the metro station, noticing the constant reminders of PetroSynth everywhere he looked. It was fascinating to Wilfred that PetroSynth had managed to change so much, yet so little was different. It had cleaned the air, but had society changed, had people evolved? Even in a densely populated city like Athens, inhabitants still pre-ferred to do battle with traffic and drive their cars than use the expanding metro system. At least pedestrians wouldn't die of lung cancer as they had in the fossil fuel days. It occurred to Wilfred that something was terribly wrong with what they had done, what he and PetroSynth had achieved. They had given humanity the easy way out. Change had occurred around people, but not to people. Their wasteful habits had continued. Consumerism had not been curbed, only further exulted as a virtue. His own life choices suddenly didn't make any sense. Was there another kind of happiness he could've had. One not based on money, power and the fulfilment of all his desires, all the desires he thought were his. He thought again of the kind of happiness he saw on his mother's face after she had returned to the simple life in her village in China, how he'd ignored her refrains over the years about returning 'home' and had never understood until now what it had meant to her. A simple desire but once it had been fulfilled it radiated her very being.

Wilfred stood at the edge of the platform, feeling assured now that he was doing the right thing, that his next course of action was the right choice, not just for himself, but for all his fellow human beings. The significance of the document in his briefcase grew in importance with every new thought that filled his head.

The seemingly endless sea of humanity that struggled its way through history, never really learning, never really changing – the scope of it engulfed Wilfred and his tiny life, his minor collection of moments so lost in the history of space and time that his mind swooned. He stood close to the edge of the platform and leaned out to see the front of the train. It was a habit he suddenly realised he didn't like anymore. It was only so that he could see the glowing red text above the driver-less front carriage: 'Powered by PetroSynth'. Once it had meant so much to him that he'd given people the gift of clean energy, but for what? Look at them, going from place to place with wires plugged into their ears and their heads turned down, glued to screens, no time or words for each other, just a collective desire for the latest technology or time-saving device that only gave them more time to do nothing of any significance. Why was he suddenly so repelled and at the same time so compassionate for the people around him? They knew nothing of their fate, they only concerned themselves with their own lives, their desire for objects and status, following ideas planted in their minds from birth and reinforced every waking moment by the relentless outpouring of banal communications.

It no longer mattered to Wilfred, the emptiness of it all, the very nothingness of everything infected him, the meaning of the world suddenly all just a human projection. The words on the front of the train once giving him pride, then resentment for the lack of gratitude, then acceptance of doing the right thing regardless of how it was received by others. He realised all these emotions he was experiencing were projections too, all just made up in his head. His clever human brain doing what it did best. Every single little thing around him vibrated with his label of what it was. Still he knew, through this feeling, through this emptiness, through this projection, through this fog, through this clarity, that what he did next would be right. Reactions no longer mattered; if they praised him it was right, if they condemned him it was right, if they didn't even stop to notice, it was still absolutely right.

A short, shabby man in a crumpled seersucker suit pushed in behind him. There was always a shuffle for seats on the train and it began as the carriages reached the platform. Wilfred tried to resist looking out to see the front of the train, but he couldn't resist this particular pattern of behaviour, even though he recognised it as being part of his former feelings of self-worth. He felt a hand on his back, felt his briefcase being pulled away from under his arm. Then a firm shove and his arms flapped helplessly as he fell in front of the train. The last thing he saw before the train carved him into pieces were the words, Powered by PetroSynth. Clutching firmly onto Wilfred Fong's briefcase, the shabby little man in the crumpled seersucker suit pushed his way back through the gawking crowd and calmly made his exit.

FIVE

Klondike Khartu's fixed stare encompassed the room. Although his youthful brown eyes did not move, everyone in the room felt the intensity of his gaze, each suspecting he was looking at them individually, assessing their loyalty and confirming their resolve to the cause. Klondike's rich, dark hair sat still on his shoulders, unmoved by the light breeze that blew in through the open window of the neat inner-city London office.

The grin on Klondike's portrait seemed to widen as General Franklin, Commander-in-Chief, called the small group to order. General Franklin stood at the head of the boardroom table with his two deputies on either side. To his right was Wilma, her bony features and shoulder length grey hair made it hard to determine her age, many mistaking her for a septuagenarian when she was only fifty-five. Believing the solar crisis to be a PetroSynth conspiracy she had ignored planet-wide exposure warnings and spent too many hours enjoying the warmth of the sun on her face and body. Her dry skin, stretched and mummified clung tightly to her frame. Her dark eyes were set deep into their sockets and the ring that pieced her eyebrow looked as if it was wedged in the bone of her skull. When she moved her arms or legs it was with the jerkiness of a marionette rather than the grace of a human being. Wilma's skeletal features often frightened new recruits so Franklin preferred she didn't interact with those outside the Order until they'd been well and truly accepted. As she was living proof of the damage the industrialised age had wrought on humanity he would often orchestrate her appearance at an appropriate time for dramatic effect. This was not always a successful move as she had an annoying tendency to speak her mind, and in Franklin's view, she held an inflated sense of her own status within the Order.

On the General's left sat Johnson, a plump man in his mid thirties. His thick bottle glasses were disconcerting and Franklin often thought of offering to pay for him to have laser surgery but didn't want to risk offending his gentle nature. Johnson was the perfect balance for Wilma's hardness and someone Franklin could count on to do his will. Between these two less than perfect specimens, General Franklin looked like the model human being, his handsome features not dissimilar to those of the portrait of Klondike Khartu hanging on the wall behind them.

The ragged collection of Khartuists sitting around the table came to silence and honoured him with a few moments of attention before returning their collective gaze to the portrait of their hero and saviour, Klondike Khartu, that loomed authoritatively over the General.

"The wisdom of Khartu is spreading." Franklin spoke confidently to the group, opening a file that lay on the boardroom table before him.

"Our efforts to have *The Cycle* and *The Wisdom of Khartu* widely distributed are beginning to take effect. Distribution of *The Truth about PetroSynth* is up, with over ten million hits to our website this month. It is encouraging that one of our main goals – to subvert the power of PetroSynth Corporation – is beginning to take hold."

"But surely we must focus on our other problem!" Wilma said, waving a bony arm in the air. Franklin immediately felt his anger rise. The meeting had only just started and already he could feel the blood pounding at his temples. He wanted to scream in frustration at this pathetic collection of losers in front of him. Why couldn't they just let him speak, why did they always have to cut him off and undermine his every word? Hadn't he created and founded the Order? Hadn't he single-handedly made it a household name alongside its nemesis the evil PetroSynth Corporation? Hadn't he grown the Order from a small band of dedicated followers to a million strong international movement while at the same time protecting their own personal anonymity? Where was the respect, for god's sake, for Khartu's sake?

Franklin took a deep breath, resisted the urge to rip out the piece of metal that pierced the older woman's eyebrow and he let her continue speaking, her bony jaw moving up and down in her familiar marionette fashion.

"Klondike Khartu is out there somewhere and we must find him. What good is a movement without a leader?"

The frustration now gave way to a wounded inadequacy and he could not stop his face from betraying his feelings. The woman continued. "No offence General Franklin, but you're not Klondike. We need him."

Franklin scowled but took advantage of her pause to regain control of the meeting.

"We have operatives all over the globe looking for Klondike Khartu. He will surface and when he does we will convince him to take his rightful place as our venerable master. The very nature of Khartu philosophy dictates the inevitability of his return to us. Look," Franklin said, trying to dispel the doubtful looks of his followers, "we are only at the beginning of awareness. Our numbers are small but they are growing every day. The founder must be located and given his place in history. His own words tell us of our journey. In his own text

The Cycle he clearly tells us of our future, not just that of our collective future but our own personal path, one that we will all inevitably follow.

"One of you may be lucky enough to locate the Founder. Joining the other operatives, as you will shortly, in the international search for the Founder, is one of the two great missions charged to a true Khartuist. The other is, of course, the subversion of the PetroSynth Corporation. Need I remind you that it is the Founder's wish that PetroSynth Corporation be exposed for their misuse of trust and power, their greed, self-interest and disregard for humanity?

"Don't ever forget our basic philosophy. We are you and you are us. Of course we are also the Founder. You could say it is unfortunate that we are also everyone who works for PetroSynth but, my friends, that will ultimately give us an understanding of how and why things are the way they are. It is to our movement's greater glory that we find Klondike Khartu."

The group seemed more focused now and Franklin felt a rush of confidence.

"If you are blessed with the honour of discovering the Founder you must report to HQ immediately but never lose sight of him. He must be approached with due respect by myself and the other leaders of the movement, if there is to be any hope that he will lead us."

"Why?" a small voice from the group piped up.

"Why?" repeated Wilma indignantly. Franklin placed his hand on her shoulder to silence what he knew would be a ridiculous rant.

"Why, indeed," Franklin began, "Why has the Founder hidden himself in the sea of overpopulation? Is it because he is consolidating his works in a mountain retreat or perhaps just living a simple life out of the spotlight? No, the answer is clear, he has withdrawn because he wishes to be found. He wants his followers to show how much they care for his teachings, he wants to know that those who believe in him do so with the entirety of their hearts, minds and souls. To do that, to discover that commitment in others, he has left his words, his writings, his teachings, so that we may discover the beginnings of his truth. And when we are ready he will emerge to give us his blessing and complete, not only our Order, but our very understanding of reality."

"Now before you leave tonight and take up your assignments we are going to read the first chapter of *The Cycle* together."

The Khartuists opened their copies of the sacred document. General Franklin took a deep breath and then began to read.

THE CYCLE

By Klondike Khartu of the Fourth Incarnation

I remember the feeling of the sun's rays falling on my outreaching appendages. The warmth moved me with a seminal flux of energy. Like a breath, I took in the light; like a lung I released the oxygen from my porous cells.

I was but a mere shrub in some garden somewhere, sometime.

That was my first incarnation.

I now realise after considerable contemplation, deep relaxation exercises and self-induced regression that the universe repeats itself. It goes through its cycle of trillions of years, ever expanding and thinning its resources until it comes to a stop. At that moment there is no space, no time, in fact no moment. But it does not stay stagnant, there is a small flicker of energy and in a moment what seemed to take forever to expend is suddenly reset, ready to start from the very beginning.

But something minor has changed, something so minor that we barely notice. As this process reoccurs again and again, more and more of us will notice that which now seems unrecognisable. What I have come to realise, and what you too will one day see and feel, is that it is we who change. The universe teaches us by giving us a new role in each reset. My first incarnation was a plant, my second was a worm in a dog's gut, my third a high priestess of our own movement a thousand years from now, and the fourth as Klondike Khartu.

We all have our turn to live as every other living thing until we have experienced everything there is to experience. We will all be the first cell to divide, the first fish to walk on land, the first primate to find fire. We will be tortured and be the torturer, we will conquer and be conquered, we will have grand lives and poor lives. We will be plants, birds, dogs, cats, reptiles, insects and microscopic bugs. We will love, we will hate, we will have everything and we will have nothing and in the end we will understand.

The group looked up from the pages before them, filled with the pride of being chosen for this important mission and rose to their feet.

General Franklin, flanked by his deputies, also rose to his feet. He wished the Khartuists well for their mission and instructed the fledglings to leave immediately.

Franklin was alone with his offsiders now and allowed the glory of the reading to be replaced by his previous irritation as soon as Johnson spoke.

"Franklin, what if they fail and we never find the Founder?" Johnson asked.

"They will not fail," he said slamming his fist on the table. "He will be found! We have now sent over 200 operatives into the field."

"We should have a contingency plan," Wilma said.

"Like what exactly," Franklin snapped. "A crash test dummy with a wig?"

"Martyrdom, or if we could clone him, or a hologram," Wilma replied. "It's the next best thing to the real Khartu. You should see what they can do with 3D printing now."

"How do we get Klondike to be a martyr if we can't find him?" Johnson asked.

Wilma's bony features slipped into something resembling a smile. "We don't, we just put it up on the internet that he was killed somehow. We could say he languished in an Australian prison, persecuted for his beliefs, or that he was shot by an assassin in a mountain retreat in Nepal," Wilma said.

"What mountain retreat?" Johnson asked.

"I'm just making it up, you idiot. It doesn't matter what we say as long as people believe it. Don't forget Khartu's own philosophy. We are all aware of this because we have been here before or will be here again, or something like that. Maybe you should brush up on your Khartuist teachings. Or listen more instead of looking for online hook-ups?"

Johnson placed his phone on the table sheepishly. "Perhaps it is the Great Khartu's words and ideas that are important, not his physical being. His ideas, his writings and teachings form the basis of our belief system. Isn't that already a solid foundation for the future?"

"No," barked the General, "we must find him and we must find him alive. There'll be no martyrdom, no clones. Do I make myself clear?"

"Yes, General," the two replied.

"Now leave me. I have important work to do that may lead to the discovery of the Founder."

To Franklin's surprise, Wilma and Johnson obediently left the room and he moved from behind his desk. He stood looking up at the portrait on the wall, its imposing figure overpowering the room, overpowering his thoughts and feelings. The gaze between the two, between the man and the impression of a man was as real to Franklin as if Klondike were standing there before him. They sized each other up, they were testing each other's resolve, issuing each other a challenge as real as if spoken.

"You think you can hide from me forever you bastard but I will find you?" Franklin broke the stare, turned his back on the portrait and walked from the room with conviction and pride, as if he'd already won the challenge. After all it was he who had broken the stare, he who had named the challenge and brought it out into the open where it belonged. Klondike could hide behind the painted image of himself if he liked, but Franklin knew there was an understanding between them that lived beyond his own imaginings. Klondike was aware that he was being searched out, every bit as much as Franklin was aware that he was hiding. They understood each other, the hunter and the hunted, and Klondike could look down as smugly as he wished from the boardroom wall. It would not change anything for Franklin, his intent unwavering, his focus as clear and as acute as those immovable painted eyes.

SIX

By the time Angel was five she'd come to understand some of her capabilities. It was already clear she was a gifted child. She could complete advanced mathematical calculations in her head within a fraction of a second. While this seemed terribly exciting to all the adults around her, to Angel it was rather boring. Mental accomplishments were trivial. It was physical wonders that Angel liked to conquer. She was tired of everyone asking her to recite the first hundred prime numbers, or working out special differentials, or explaining the paradox of $\sqrt{2}$. Even Einstein's Theory of Special Relativity wasn't looking particularly special.

So for her fifth birthday, Angel had something unique planned. Something she had practiced a dozen times. Something she knew would truly impress not only those over-excitable adults but also her five-year-old friends who cared little for Fermat's Last Theorem or Kepler's ellipses.

Angel sat at the end of the brightly decorated table.

"Happy birthday to you," her friends and family began to sing. "Happy birthday to you!"

The lights went out and Angel's mother came into the room holding before her a large chocolate cake with five birthday candles burning in a circle.

"Happy birthday, dear Angel!"

The cake was placed in front of her.

"Happy birthday to you-uuuu!"

"Now blow out the candles, Angel," her mother instructed.

This was her moment. Angel got up on her chair, leant over the cake and put her lips around the naked flame of one of the candles and extinguished it by closing her mouth. No one moved to stop her as she proceeded to put out the remaining flames in the same fashion.

Angel sat back down on the chair, triumphant in her mastery of this physical feat. She surveyed the room of shocked adults and wonder-struck children.

"Help me cut the cake, Mum, so I can make a wish," Angel directed.

Angel's mother responded obediently.

SEVEN

The old man's truck skidded off the highway and onto a dirt road. Patrick was under the misconception that they had been heading into town and as they bumped and jerked along this deserted path that could barely be described as a road, the thought crossed his mind that his luck at being picked up in the middle of the day was going to turn out horribly wrong.

He looked over at the old man and no longer saw a dithering fool; now he saw a psycho serial killer who enjoyed stir-frying people's internal organs in the heat of the sun and eating them with noodles and sautéed vegetables while the semi-conscious victim looked on in horror.

He looked around the cabin of the ute, trying to locate some type of weapon for self-defence, trying to make a last-ditch plan to stave off the inevitable attack. The driver was old but he didn't look frail. He might be just as strong if not stronger than Patrick. He slid himself to the far side of the cab and pushed all his weight against the door. He slipped his hand discreetly down on to the handle and rested his fingers on the latch. Any sudden movement from the old man and Patrick would pop open the door and roll out.

Patrick relaxed a little, now that a plan of escape was in place, and the gentle roll and jerk of the ute as it trundled along the path dulled his senses. Strangely the thought of his guts sizzling on stainless steel cookware seemed less alarming. He was exhausted and like a rail commuter being lulled to sleep on the way home from a long night at the office, Patrick was having great trouble keeping his eyes open. He drifted in and out of a soft numbness, a pleasant space between sleep and consciousness, a little bubble of twilight where there were no imperatives, not even to survive. He became too ready to accept his fate. As all life on the planet must end, why fight it when it was your turn. As far as Patrick could see, he'd already lost everything. All he had apart from the terrible truth hidden beneath each and every word he uttered, was his life, and without Kirby he wasn't sure he wanted it.

The truck skidded again and jolted to a stop. Patrick looked out the window and thought it did not look as if they had arrived anywhere in particular. It was just a dirt road.

"We have to walk from here!" the old man said.

"What about my car, I need to get some PetroSynth."

"You don't want to put that shit in your car. I've got something much better. Anyway we have to get out of this heat for a few hours. Don't worry, I'm not going to cut your balls off and eat them for lunch."

Patrick was somewhat relieved that his testicles would be safe but was still a little apprehensive. Despite his ambivalent flirtation with a possible demise the natural instincts rooted deep in his reptilian brain held firm and kept him on alert.

Patrick followed the old man down a dirt track through large rocks and old growth trees.

"I don't usually bring people here, but I have a good feeling about you. What was your name again?"

"Patrick. And sorry, what is your name?"

"Oh I have many names; perhaps the one I started with is the one I'll finish with, but perhaps not. It all depends on the lights."

"Very interesting," Patrick said rolling his eyes. "But what can I actually call you, other than 'he of many names'?"

"Most people round here call me Ancient."

"Ancient?"

"You know, very old, antiquated, antediluvian, prehistoric..."

"I know what it means. It's just odd to have it as a name. Don't you think?"

"Odd? Odd is relative. You'll get used to it."

"Get used to it. I'll be out of here after sunset. Won't I?"

"Well, you see that all depends on how the conversion goes."

"Conversion, what conversion? I'm quite happy with my individually derived belief system thanks."

"Not you, your car! Once we get the rest of the kangaroo out of the radiator grill we have to get it off that PetroSynth crap."

"Well maybe I could make a phone call. Then I wouldn't have to trouble you at all."

"Oh it's no trouble; in fact it is my duty to fix your car. Anyway I don't believe in phones; there are much better ways to communicate."

"Yes of course, like smoke signals, or perhaps you prefer telepathy."

They arrived at a clearing and Patrick was surprised to see a large mud-brick house with a giant satellite dish out front.

It was cool and pleasant inside and the old man told Patrick to make himself at home before opening a side door and disappearing. Patrick caught a glimpse into the other room and thought he saw what looked like last century communications equipment.

The door opened a fraction and the old man stuck his head out.

"You can take a shower. We'll go back for your car in a couple of hours when the sun's down. Here read this." The old man threw a book at Patrick.

"The Truth about PetroSynth," Patrick read the title, "What a load of crap!" and tossed the book to the side.

The cool water of the shower was refreshing and Patrick decided to linger in its stream. He knew he was in a very remote location and that water might be scarce but he didn't care. The old bastard hadn't given him a time limit for the shower so fuck it. It wasn't his fault if he stayed in there too long. He needed it. He deserved it. It was the least he should have for letting the old fart muck around with his car, an event that seemed inevitable. At least all this took his mind off Kirby and the depth of her deception. How could she have betrayed him? And not only him; she had betrayed herself, her entire species and every living thing on Earth. The image of Kirby stayed in his mind, her beautiful soft skin, her long fair hair. He imagined her in the shower with him, the cool water running over her taut body, the coolness hardening her nipples. How many times had he kissed that delicious naked body? He soaped up and took his swelling penis in his hand. He thought of Kirby's perfect mouth, her tender lips wrapped around his cock. He thought of her moist opening as he penetrated its warmth, slowly at first, tenderly, then faster, more urgent.

As the semen shot onto the shower floor so too did the reality that Kirby was not there; and in that moment she had never seemed so far away. Patrick wept, unable to reconcile still being in love with someone who'd betrayed him so completely? After all she'd said, after all she'd done, he still wanted her. He turned the water on harder to conceal his tears, to wash them away along with the feelings that caused them to flow. He pushed his face into the hot jets of water as the semen, the dirt, the sweat and the grime of the past four days swirled about his feet and spiralled down the drain.

EIGHT

Kirby walked into her quarters and dropped her bag by the door. She raced over to the communications console embedded in her desk. The little light was flashing. 'Thank God', she thought, 'he's finally come to his senses and fucking called.'

She hit the play button and leaned excitedly over the console. "Hello, sorry to disturb you when you're off duty, Kirby, but that work matter has now become quite urgent. Can you please contact me at the lab?"

"Fuck off, Professor!" Kirby yelled. She hit the buttons on the touch screen and dialled Patrick's mobile number.

"The mobile number you have called is either switched off or out of range. Please try again later." The same recorded message Kirby had heard a hundred fucking times. Why didn't the cheap bastard have message bank like everyone else on the planet. Kirby wished she was on Earth; not just because it would be easier to track Patrick down but because if she were in her apartment she could've ripped the phone from the wall. All this trendy space age wireless gadgetry really pissed her off because she couldn't smash it to pieces when it didn't do what she wanted. And now what she wanted was for this fucking communications console to communicate with the man she loved, who had disappeared somewhere on the face of the Earth for some stupid unknown reason, that he called 'the truth'.

The incoming message light flashed in sync with the simulated phone ringing. Kirby quickly hit the answer button.

"Patrick!" she said.

"It's Professor Gardener. Did you get my message?"

"I just got in."

"The project's been advanced. We need to start reconstituting the children immediately." She hated the way he referred to them as 'the children'. No human would do what the professor had done to their own children. They were an experiment, to date a very successful one, but an experiment nonetheless. They were not his little children, not unless he'd fathered 200 chimps in a previous experiment. A possibility, she thought, she wouldn't put past him.

Patrick's words of disbelief were beginning to penetrate. How could she be working for these bastards?

"I'll be there as soon as I can," she said and quickly hit the disconnect button before the Professor could say another word.

'Ring, Patrick!' She willed the communications console to respond but it made no sound. "Ring me, you bastard!"

NINE

Mrs Fong sat calmly in her favourite armchair, an orange vinyl antique from the 1970s preserved in pristine working condition. Her favourite feature was a retractable footrest that she couldn't resist using. She loved the fact that there were no buttons, voice controls, computer chips or hydraulics. She had to actually pull a lever on the side of the chair and the footrest would slide out as she was reclined into relaxation. At the moment the chair was in its upright position and its bright orange vinyl clashed dramatically with her otherwise inoffensive black leather lounge suite. Her face betrayed little emotion and her elegant little black dress was the only hint to her newly acquired widowed status. In fact she had no genuine widow attire in her collection. Despite the age difference between them she'd not been prepared for her late husband's passing. Mrs Fong simply followed her life's motto: 'When in doubt, wear black'.

Detective Costas Paradisos sat opposite Mrs Fong and tried to listen carefully. As she spoke of the rising wave of insecurities now that her husband had gone, Costas could not stop his mind and eyes from wandering over her shapely form. There couldn't be much difference between them in age. And at 44, with a well-maintained physique, Costas thought he was more or less irresistible to anyone he decided to grace with his attention. It bothered him a little that her late husband had been almost 30 years older, but he was dead now and out of the picture, and she had such strong looking shoulders and firm, defined legs. Her tight fitting dress clearly outlined her toned, athletic body. She must work out, he thought, a personal trainer, yes definitely a personal trainer. She probably fucks him as part of the workout. He pictured her perspiring as she climbed endlessly on the stepper machine. How he would love to take her in his arms as she moved off the stepper, pull off her pungent gym clothes and press his mouth against her sweaty hot skin.

Mrs Fong stopped talking and seemed to be waiting for the detective to speak. Costas took in a deep breath and a guttural sniff and adjusted himself on the leather lounge. He crossed his legs to cover the swelling and tried to look charismatically into Mrs Fong's eyes.

"Mrs Fong, I'm very sorry about your husband's untimely death."

"Thank you, Detective Paradisos."

"It's okay, and please call me Costas. Mrs Fong, I don't believe your husband's death was suicide. No note has been discovered and it seems quite uncharacteristic. He clearly had much to live for. Unfortunately there is no CCTV due to some kind of computer error."

"I too believe my husband was murdered."

"I see, but why would someone want to kill your husband?"

"He was a very wealthy man; perhaps someone owed him a lot of money that they couldn't pay back. Perhaps someone was blackmailing him for something he did in his youth. I'm really not certain. He never involved me in business matters. All I know is that he would never have killed himself and he would never be so careless as to lose his footing. It may just be my woman's intuition."

"I see," Costas took note of her flirting. It was not unusual for a woman in an unhappy marriage, finding herself suddenly free, to be drawn to him.

"I am pleased you are on the case, Costas, you have a very good reputation."

"This is true, Mrs Fong. I have a nose for this business," he said tapping the end of his schnoz. "We will find who murdered your husband, Mrs Fong, rest assured."

"Thank you,"

Costas stood quickly and adjusted his erection. A slight movement of the hand and leg that he knew Mrs Fong would detect. It was his first step in seduction. He liked his prey to know they had aroused him.

"Here is my card. If you think of anything that may help please call me."

"Of course. Would it be too much to ask to be kept informed of your progress?"

"Certainly, Mrs Fong, I'm sure you will be assigned a police liaison, however I'd be most happy to do that when I can directly."

"Oh and please call me Virginia."

Costas took her olive skinned hand in his, brought it to his lips and gently kissed its smooth surface. His nose twitched slightly at her scent and he wasn't at all sure if she could be trusted. However the blood rushing to his groin soon took with it any doubt that lingered in his mind.

TEN

Franklin placed the key in the lock of his London flat and turned it gently. He felt the click of the lock's bolt as it moved from its secure slot in the notch of the door-frame to rest inside the mechanism. He felt the vibration move through his fingers, into his hand, up his arm and through his chest. He breathed in the feeling. The door was open to him, and him alone. This was his space, his place, his world. He removed the key and walked through the open door.

As the bolt returned to its secure slot, Franklin's mind raced through the many times that door had been opened and closed to him. His mother had used the very key that was now in his hand to take them from the safety and security of their world behind this door to the world outside. Firstly as a babe in her arms, then in a pram, then holding his hand, then walking beside him. His life, its many stages and changes all anchored to this modest two room flat. If not for the bricks and mortar this defined area of space would simply be a pocket of air three storeys off the ground. But more than the walls, floors and ceilings, it was defined by his mother's tastes, established by her presence and her personality.

He remembered blissful days playing in that space; quiet times together, just the two of them – mother and son. Franklin knew no father, only the concept of one, something his friends had that he didn't. Franklin's father was a scientist his mother had told him, a great man of science who had given the world something tremendous and wonderful. But he was only good at being himself, at being a scientist, he wasn't able to be the great man the world needed and a father at the same time. Franklin had to understand that the world needed a great scientist more than he needed a father. And after all Franklin had his mother and they were happy playing together or existing in parallel, reading quietly in their separate rooms or her cooking while he played games of adventure in his room. Building tents and forts and great cities where he was always the master and chief, the lord of all he surveyed.

Then it was taken away when his mother announced she would soon be returning to work, her career at PetroSynth. An opportunity too great to refuse had been offered, and, as always, only the best solution that money could buy would make everything alright for Franklin.

Going to boarding school was like being ripped from the womb prematurely. Leaving the safety and security of his mother's calm and giving presence but also leaving his domain, his entire world taken away. During holidays he would visit and soak up as much of what made his world special and take it with him to the empty and sterile environment of his state of the art boarding school. He refused to decorate his rooms there, preferring to keep the walls clear and his belongings tucked away. His various room-mates over the years filled their spaces with pictures and calendars, favourite bands, pin-up girls and family photographs. Franklin needed the walls blank, a clean surface on which to project his imagination. There on that empty wall he recreated his London flat, his mother in the room next door, the bathroom one door to the right and the hallway leading to the large living space with open kitchen, dining and lounge. And at the very end that door, a portal that led to another world, a world he was happy to visit sometimes with his mother, but a world that had ultimately taken him away from the space he loved most.

He remembered lying in his boarding school bed for the last time. He had finished his final exams and in the morning he'd be packing and going home to be with her. They hadn't discussed what would happen next. He had just assumed he'd go back to his room, back to it being the two of them again, as it was several years earlier. He gave no thought to work or earning money. Everything had always been provided. The best schools, the best food, the best gadgets.

It was odd to see the headmaster enter his room after a gentle knock at his door. He never came to the boys' rooms after dark, not unless there was something wrong. The headmaster beckoned and Franklin followed the older man's instructions. He got out of bed and put on his dressing gown and the two moved into the silent hallway.

There amidst the sound of two hundred sleeping boys the headmaster gently placed his hand on Franklin's shoulder and told him of his mother's unfortunate and untimely end. An accident at the PetroSynth labs had occurred and his mother, a PetroSynth energy specialist, had been killed. There were no remains. An experiment the company was not willing to explain had somehow not gone as planned. He was presented with a copy of her signature that waived the company of any liability in the event of her death. He was also given a substantial lifetime annuity, transferred to him on condition he never spoke of her death in relation to PetroSynth. He later discovered that the headmaster, soon after passing on the news to young Franklin, had taken an early retirement.

Franklin at the age of seventeen, found himself alone in his London flat. Yes it was his now, his world finally. Not the same without his mother in the next room reading, but it was his and always would be his. He scanned her room as never before taking in every detail, cataloguing in his mind every item of clothing, every ornament she had on her dresser, her collection of Buddhas and eastern artefacts strangely comforting. He lit an incense stick, Sandalwood, her favourite and placed it in a holder to let it burn. He pulled open her drawer of private papers that he'd never dared to look at before. He found himself fishing through a stack of papers, old bills, meaningless bank statements, payslips, tax returns and receipts. He had purpose, there was something in this pile of printed details that was meaningful, something pulling him in.

The moment his hand touched the folder he knew it was what he'd wanted to find, what he'd always wanted to find. More than the mere fragments of speech his mother had given him, here were words from his past, from a time that existed before his conception. As he read, page after page, it became clear to him what he needed to do; it became solid in his mind, as real as any object he'd held in his hands. These were words from Klondike Khartu, these random musings from the mind that gave the world PetroSynth, the man with so much to give to humanity but no time to give a single day to his son, this man who left these ideas, these literary oddities. He would be forced to resurface and take responsibility for what his mistakes had left behind.

At that moment, at that very instant Franklin was no longer a boy, no longer an adolescent, he was a General, he was once more the commander-in-chief of all he surveyed. Moving beyond the restricted playing fields of his imaginings, he would bend reality to his will. In the same way he had commanded the forces of nature, led countless armies in victorious battles, fought long and hard in campaigns that spanned the confines of his room and his mind, so now he would use those very skills to conjure Klondike Khartu, to bring him into the light, to force him to speak the truth. And he would make PetroSynth pay for taking his mother.

He stood at that door again, the years between a blur and yet he was acutely aware of how one moment had led to the next. They had all brought him to where he stood now. The purpose so strongly formed in his seventeen-year-old self still vibrant and clear to his middle aged mind. He could feel the fruition forming around him. A little more patience and all he had been planning for would soon be his.

ELEVEN

Having already obtained her doctorate in advanced mathematics at 15 it seemed a logical step for Angel to commence a PhD in astrophysics. She had much to celebrate on her 16th birthday with both degrees completed with honours.

Angel looked around the large back room of the house, especially converted with ultra UV-resistant glass, so the party could go well into the daylight hours, and realised she had only a few friends her own age. Reflecting her advanced intellectual standing the room was full of university academics, fellow students and her parent's colleagues.

It would be easy to impress this crowd with her knowledge and speed of mental agility. As with her fifth birthday she had something better in mind.

On cue, Angel's mother appeared in the room holding a cake ablaze with candles. They all knew what was coming. Angel's famous party trick was well documented. She quickly covered each candle with her mouth, smothering and consuming each flame, before finally taking hold of one resistant flicker between her fingers and stubbing it out. The crowd marvelled and clapped, then suddenly jumped back as Angel breathed giant flames into the air. Fire shot from her mouth like a dragon. She sprayed her hands with flames, waving them in the air as they remained alight.

As quickly as they had ignited, with a few brisk movements, Angel snuffed out the flames.

Her guests' delighted chatter drifted through the party as Angel's mother passed around pieces of cake.

A cool breeze blew through the enclosed room and she shivered. No one else noticed the distinct change in air temperature. A pair of soft hands touched her shoulders and she felt a cool steady breath on her neck. The hands were the same temperature as the breeze that had just blown by. The skin strange, supple and electric. Angel tried to turn but the hands held her still. At first she thought it must be someone she knew, wanting to wish her happy birthday, but as the man began whispering secret intellectual possibilities she realised the voice was too exciting to be familiar.

Angel nodded her head in agreement with everything he said. As he spoke she continued to look forward. None of the other guests approached her. No one even acknowledged her presence. It was as if Angel and this man, with his deep resonating voice and smooth-skinned hands had stepped out of time and space and were looking at the world through a portal. And even though her head swam with the dizzying amount of technical and scientific wonders the voice pumped into her head, she was readily able to absorb it.

Suddenly the words stopped and the hands moved to turn her body. She spun on her heels, eager to match a face to that voice. He looked into her piercing angel eyes. She looked back into his. Their colour, their depth, their similarity seemed natural to her. He removed his hands from her shoulder and time and space were restored. The man was gone. Had he turned and walk from the room or had he simply vanished? She could remember his voice, all the amazing things he'd poured into her thoughts and she could remember those eyes. How could he have her eyes? But the moments of his arrival and departure were not available, as though edited from her memory.

"Happy birthday, my Angel," Richard broke her thoughts as he took her in his arms.

"Thanks Dad." Angel replied, uncertain what was real, her moments with the stranger, or this, her father's warm embrace.

TWELVE

Patrick held the torch for the old man as he hunched over the engine. The evening air was cool and refreshing but Patrick could still feel the heat of the day rising from the ground and the faint smell of charred kangaroo from the radiator wafted intermittently into his nostrils.

"It's actually a very simple process," the old man said from under the bonnet of Patrick's car.

"Really?"

"Oh, yes. A little twist here, a little turn there."

"Great."

"Once we've done this, not even the second law of thermodynamics will stop her from running."

"You don't say."

"You ever heard of the Second Law of Thermodynamics?"

"Actually, yes I have." Patrick replied. "My wi... Someone I know is a physicist."

"Your wife, eh?"

"Possibly."

"It's a nasty one that Second Law of Thermodynamics. Even that glorious saviour of humanity, PetroSynth, can't stop the end of the universe. No, one day all energy will be expended. But even when that day comes, there will be a little hum in the universe, and that my friend will be coming from your car."

"What are you going on about?"

The old man picked up his canvas pack and put his hand inside. He felt around a bit and then slowly withdrew his clenched fist. He held it up in front of Patrick's face.

"If PetroSynth Corporation knew what was in the palm of my hand they'd be tearing their collective hair out, those with any left. Which is exactly what they are going to do, far sooner than they think!" The old man chuckled to himself.

Patrick looked at Ancient's clenched fist. A faint glow seeped through the cracks in his withered fingers. Patrick was momentarily distracted by the state of the old man's digits. Their frail exterior deceptive given the work they were being put to.

"What is it?"

"A gift," Ancient replied and he walked over to the side of the car. He removed the fuel cap and dropped the contents of his hand into the tank.

"Now start her up," the old man directed.

Patrick got into the car and tentatively turned the key. It chugged a little, coughed and spluttered.

"It's just adjusting," Ancient said.

Soon it was running smoothly and humming quietly. Patrick got out of the car as Ancient soldered the exhaust pipe closed. "You won't need this any more, emission free!"

"Well, thanks for everything," Patrick said as he shifted the car into reverse. He put his foot on the accelerator and gently lifted the clutch. The car shifted slightly, but didn't budge. It was not the incline of the small gully that was the problem. The engine, thanks to Ancient, was purring nicely and it was definitely in gear. Patrick tried again, pulling into neutral and then back again into reverse. The car wouldn't budge.

"Looks like I'll have to give you a tow back to my place. Probably the axle, but we can have a better look at it there."

Patrick slammed the gears back into neutral and turned off the engine.

"Back to Neverville! Fucking beautiful," he said and hit the wheel in frustration.

THIRTEEN

Kirby dreaded the lift down to the freezer. Not because it was a confined space, or because it was the only way to the secured lab twenty storeys below. She was not claustrophobic; being in a small, enclosed space did not particularly bother her. It was the Professor's stale breath and body odour that she could not tolerate and the incessant flirting.

Kirby usually found a creative way to avoid getting in the lift with him. Deliberately forgetting something vital that would require a few minutes to pull together, forcing the Professor to go on ahead without her. Not an easy task to achieve on a regular basis especially considering that while she was doing her utmost to avoid getting in the lift with him, he was doing his best to try and corner her there. For the Professor, the more time he spent alone with Kirby the better. Surely a rapport would develop between them, a rapport that would sooner or later lead to carnal experimentation.

A more vile thought could not cross Kirby's mind than the fetid mouth of Professor Gardener slobbering over her body. Such an encounter would undoubtedly leave an indelible smell that would prevent her from ever having another lover. Not that she was looking for a lover. She only wanted Patrick.

Kirby relaxed as the lift approached, feeling fortunate that Gardener had gone down earlier with the rest of the team. She would not have to put up with his leering smile or foul stench.

The lift door opened and Professor Gardener stood smiling at her. 'Fucking great,' she thought.

"Just, thought I'd pop up for my sandwich. Can you hold the lift for me Kirby, I won't be a moment."

Oh, beautiful, Kirby thought. Not just the body odour but the progenitor of the stench as well, the dreaded garlic salami sandwich.

Kirby dutifully held the door open as Professor Gardener rummaged around in his office. He jogged back into the lift smiling warmly at Kirby.

"There's plenty of excitement in the freezer."

"Great," she replied trying not to gag on the almost visible globs of stench emanating from the Professor's pores. It seemed worse than usual today, confirmation the sandwich was the cause of the man's downfall. His little jog across the office triggering his sweat glands didn't help him any.

"You know, over the past few years and particularly the last couple of months I've come to greatly admire you, Kirby."

Outright flattery. The man was getting bold, Kirby thought.

The Professor lifted his arm and scratched his head nervously. A few flakes of skin fell onto his shoulder and a wave of body odour shot from his armpit, hitting Kirby square in the face and saturating her nostrils with burning intensity. This had gone too far. Not only did he smell as though he had rubbed his armpit with a slab of salami instead of deodorant but he was outright trying to hit on her. Kirby held her breath and winced.

"Is something wrong?" he asked.

"Look Professor, don't take this personally, but you need to think about getting something else to eat. That sandwich stinks. And frankly you smell as if your system is seriously backed up. Can you go easy on the salami for a few days? I mean we've all got to work together here. And by the way I don't find you remotely attractive. So just give it a rest. Okay?"

"Oh, okay." Professor Gardener replied, almost dumbstruck.

Kirby couldn't believe she'd laid it on the line, but with Patrick gone and the project being advanced she had to take the pressure out on someone. The Professor was in the wrong place at the wrong time eating the wrong rancid sandwich.

The lift door opened and as they walked out the Professor dropped his sandwich into the small bin next to the door.

"I'll be with the team in a minute, I just have to go freshen up," he said.

"Good idea!" Kirby said as she joined the others.

The team greeted her with wide grins, some unable to hold back incessant giggles. Kirby noticed the lift camera was showing on one of the screens and it was clear they had hacked in and overheard.

"Okay, let's get to work. We've got a lot of primates to reconstitute," a small smile appearing in the corner of her mouth.

FOURTEEN

Costas sank into the comfort of Wilfred Fong's executive chair. He surveyed the former trillionaire's office, both contemplating life as a PetroSynth executive and waiting for clues to the man's death to spring out of the furnishings. He leaned forward and put his head to the desk. He sniffed along the edge of the mahogany surface like a dog looking for a scent. His olfactory sense was his secret weapon. It was a talent that had helped him solve many cases but had also led to him being widely misunderstood by his superiors and colleagues. No one believed that his nose could be so sensitive or in fact that he was anything less than a total fruitcake, and no detective in the Athenian police force would work as his partner. Costas mistook their embarrassment for envy as he would take vital clues and press them to his nostrils. As such he was ostracised by his peers and forced to work alone, usually on smaller cases. Homicides of deadbeats, drug addicts and hit-and-runs were his mainstay. Indeed he'd been surprised by the chief's insistence that he take the high profile Wilfred Fong case. He was mindful of the opportunity and determined to achieve a quick and successful outcome.

The fastest way to the truth was to sniff it out. He would stand by his nose and vindicate its powers. Now, as he sniffed around the desk nothing criminal registered. He could smell paper of various weights and textures, ink, Biro and fountain pen. As he moved along the desk nothing had any abnormal impact. Then his nose touched the edge of the computer keyboard. He sniffed deeply, his eyes rolled back into his head and his eyelids fluttered violently. This was it.

He sat up sharply and turned on the computer, unsure exactly what to look for. No password. That was strange and a quick scan of the file structure showed nothing unusual; there were no personal files at all. Costas picked up the phone and buzzed Wilfred Fong's secretary.

"Hello."

"Hello, Alix is it?"

"Yes, Mr Paradisos, can I help you?"

"Yes, can you tell me did Mr Fong keep any personal computer files?"

"He saved them all onto flash drives, in the drawer to your right, under the monitor."

"Thank you, that's most helpful," he said, turning on the Costas charm.

"The only personal information on the computer would be his address book. Nothing is encrypted so you should be able to access what you like. Mr Fong hated codes and passwords," she added.

'Thank you, you've been very helpful indeed."

"I just hope you find whoever did this to Mr Fong."

"I will," Costas replied and returned his attention to the computer.

Wilfred Fong's address book was extensive and Costas became irritated with it fairly quickly. He hit the print button and looked in the drawer under the desk as he waited for the twenty or so pages to print out. He took the handful of flash drives from the drawer and examined their labels. It was mainly business correspondence but he decided to take them with him for further investigation. The printer was still going so he opened the box and sniffed each memory stick thoroughly. One made his eyes roll back and his eyelids fluttered.

He plugged it in, examined its list of files and opened one dated two days earlier.

> My dearest Eko,
>
> *I long to hold you in my arms again. Your sweet young body replenishes my soul and helps me forget that my own decaying form will not serve me forever. You are the only vice I have. The only secret I keep. While I have you, I have no fear of death.*
>
> *Love always,*
>
> *Daddy Fong.*

"The Fates have proved otherwise, Daddy Fong," Costas said as he picked up the printout. He turned the pages, ran his finger down and stopped at Eko, a single simple name with mobile phone number.

Costas brought the pages to his nose. He sniffed and it triggered the indisputable facial ticks of success.

"Thank you," he whispered as he gently tapped his nose.

FIFTEEN

Franklin closed the door to his office quietly and rested his back against its cool firm surface. He could hear the footsteps of his agent grow softer as she walked away from him, down the narrow tiled corridor. In syncopation with each breath he exhaled, the volume from the click-clack of her heels lessened until she came to a stop. Closing his eyes, Franklin held his breath and focused only on the sounds around him and the firmness of the door that held him in place. The lift arrived, and its soft predictable rhythms, though faint, brought him comfort. Soon the girl would be gone and the living reminder of what he'd done would be out of sight and out of mind.

In his hands he held his future. Did that poor girl, clouded by the lies he'd fed her, have any idea of what she'd just delivered into his hands?

He looked through the folder and sensed the paradox of creation sweep through him with all its complex glory. He'd been feeding lies for so long now that it was sometimes hard to keep hold of how this had all started.

Creating a religion from the works of Klondike Khartu for his own singular needs had come so easily. It was pure emotion that had driven his actions and worked every detail into place.

Klondike Khartu was innocent and perhaps even ignorant of his status. He'd simply written stories, stories that explored the nature of life, consciousness and meaning, but stories nonetheless. Fictions born of a man's mind that he had no use for once he'd penned them. And what had Franklin done? The thought of it now seemed ludicrous, taking another man's creative works, reorganising, rewriting, reshaping into a religious text, into an organised and mobilised group of people. A group at his personal disposal, established to weed out a man who was hiding from the world, hiding from him.

Franklin took a deep breath and moved away from the door. It took all his energy to release himself from the support the surface gave him, but there was no more time to waste. He turned, locked the door and slumped into his office chair. Countless souls looking for meaning in a meaningless world, and what had he given them? Another sweet lie in a long history of lies aimed to control people and their lives. Was what he'd created any different from any other religion the world had known? Perhaps only because its cynicism was there from the start rather than evolving over time.

By giving people hope that if they found Khartu they would somehow give rise to a new dawning of human civilisation was only one part of Franklin's lie. He'd also used Khartu's attacks on corporate globalisation, the monopolisation of power, the destruction of individuality and cultural difference in the name of a single economy. Khartu celebrated difference and loathed conformity and Franklin had used these potent ideas to further strengthen his movement, attracting many who wanted to buck the system, fight a war or feel the intoxicating power of making a stand. Franklin made it a personal attack on PetroSynth, the largest global organisation in history. At all costs they must be exposed for the lies they were telling and for the disregard for human life that underpinned their corporate greed.

He couldn't escape the irony. After many years of convincing others of the great pursuit of Klondike's teachings and the imperative of finding and honouring their founder, Franklin had almost come to believe his own lie. But it was the man he sought, pure and simple, the man he wanted to converse with, the man he wanted to look in the eye and ask one single question. A question that had nothing to do with his writings or with his hatred of corporate globalisation.

To make that moment happen, to create that space and time where he and Klondike existed together, Franklin had lied and cheated and convinced thousands that Klondike was more than a mere mortal. And that creation, that lie, the fruits of his labours were ripening and they stared Franklin in the face.

But what of those people he'd used to create this one moment for himself. Despite his selfish intent he'd given meaning to countless lives that previously had no meaning, given purpose to those who had none, faith to those who languished in a dull existence. He'd turned an obscure creative genius into a household name, but did anyone recognise his own genius, did anyone stop to thank him for bringing Khartu's words of wisdom to them? Those sad little lives, those people devoted to the cause, the cause he'd laid out before them, the cause he'd created. He was the genius, not fucking Klondike. Klondike was a coward who'd run away leaving everyone behind, escaping from everything and leaving only words, useless fucked-up phrases. Sure his words made people feel better, but if they looked in the mirror for five minutes they might just see their lives for what they were.

Why didn't they see the choice, a choice in every single moment of their lives. A choice to continue, knowing full well that tomorrow will be just the same, that standing in front of the mirror then will be as it is now, or choosing something different; not going to work that day and picking up that thing most valued, an instrument, a pen, a paintbrush, a pack of cards, a song book, that dream lost beneath thousands of moments of doing what they were told instead of what they felt. Accepting conditioning without question, accepting the lie that choices had already been made for them before they were even born. Going through the motions of life without realising their unhappiness might be a simple side effect of simply not doing what they felt most inclined to do. Repeating the mistakes of humanity by spending their entire lives doing what they were told, what was expected, what was normal, what was appropriate, what was safe and what ultimately was not them!

Instead of having a choice they listen to all the messages contained in every movie, book, TV show, advertisement and casual conversation around the water cooler. Get married, have kids, go to work, desire stuff, buy stuff, stuff makes people happy, stuff makes people feel better, the more people have the happier they will be. Fuck why can't they see that the less you have the better off you will be, the less shit you have, the less shit you have to think about, the less you have the more you have. But no they work harder to pay for things they don't really need and they don't question if they are things they truly want. Keep reading giant billboards and watching TV commercials and cinema advertising and web-page banners and magazine articles all conspiring to sell a slice of happiness, a moment of bliss. Desire it, strive for it, grasp it, pay for it on credit, then wake up the next day and go to work and do things they hate to get things they think they love.

Then they hold that thing in their hands and they love it and love it and love it, then they look around and think they don't love it so much anymore, they start to think about that other thing they have been told to love, they want that other thing now, they need that other thing! Earn more to buy more to earn more to buy more to earn more and then they die and someone has to earn more to pay for the expensive funeral they wanted.

People annoyed Franklin, really annoyed him. He could read their lives like signposts, examples of ways not to be, like giant 'Wrong Way, Go Back' warnings . If they couldn't see it, then who was he to tell them. At least in his teachings, in the Khartuist tradition that he'd created, that he'd moulded from Klondike Khartu's words, the signposts for change were there. All anyone had to do was learn to read them.

Taking another breath and holding the folder in his hand, Franklin suddenly began to feel tears fall from his eyes. What was he feeling? He'd waited so long for this moment, the best lead to the Founder he'd ever had was in his hands and all he could think about were the millions of people he'd misled. But it was more than that. It was the sad lives, the suffering, the unnecessary suffering. That so many lives could have been lived differently if only people had seen how easy it is to choose otherwise. Franklin was overcome with compassion, overcome with gratitude. They might not read the signposts but he could only be grateful to them for the insight their lives afforded him.

Damn, it was Khartu who had written:

"Be grateful to the ignorant and small minded, the intolerant, the unhappy, the insecure and self-loathing masses. Read them as you would a signpost, a warning to head in another direction. Be grateful and thank them for their message. They have suffered to bring it to you and deserve your compassion."

How much of that Franklin had rewritten, he could no longer remember. Having subverted Klondike's words for his own purposes, Franklin knew that PetroSynth was not all bad. As a product it had certainly done its part to stop global warming. It was the company, the capitalist structure that Khartu hated so much. They had taken a simple genetically engineered plant and turned it into a global monopoly. So now they weren't just a multinational, they were the Multinational. God forbid anyone should discover his annuity from the very beast he fought.

If the company had stopped at solving the energy crisis Khartu would not have been so riled, but they had gone on to use that power to control nations, manipulate governments and control the structure of the average person's everyday life. The head PetroSynth executive in any given country vastly more powerful than any elected representatives of the people.

Here he was walking home in the early hours of the morning, enjoying the twilight but wondering if the switch from daylight existence to that of a night prowler was ever truly required. Was it just the PetroSynth corporation implementing a policy it thought best? The company didn't care if it was safer for humanity to be indoors during the day and out at night. The decision was more likely made to simply test how compliant the human race was. Given the right set of circumstances, they could be made to believe anything; they could be controlled and PetroSynth wanted to exercise that control.

Franklin, on the whole believed the change from day to night had saved lives. It was certainly safer and more sensible for human activity to become nocturnal, when the Sun, the giver of life on this Earth, was so hot that any living being would receive second degree burns after only a few minutes unprotected exposure. But when could humanity's nocturnal behaviours be abandoned, when would it be safe to walk the streets in daylight again? When PetroSynth Corp decreed, and that's what angered Franklin the most.

As he reached his front door and turned the key another reality hit him. This new opportunity would take him away from his precious private space. No other living being had walked through this open door in the 25 years since his mother's death.

He dropped the documents on the table. All the paperwork, all the photos, all the lies all the bribes, everything was in place. He could finally infiltrate the PetroSynth corporation at the highest level. No one but he could take the mission and its success could lead to the undoing of the most powerful multinational in history and potentially weed out the founder Klondike Khartu. The running of the Khartuist movement left in the less than capable hands of his deputies. The thought initially filled him with unease, but that soon evaporated as he realised he no longer cared if the organisation grew or floundered under their control. It had served its purpose.

All he had worked for was threatened either way. It would be impossible once he took up his new identity for any Khartuist to have access to him or for him to have access to them. He would only break his cover if they found Klondike before him.

Franklin set to work busily typing instructions to Wilma and Johnson but his mind raced with other concerns. In the early evening they would wake to find their commander-in-chief gone, leaving only a few suggestions as to how to continue and a hint as to where he had gone. Perhaps they would feel his absence as much as he felt the neglect of Klondike Khartu, but it was unlikely.

Franklin accepted his destiny, self-created as it was, with a bitter-sweet understanding. His new identity would give him top-level access to a major operation being undertaken by PetroSynth and place powerful resources at his disposal.

Franklin sent his last email to his deputies and shut down his computer. He contemplated what it was going to be like in a few short hours when he would no longer be General Franklin, with a new name and a new face.

He looked longingly at his father's portrait. Its ingratiating grin beamed down as if revelling in having thwarted attempts to be discovered.

Franklin ceased any remaining flirtation that any of his lies could be believed. There was no illusion about wanting to find Klondike Khartu, the great man of thought and action. He didn't want to see the man who had written a simple story that had so easily been turned into a religion. He didn't want answers to universal questions; he just wanted to see his father, and perhaps then learn something about himself.

"I'll find you, you bastard," Franklin said, before closing the door on his old life and falling into the insulating comfort of a new and false identity.

SIXTEEN

Angel sat on her bed and watched as a few rays of light crept in through a broken blind. Why should she go to bed? It was her 17th birthday and there was no reason she couldn't stay up. She could wander the empty streets all day if she liked, the sun wouldn't burn her skin as it did everyone else. The streets were there to explore as long as she kept her sunglasses on. A freedom she'd regularly exploited, mindful of how precious it was to be the only human walking the streets of her city by day. The experience sometimes tinged with sadness, the vacant spaces singing of loneliness, the absence of people making the structures appear pointless. She didn't feel like chancing that melancholy today.

She moved her hand into the beams of light and the warmth danced across her fingers. An amazing proposition occurred to her. It was such a simple and easy experiment she could hardly believe it hadn't presented itself before. The theory was sound, based on years of experience. If she could withstand boiling water on her body and could put out birthday candles with her mouth, if she could expose her skin to naked flames, then the experiment she had in mind would undoubtedly prove successful.

There had been many experiments over the years, but she had never tried anything quite like this. She'd often take things out of the oven when they were too hot for normal people to touch. She'd held her hand in naked flames, dipped her fingers in methylated spirits and set them ablaze. It was magical the way the flame would dance around her beautiful white skin, never leaving a mark and causing only the faintest sensation of warmth.

All this playing with fire had proved little other than her skin's unique heat-resistant properties. She had read books and seen TV programs about other people who displayed similar talents, people who could walk on hot coals or eat fire. Angel assumed these feats were mind over matter rather than an esoteric cell structure. This new experiment would prove her mind had little to do with the properties of her skin, and that she was more unique than she'd previously conceived. If the experiment failed then she would be left blinded by it. A risk she felt worth taking.

Angel got out of bed, put on her swimming costume, usually saved for evening swims, and went into the backyard. She flicked her folded towel into the air holding it firmly by one side and laid it out on the already warm patch of grass. Lying down so that she was facing the sun, her hands rested on her sunglasses for a few moments as she contemplated her intended action. It was not the sun's rays burning her skin that she intended to verify, that she had tested on numerous occasions. While other people burned within a few minutes, her skin had never even reddened. No, this time it was her eyes, her precious angel eyes that she was going to put to the test.

Angel removed her sunglasses, tentatively opened her eyes and then stared purposefully into the burning heat of the sun.

SEVENTEEN

Patrick sat calmly in his car, resting his hands gently on the wheel as the old man's ute towed him steadily along. What else could he do but go with the situation. He wound down the window and allowed the cool night air to blow in. Its crisp freshness chilled his skin and the black openness of the night helped him forget. Hopefully it would not be long before he was back on the road and travelling towards oblivion once more; or had he already reached it?

The ute came to a stop and Patrick remembered he was still required to brake. He slammed his foot down and the car jolted to a stop, a few millimetres to spare between the two vehicles. Both men got out and met at the hook-up point. Ancient removed the tow-rope, placed a hand on his lower back and straightened up. It was the first sign of age Patrick had seen the older man display.

"We'll put her in the work shed." Ancient pointed to a shed that sat at the back of his house.

"Didn't we have to walk before? How come we can drive here now?"

"I didn't know you so well then," the old man answered and then moved his truck. Together they pushed Patrick's car into the large shed.

"Won't take us long to get this worked out. It's probably just a bit of roo meat jammed somewhere. Don't worry, you'll be back on the road to nowhere soon."

Patrick was a little peeved at the old man's perception.

"Who says I'm going nowhere?" he asked.

"It's a long way from anywhere out here."

"Maybe I just wanted to see the Mini lights."

"That's Min Min lights," Ancient corrected. "Anyway, nothing wrong with escaping."

"Escaping! Who's escaping? I'm on holidays."

"Oh, I see, well then you have nothing to worry about."

"Who said I was worried?" Patrick said.

"No one, certainly not me."

"Well I'm glad that's clear."

"Oh yes, very clear." The old man hit a few things around the radiator.

"Is it going to be okay?" Patrick asked.

"Once you get some sleep everything will be fine. You'll have to help me fix the car tomorrow. We start early, before the sun comes up. You can sleep on the lounge."

"Don't you sleep during the day?" Patrick asked.

"That nocturnal nonsense never did anyone any good. No I'm a traditionalist. I sleep at night and work in the day like people have always done. I'll wake you at five." Ancient dropped his tools and walked into the house.

Patrick began to follow him but stopped as a cool breeze blew past. He looked up into the clear night sky. There were more stars than he'd seen in his lifetime of living under city smog. A bright light moved quickly across the sky and for a moment the multitude of tiny stationary bulbs lost their significance, Patrick's thoughts turning to Kirby and the PetroSynth space station. Of course they'd used some technical wizardry to mask visibility from Earth. The station couldn't be detected by the naked eye. And Patrick's naked eyes felt tired, more tired than ever before. His lids drooped and he stood ready to be consumed by what had been chasing him, what he thought he was running from. Instead, it all faded as his mind filled with the idea of Kirby gently hovering around him as she orbited the globe.

When he lay down on the lounge his eyes quickly closed. He could feel the comfort of sleep gently consuming his mind and relaxing his fatigued body. The cool darkness of night had never seemed so perfect for rest.

EIGHTEEN

Data, graphs and charts filled Kirby's screen. While it was clear to her what each component of information meant, how they all worked together to create an informed opinion, they momentarily blurred, becoming the background to her thoughts, to her brain's desire to process. She didn't need the computer any more to rewind and replay the last message from Patrick. It was ingrained in her memory and she could add layers to it in a way the computer never could. She could hear and see him speak those accusing words while recalling the smell and feel of his presence. The warmth of his body close to her, the comfort and joy she felt in his arms. That feeling of belonging she'd never had with anyone else. Was it really just a chemical reaction – his pheromones playing havoc with hers – or something beyond the physical?

She was a doctor, a physicist, computer specialist and above all a scientist. She didn't ignore ethical issues; on the contrary, it was her responsibility to utilise her expertise to advance humanity. These were all aspects of her that Patrick loved, or so he'd told her many times over the past 10 years. Much of that time her professional life had been engaged on a project that would send the human race into the far reaches of space and perpetuate the species beyond the confines of its origins. Patrick had always been there, whispering his support in her ear, telling her how much he admired her for the work she was doing. Okay, so there were a few grey areas, as Patrick had annoyingly pointed out. Darwin had taught her it wasn't the fittest that survived, it was those more adaptable to change. Where did Patrick and his moral sensitivities have their place? She could hear his voice whispering in her ear still, 'What was survival if its cost left you spiritually bankrupt? As a species shouldn't we not only strive to survive but also strive to evolve?'

Was that just Patrick's idealist nature, his narrow perspective of what he considered to be the big picture. PetroSynth had spent billions on this project when that money could have been used to feed millions of people, to relieve poverty, wipe out third-world debt, give education to those whom society had otherwise abandoned. In the immediate future Kirby's work would only help a few hundred people, but long term it would ensure humanity's survival. Failure to participate in an endeavour of such historical significance would have been an immorality of its own.

How could she stand by and watch the human race be trapped on a planet that would ultimately cease to exist, when she had the opportunity to send them into eternity? The notion of eternity made her pause. Who was she kidding? There was no real eternity – not in the physical world, nor the scientific one where she lived and breathed, not even in the artificial life of the space station. The second law of thermodynamics made that clear enough. Everything would cease at some point. Everything would expend the energy it had and move to a state of inactivity. We were so clever in our constructions, Kirby thought, in our science, in our minds. So clever we were making our one and only home unlivable.

'Bloody Patrick,' Kirby thought. How dare he place uncertainty in her mind when she'd been so focused and clear? Now, as she checked the data on the reconstituted primates, with everything working to plan, all results positive, his words tugged at the edges of her thoughts, slowly but surely undoing the threads that held it all together.

Kirby detected a cool minty smell blow across her shoulder and turned to see Professor Gardener.

"How does it look, Kirby?"

"One hundred percent survival, all the data storage and reconstitution systems are working perfectly. As long as the power source stays stable, I can't see why people in data storage wouldn't stay intact indefinitely. Even without a power source the data records would still be stored. To verify we've shut down power for twenty-four hours on data bank Delta. We will reboot and attempt to reconstitute the digital code to living tissue at eight hundred hours." Kirby wanted to feel pleased with her answers but kept imagining Patrick's disapproving face.

"It is an ambitious project, but colonisation of the stars is a worthy ambition," Professor Gardener said, trying to sound grand and authoritative.

"We could be ready for the final stage within days. It seems premature but we will do a human trial tomorrow."

"Excellent." His eyes glowed with success.

"Of course the time scale we've had is minuscule. To test this properly we'd need a thousand years or so. Frankly I'd have liked another twelve months before the human stage," Kirby added.

"We'll just have to make do with the ten years we've had. The human test will be the same as the primate, you'll see. Theoretically there is nothing wrong with the system."

Kirby thought for a moment about the system. Not the technical system; that was working fine. It was the social and political system she felt had let her down. The system that had promised so much knowledge and so much reward. Now all she seemed to have was a lost husband and a foul smelling, mint-laced suitor.

"Have you thought more about whether you will join the crew?" the Professor asked.

"I don't know. At this point I really don't know," Kirby replied. She swivelled on her chair, turning her back to the professor and returning to her work. Professor Gardener took the hint; the conversation was over. He allowed a flashing light on one of the lab consoles to take his attention and he moved to investigate. From the corner of her eye Kirby recognised his actions as another haplessly disguised attempt to cover his incessant interest in her. She tuned out the professor's lingering presence, allowing the details before her to take precedence in her thoughts. Still Patrick and the uncertainties he created loitered there, resistant to her focus.

NINETEEN

Costas pulled his chair into his desk, stubbed out his synthetic tobacco cigarette and looked at his computer.

"Phone, audio only."

"Number please?" the computer prompted.

Costas typed in Eko's number from the printout. He hit the Enter key, sat back and waited.

"Hello, this is Eko."

"Hello, Eko," he said. "A friend gave me your number."

"Really, and which friend might that be?"

"Daddy. Daddy Fong."

"Daddy Fong is dead."

"Yes, I know. He gave me your number before he passed on. Can we get together, or is your schedule too full?"

There was an awkward pause. "I'll meet you at midnight at the Paper Moon. Do you know it?"

"Well enough to say let's meet somewhere else. I'm not interested in buying you a drink for five hundred Euros. I'm interested in you."

"My apartment at midnight. I'll transmit the address now."

"Thanks. See you tonight," Costas said, but only the dial tone heard him.

The address came up on his screen along with a seductive photo of the young Eko. He may well have to list this under 'miscellaneous' on his expense account.

TWENTY

Angel had been staring into the sun for at least an hour and she could still see perfectly. As far as she could tell her sight had not faltered. Not only had she not been blinded but there were no spots, no blurring, no perceivable damage at all. Confirmation her theory had been proven and her heat-resistant properties were more than skin deep. Every molecule in her body displayed the same remarkable qualities.

Satisfied, Angel put on her sunglasses and got to her feet. Her skin was warm and tingled softly from the direct exposure, but as always not a blemish. She flicked her glasses back on to her forehead and turned once again to the sun. It seemed impossible but there was no mistaking what her eyes saw. An object of some kind flew directly into the sun. A comet or asteroid would burn up before getting that close. Millions of objects were on a collision course with the sun, all of them would disintegrate on approach. How could something fly into it like that, as if penetrating its surface on target for the core?

Angel got up, threw her towel over her shoulder and moved out of the heat with purpose. She had some serious calculations to do.

She sat at her computer, the heat of the day poured through her open window and she could hear the soft sounds of the house's occupants sleeping in their cocooned rooms. Angel's fingers caressed the keyboard as she began to consider the possibilities and repercussions of what it was that made her different. It blurred and mixed and swirled with what had just happened, with what she had seen, what only she could have seen.

TWENTY-ONE

"There are only three things you need to worry about. What you were, what you are and what you'll be."

Patrick comprehended the past, present and future concept, but wasn't sure where the old man was heading with what he presumed was advice.

"For me, what I was now consumes what I am because I didn't think about what I would be. Don't despair, there is hope," Ancient continued. "If I can put right the disasters that came from what I was, then what I will be, will be ...."

"Good?" Patrick suggested.

"Perhaps 'good', but I'll accept better," Ancient replied. The old man placed his hand on Patrick's shoulder. He tightened his grip and Patrick was surprised by the strength in those old fingers. The digits dug in deeper and the old man began to shake Patrick vigorously by the shoulder. Patrick could feel the old man's nails begin to pierce his skin and the pain startled him awake. The old man was leaning over him, gently rocking him awake, his hand resting lightly on his shoulder.

"Time to work on your car. Let's get you back on that road to nowhere." Ancient straightened up.

"I'll see you out there," Patrick mumbled. He moved his hand over his shoulder, unsure where his sleep had ended; what part of his conversation with the old man was his dream and what was reality.

The old man moved to the door of the secret room he'd entered the previous night. Patrick caught another glimpse of the old communications equipment as the door slid shut. Patrick got to his feet. He pulled on the door but it was locked. Glancing around, he saw the door he'd entered the day before. Somewhat relieved that it was unlocked, he moved into the early morning. It was still dark with a faint glow of dawn and the air was fresh and cool on his face. He could just make out the figure of the old man walking towards the shed and so he followed.

Halfway across the lawn Patrick stopped walking and looked to the east. He saw the first glimmers of light appearing on the horizon. The warm rays of sunlight stretched across the clearing, as if striving to reach him, longing to touch him. And when those mild morning beams finally caressed his face, they illuminated the truth he'd been hiding in the dark crevasses of his mind. The injustice that he should know what billions did not distressed him. For a moment he was uncertain who was worse off – himself for knowing, or the billions in their ignorance. Perhaps they were all doomed and it did not matter what was true, what was false, who knew what or when they knew it.

The old man stopped up ahead and turned around. He saw the look of despair on Patrick's face. It was an expression he knew far too well, one he'd seen reflected on many surfaces. Ancient forced his own face into a smile, deliberately contradicting the instincts of his facial muscles to contort into the same gloomy display. It distressed him to see Patrick look so defeated but he was not going to allow it to overwhelm them both.

"Is it really that bad?" the old man asked.

Patrick dropped his head, unable to answer.

"You know, there are only three things that you ever need to worry about. What you were, what you are and what you'll be."

Patrick looked up: "Haven't we had this conversation, or was that a dream?"

"Maybe both, so I guess I don't need to repeat myself."

"No, you don't," Patrick replied. "What did you do that was so terrible?"

"I don't know if I can say. I've buried it so deep. It underlies every thought and instigates every action, but it chills my soul to think of saying it."

"It can't be that bad," Patrick replied.

"Well, what is causing you such despair then?"

"Truth."

"Truth?" Ancient said. "Truth is like time; it's relative. It only takes a small movement or gravitational force for two people's relative times to lose sync, even by one billionth of a second. It takes even less for two people's perspective of truth to become unsynchronised."

"What about a world truth? Is that relative too?" Patrick asked.

"World truths are harder to rationalise, and sometimes harder to live with, but yes they are relative too."

Patrick looked up as the sun appeared on the horizon, its eight-minute-old photons creating long shadows on the open landscape before them. He could feel the warmth growing stronger on his troubled face and he wanted to smile like the old man but his jaw would not cooperate.

"Let's forget about the car, go have something to eat, and tell each other these world truths we think we know. How does that sound?" Ancient asked.

"Like a good idea," Patrick replied.

The old man put his arm on Patrick's shoulder and guided him out of the morning light and into the house.

TWENTY-TWO

Staring out the window of her quarters, her arms around her legs and her chin resting on her knees, Kirby allowed her eyes to soften their focus as a large luminous moon came into view. She liked the moon. She liked what she knew about it. She knew its diameter was 3476km and that it orbited the Earth at a distance of 384km. She appreciated the moon's historical femininity. The Romans had called her Luna but to the Greeks she'd been Selene and Artemis. On this populated but lonely space station she was thankful for the illuminating presence of what had become a sort of surrogate sister. Someone Kirby could turn to, depending on the time of day and the orbit of the space station, when she craved distraction, when a beam of comforting light was all her soul needed to feel a little better. Her lunar sister was a reminder of stoical loneliness and dependability, seemingly alone yet locked into orbit around her ever-present partner, the Earth.

And while she contemplated the moon Kirby did not have to think of Patrick. But then she realised that the idea of not thinking of Patrick was actually a thought of Patrick. There wasn't much now that didn't remind her of him. The Earth reminded her of him, because he was down there, and the station reminded her of him because he was not there.

She could feel her anger rising. She missed him, she loved him, and all she had left were his aggravating last words spoken five days earlier, words that resonated in her head as she got to her feet and paced the room. How could he say, 'have a nice life'. How could she possibly have a nice life with him down there, somewhere, and her up here, nowhere, with the moon as her only friend and a rabid professor intent on pursuing and possessing her secret joys?

The door buzzed.

"Come in!" she yelled.

The door opened and Professor Gardener nervously walked in.

"Kirby, sorry to bother you."

"Professor?" Kirby said, doing her utmost to contain her mounting anger. "What do you want?"

"Well, I was wondering if you've thought more about staying on with the colonisation crew."

"I told you, I haven't decided yet."

"I see. Well, I wanted to share something with you. Your honesty earlier impressed me and I have taken steps to rectify the situation." He casually popped a mint into his mouth.

"Yes, I've noticed. It's a refreshing change."

"Thank you. But what I really wanted to talk to you about was the future. You see I want more than anything to be part of the crew. I'm a little old but still very healthy. The problem is that for the project to work we need couples on the crew. People who intend to have children. Well, my wife is not interested in having children or ending her days in space. So I will be looking for a younger partner."

Kirby could not believe what she was hearing. Hadn't he got the hint during their altercation in the lift? It wasn't just the smell of him she disliked; it was everything about him. His greasy hair with visible dandruff, his pasty skin, leering eyes, sour mouth, and coated tongue. His protruding pink nose swelled with ripe blackheads and puss-filled pores. And that was just his physical characteristics. There was no end to the personality traits that offended her. The very idea of him was feeling like an infectious thought, distracting and deflecting her mind from the things she wanted to resolve.

"Anyway, take a look at these papers and let me know what you think. I won't say another word on this matter unless you bring it up. Oh and please keep these documents under lock and key. They are highly confidential and I will need them back." The professor handed Kirby a folder. He backed up to the door, pressed the open button and was gone in a flash, leaving a mild minty aroma.

Kirby slumped into her chair, and opened the folder. There was a handwritten letter on top of some other papers.

Dearest Kirby,

Writing this is very difficult; however I am driven by your beauty and the overwhelming desire to possess your fiery soul.

Kirby slammed the folder shut and threw it into her desk drawer. The last thing she wanted was to read a soppy love letter and proposal of marriage from Professor Gardener. How could he have failed to get the message? Did he have no dignity at all? Was he so obsessed that he was prepared to lower himself ever more at each encounter? Evidently.

Kirby re-established herself at the window. Earth was now in view. She willed Patrick to communicate with her. But the small light on her communications console remained dormant. She pulled her knees back into her arms and stared blankly into space, the comforting light of the moon already out of view. She resolved to clear her mind, keep herself still and at peace until the synthetic phone chimed. She felt her anger stir and wasn't at all sure she could keep it below the surface for long.

TWENTY-THREE

Costas woke, surprised to find himself in his own bed. He tried to sit up but the movement sent a shaft of pain racing through his head. He couldn't remember ever having a hangover this bad. Even the slow opening and closing of his eyelids hurt, sending dull waves of pain back into his brain.

He lay motionless and thought of the night before. He remembered arriving at young Eko's address, an old building in the Plaka. He'd stood at the entrance and looked for the intercom. It was dark, the entrance in a quiet back street, away from the crowds of tourists and locals parading in the warm night air.

He remembered pressing the buzzer.

"Hello," said Eko's voice through the intercom.

"Hi, it's Costas, your midnight appointment."

"Come up." The memory of the buzzer pounded in his aching defenceless skull. Quickly he moved his thoughts to the next thing he could remember – pushing open the door and inspecting the ancient lift that was out of order, climbing the narrow stairway to the top of the building, arriving a little out of breath at the top.

It was getting foggier but some elements were still clear, like Eko waiting at the door of her apartment, looking younger than the digital photo he had seen. Perhaps only sixteen, but as he'd walked in and brushed past her, his nose took in her aroma. The smell at least was clear in his mind, even if the image was frosty round the edges. He had sniffed discreetly; she couldn't have noticed the microscopic twitch of his nostrils. From her scent he concluded that she was in her early twenties.

Costas waited for her to close the door and lead him inside. She walked slowly in front of him. He watched her slender yet shapely body mince from side to side. Her skin-tight black pants and psychedelic midriff top contrasted nicely with the Eshure floor tiles. The apartment had modern furnishings and though small, it looked comfortable and well lived in.

Eko gestured for Costas to take a seat on the lounge and she had sat on a chair opposite him, curling her fine legs together and waiting for him to speak.

"Is this a test?" he asked.

"I'm just wondering what you want," she replied.

"As I said on the phone, Wilfred Fong gave me your number."

"I know you said that. That's why I'm wondering what you want. You see Daddy Fong would never have given another man my number. Daddy Fong loved me. He'd never share me. I'm not what you think I am."

"Really?" Costas asked.

"I only ever have one client at a time. I am faithful to that client until we mutually decide to end the arrangement or, as in Daddy Fong's case, there are unforeseen circumstances. So I know he didn't give me my number. You must have found it somewhere. Did his wife hire you to see if he had been unfaithful?"

Costas shook his head. The memory was getting patchy. She had made some good assumptions and was getting the upper hand. He recalled having decided to tell the truth; his keen sense of smell told him he was not going to get anywhere playing games.

"I'm a detective with the Athenian Police, Homicide Squad, investigating Wilfred Fong's death. I interviewed Mrs Fong and have no reason to believe she has any idea about you. She simply wants to bring her husband's killer to justice."

"Justice? A woman who lives her kind of life wants justice?" Eko's young face flushed with anger. "I'm afraid I can't help you. I wasn't with Daddy that night and hadn't seen him for about three nights. You can check my diary and phone if you like."

"I see. I was hoping you would be of some help. Can you think of any reason anyone would kill Mr Fong?

"Our relationship existed in this apartment. He didn't bring his outside life with him. This was his escape, his oasis."

Costas shifted his weight and moved to stand. His nose told him this was going nowhere.

"I see. I won't take up any more of your time." Once on his feet the height advantage gave him a clear view of her cleavage.

This was a strong memory. It was a clear moment. A moment where he understood if he stayed any longer he might regret it. He was attracted to her and his nostrils quivered with excitement. Sex was out of the question, he was on a case and she had been intimate with the deceased. Best to keep a distance until the case is settled.

"Would you like a drink?" Eko asked.

"No thank you, I really must go."

"You've come out of your way. You know I was quite fond of Daddy Fong. The least I can do is give you a drink."

"All right, I'll have a drink."

Eko fetched two beers from the kitchen and sat on the lounge next to Costas.

"Why did you call Mr Fong 'Daddy'?" he asked.

"That's what he wanted to be called. I don't know why." Her naiveté surprised him.

"You know, you can sleep with me if you like," Eko said.

Costas choked on his mouthful of beer. "Really?" he asked incredulously.

"I'm between clients. And I need some company. Do you have something better to do?"

"Not that I can think of."

"Would you like to try something new?"

Eko put her beer on the coffee table and disappeared behind a door. Costas took the opportunity to check his breath and sniff his armpits. They seemed okay so he assumed a relaxed position.

She returned to the room holding two pills, one blue and one red. The images were getting very frosty. The words were now unclear, the memory hard to hold.

"This one," she said, holding up the blue, "is for me. And this one," she held up the red, "is for you." Eko popped the blue pill in her mouth and swallowed it with a gulp of beer.

"What is it?" Costas asked.

"It heightens your orgasm. It makes both men and women have multiple and lasting orgasms."

"I don't really need to take that," he said, his manhood a little bruised.

"Oh, I'm sure you would be fine without it, but the effect is quite amazing." She smiled enigmatically, then added: "Daddy Fong was also too scared to try it."

"Give me that." Costas took the pill and popped it into his mouth.

"There can be some side effects for men," Eko said.

"Like what?"

"A hangover and maybe mild memory loss, nothing serious."

Costas tried to recall what happened next, but there was nothing but black, empty thoughts. That was all he could remember. He tried to sit up again. The pain in his head was receding, but as he bent to sit up in bed he felt a sharp jab in his abdomen. He threw off the sheet and looked down. His bellybutton was red and swollen with a fresh ring piercing. Dangling from the ring was a small charm. He bent forward, wincing with pain, and examined the violation more closely. The charm looked like the face of an ancient god with sharp strands of hair shooting out in all directions.

Costas touched the wound tentatively, not seeing any way to remove the ring. He gently pulled on a shirt, bending over painfully to pull on his pants, socks and shoes.

He glanced at his watch as he strapped it to his wrist, and discovered he had lost almost twenty-four hours. Not a good start to the case, he thought, and he hurriedly left his apartment.

PART TWO

TWENTY-FOUR

"To be precise it's the sun god Helios that you have hanging from your navel." The young body-piercing artist straightened his back and sifted through his tray of metallic instruments, looking for the correct tool to begin the removal procedure.

"Just get it out of my stomach, now!" Costas said as he tried to sit up. The young man placed a hand on Costas' shoulder and pushed him back down on the operating table.

"It looks like a home done job. Good work, but definitely amateur. You really should leave it in until it heals properly," the young man said as he lightly poked the swollen flesh at the ring's entry point.

"Can you get the fucking thing out of me or do I have to go somewhere else?"

"Okay. Relax."

Costas tried to relax but his stomach muscles tightened instinctively as the piece of metal in his navel was tugged and cut. The surroundings weren't helping him relax. They only gave further fuel to the burning pain behind his eyes. The nouveaux metallic walls reflecting the ultra bright LED operating lights in endless refractions, and the fucking artificial turf flooring. It pissed him off that they had fake grass in their fake operating room. Not like real grass, real grass was soft and flexible. It's fragrance pleasant and comforting to his sensitive nostrils. God damn artificial turf just stuck up straight regardless of being trodden on, its unforgiving new-plastic odour drove like a nail into his already aching head. It had been a relief to lie on the operating table just so he didn't have to feel that synthetic ugliness crunch under his shoes.

The foolishness of the situation seeped in, his indignation at the surroundings a thin mask covering the anger he felt at himself. How stupid and pathetic, how idiotic to be deceived by the guile of a young prostitute, a potential murder suspect no less.

His mind flashed back to when he'd woken that evening, when he'd resisted the urge to yank the offending ring from his flesh. Before seeking professional help he'd allowed his anger and shame to drive his actions, to chase down the perpetrator and catch her before she could flee.

His legs had moved speedily towards Eko's apartment keeping one hand clutched to his gut. The pain was intense but the determination to find her overpowered it. Swearing, cursing, muttering, he'd tried her mobile as he walked. Disconnected – no surprise there – suspicion growing exponentially around her. No surprise again when she failed to answer the buzzer to his repeated pressings. Aggression gave way to acceptance, as futility moved from his finger to his brain. He stopped pressing before the digit became numb. Inappropriately he'd input the police security override code known to a select few Athenian detectives. An unreasonable breach of a citizen's civil liberties in his mind until this moment. Eko had drugged him, pierced his navel and god knows what else. Strangely he'd made it to the safety of his own bed. Hard to know what had happened in between, after that red pill had dissolved into his system and taken his memory. Only Eko knew what indignities he'd suffered.

The overriding pain in his belly had distracted him from other possible injuries. What if he'd been violated in other unspeakable ways – would there be pictures of him on the Internet, the unwitting victim of femdom? He clenched his pelvic floor muscles and all felt intact. Surely he would feel something if he'd been involuntarily probed.

Eko had an old fashioned key lock on her apartment door that Costas had happily kicked in, breaking more civil liberties along the way. It had hurt like hell, a sharp pain driving deep into his gut as his boot connected with the door, but one powerful blow and the door had flown open.

As expected the apartment was empty, completely stripped of everything that Costas had seen the night before. Even the Eshure vinyl floor tiles had been mopped clean.

If only he'd been doing his job properly the night before he wouldn't be faced with this situation. If he'd been doing his job properly he would have kept her on the suspect list and run a mile when she'd suggested they have sex. What was he thinking? He wasn't thinking. That was the problem. He'd acted on instinct, on vanity, on desire.

Eko had to be pursued. Any suspect who vanishes into thin air after rendering you unconscious and piercing your bellybutton had to be hiding something? His attraction to her needed to be kept out of the equation. Still he wanted to believe they had fucked. This whole mess would almost be worth it then. His bruised ego conceded she'd simply drugged him to hasten a run for it. With no clear memory and the lack of any witnesses his report could easily leave out any fault on his part. He was drugged, end of story, a sedative unknowingly dropped in his drink. Why he was still alive was the question beginning to burn.

Before leaving the apartment he'd sniffed around but his faithful nostrils had little joy. The overpowering smell of industrial strength bleach the only thing he could register.

The pulling and tugging at this navel brought him painfully back to the moment and he held firmly onto the side of the operating table.

"Relax. Almost finished," said the young man through his sanitary mast and faux medical garb.

Costas felt a final tug and then a sharp sting from the alcohol swab. He bolted upright and glared at the young man.

"Hold this," the young man said, indicating the swab on Costas' belly. He held the swab lightly against his skin, pleased to have the ring out of his flesh.

"You want this?" The young man held up the ring and charm.

"Yes, it's evidence. Who did you say it was?" Costas asked as he took the charm from the young man's surgically gloved hand and examined it for himself.

"It's the sun god Helios."

"I thought Apollo was the sun god."

"There are many gods. Helios was the original sun god. He fell in love with a nymph named Rhodes and the island where she was born was named after her and become his domain."

"You know a lot about this shit?"

"Gotta know what you are sticking into people," he replied.

"Rhodes, you say?"

"Rhodes."

The piercing artist left the room and Costas dressed himself. He brought the charm up to his nose and sniffed it gently. His eyes rolled back and his eyelids shuddered.

"Rhodes," he whispered to himself and he crunched his way across the artificial turf.

The receptionist caught his eye with her naughty nurse outfit, her partially exposed tattooed flesh. He smiled back, contemplating that on any other occasion he would have put his great charms to use and followed up on that smile. He'd never been with someone who had multiple tattoos and piercings. An arousing and intriguing idea. But nothing would distract him from his course now, not even a seductive tangent such as the girl before him. Eko had made this personal; she had invaded his body in a way no one had before. He would pursue her until he had some answers.

TWENTY-FIVE

Kirby fell into the comfort of her high back desk chair, relieved to be in the privacy of her quarters. She tossed Professor Gardener's bundle of papers with contempt and they landed hard on the surface in front of her. She imagined palpable globs of the professor's stale breath wafting up from his love note. Had he perfumed the letter with some sort of pheromone?

There was nothing the man could possibly do to appeal to her. Was furnishing her with secret documents a last desperate attempt to force a response? If she didn't reply to his love note then she would have to respond to the PetroSynth papers. He was like a pathetic needy pet, willing to humiliate himself for any form of attention and just when Kirby felt she loathed him to the limit of her capacity to loathe another being he managed to find a way to extend it.

She'd avoided him all rotation, despite his leering half-grin and furtive glances being directed her way. He'd been clearly waiting for her to say something, to grant him some response, however minor, to the heart-felt protestations he'd laid bare. She wasn't going to give an inch, holding steadfast to her determination to prevent their eyes from meeting, even a microsecond. It had been like working two jobs, the normal duties of her rotation – evaluating data, checking computer systems, monitoring vital signs – and then the second full time occupation of avoiding Professor Gardener, with his love letters, garlic breath, pasty complexion and company secrets.

She glanced over at the incoming message light on her communications consul only to see that Patrick had failed to contact her again, its inactivity more annoying than its incessant flashing when it was active. The disbelief that he was remaining incommunicado fuelled a seething serpent of anger. Didn't he understand that time was running out, decisions had to be made. While he was off sulking, processing, or whatever it was he was doing to avoid communication with her, their future together was more and more being drawn into question.

When the colonising ships finally left Earth's orbit all she wanted was to be on one. Not like the test subjects she'd been observing, in digital stasis. No, she wanted to be amongst the active crew, part of the technical team that would spend their lives fruitfully collecting and analysing data as the ships took the necessary centuries to pass into various parts of the Galaxy suspected of containing potentially habitable planets. Naturally the crew would propagate while the majority of the human life on board would be suspended in digital stasis, only to be reconstituted when some brave new world had been discovered.

The concept of living and dying in space did not disturb her, in fact it excited her. The potential for unimagined experiences was obvious and the chance to participate unprecedented. If she had Patrick with her then it would be even more satisfying. Was that too much to ask? After all they were only going to live and die on Earth. Why not live and die in space?

She swung round in her chair knocking the professor's note to the floor. She let it lie there as thoughts of Patrick's rejection bubbled to the surface. Was it simply fear? He'd always supported her in the past, what had changed so dramatically that he could not support her now? She laughed to herself, thinking Patrick would see it more as the voyage of the damned than an exciting opportunity to explore. There was the potential for their entire lives to pass without anything more interesting happening than watching time pass and catching a few shooting stars. They would, however, be together, and the ship was large enough not to feel fenced in. It would be like living on a cruise ship. Okay, so no walking in the park, but they had an atrium, some very cool observation lounges and an unrivalled data bank. PetroSynth had spared no expense – the entire history of cinema, every book ever written, the world's collections of art and artefacts digitally preserved and available to be enjoyed in simulated three-dimensional holographic spaces. As they moved further and further away from earth they would be able to pick up the endless hours of radio and television broadcasts inadvertently sent in all directions as humanity strived to entertain itself.

Kirby imagined the day they would be far enough away from the Earth to surpass the first radio transmission. Would they mark it with a gathering? Would they dress in period clothes of the time and solemnly listen to the very first words the human species had sent over radio waves only to burst into a round of applause when all fell silent? The reality suddenly dawning on them that they were further into space than any human signal had ever been. What would that silence feel like she wondered? How would that profound silence feel to Kirby and her shipmates? The only humans listening to that complete and total emptiness the species had so desperately tried to fill.

She lent down, picked up Professor's love note and began to read. She found herself considering his offer and the sudden realisation made her retch. Had she become so desperate to achieve her goals? Professor Gardener was not the only man who was interested in becoming a member of the crew. If she wanted to find a replacement for Patrick she easily could.

Still she read on, skimming through his banal and irritating love protestations.

She threw the love note to the side and picked up the official looking document stamped 'Highly Confidential'. Well that was obvious. They only ever used paper these days if they wanted to keep it secure. It's title was intriguing, "Project Helios – The PetroSynth Priority Initiative." Kirby turned the page and read, her eyes moving quickly over the document as her mind reeled with the information. It all spun and floated around in her brain, merging with Patrick's angry words. Soon it was no longer her voice at all, but only Patrick's as if he were reading the document to her, presenting her with the damning proof of all he'd said in that last stilted conversation.

The papers dropped from Kirby's lap and she pushed herself away from the desk. She slammed her fist down on the communications console.

"Ring me you idiot," she yelled at the silent machinery. "Why don't you just fucking ring me?"

Back in his quarters Professor Gardener's tight-skinned face contorted into an abortive smile. Like the surface of the moon his pock marked face held the memory of his extreme battle with juvenile acne. His scarred cheeks hardly shifted with the broadening of his mouth. The peaks and troughs returned to their resting place as the smile faded and a sense of apprehension took over his expression. She would be reading it now, she would be understanding what he understood and she would soon be his to play with, to engulf with his passion, his ever building desire to touch, taste, smell.

Resting back in his chair he undid his lab coat.

'Computer, run hologram Kirby Alfa Zero." The professor jumped to his feet as a full bodied Kirby appeared in the middle of his quarters. His lab coat dropped to the armchair and he walked naked around the image in front of him. Stopping to face her as he moved closer.

"Computer, remove hologram attire. One item at a time!" The hologram Kirby dropped her lab coat to the floor followed by her blouse, her skirt, her bra, her panties. Professor Gardener was so pleased he'd stolen her digital pattern from the data banks.

He took a step closer, moved his face as close as he could without touching her. They stood naked, face-to-face. The professor closed his eyes and took a deep breath, then opened them as he moved another step forward. He was now inside the hologram. He shivered with excitement and allowed his hands to caresses his own body. The hologram copied all his movements as the professor touched himself where Kirby never would.

'Kirby,' he cried, 'Kirby, I'm inside you now' and he danced and touched and moved and shook and sprayed his foetid semen all over his lab coat and armchair.

The hologram vanished. Gardener fell to the floor and clutched at the semen covered coat. He pulled it to his chest then rubbed it over his body, his hands, his face, imagining his own sour scented fluids were the sweet by-product of love-making with Kirby. Tears ran from his eyes, snot dripped from his nose, urine and semen leaked from his penis as he quivered in self-contempt.

'How could you ever love me?' he buried his face in the stained lab coat and let it soak up his tears and self-loathing until his tears ran dry and self-composure slowly drifted back into his mind as a possibility.

TWENTY-SIX

Patrick and Ancient sat awkwardly on the plain but comfortable lounge in the old man's mud brick house not far from the town of Neverville, a place, Patrick wondered if he would ever get to see, if indeed it actually existed.

"So who's going first?" asked Ancient.

"Toss a coin?" suggested Patrick.

"Yes, let the fates decide." Ancient reached into his pocket and pulled out a coin. "Heads I win, tails you lose."

Patrick got to his feet and took the coin from the old man's hand. "I'll toss it. Heads for me, tails for you?" He looked at the old man and waited for acknowledgment. Ancient nodded his head and Patrick threw the coin into the air. It slavishly obeyed the laws of gravity, spinning first high up into the air on the back of Patrick's thrust, then just as it seemed to want to continue, its potential for upward motion quickly diminished and its direction sharply turned. Patrick's open palm reached out and plucked it from its trajectory before slamming it hard onto the back of his other hand. He slowly raised his cupped palm and fingers to look at the coin.

"Tails!" Patrick said.

"Best out of three?" The old man inquired.

"Not likely, you start." Patrick sat down and looked expectantly at the old man.

"Okay, but this isn't as easy as I thought it would be. You'll have to give me a moment." Ancient covered his eyes with his hands and then gently rubbed his face as he breathed in. His hands dropped to his side as he exhaled.

"I invented PetroSynth," he said quietly.

"What?" Patrick said.

"I genetically engineered the PetroSynth plant. It was my creation."

"What's so bad about that? You did a wonderful thing for humanity. You rid the world of fossil fuels."

"Yes and created the single most powerful corporation in human history and the cohort of leach-like trillionaires who feed off society. People still starve and people still fight and kill each other over money, power, perceived differences. PetroSynth may have cleaned up some of the carbon mess, but it perpetuates the way society is structured. Commerce remains the god most worshipped, humanity a constant casualty of its own ignorance."

"But you could use your money to help people?"

"I said I created the PetroSynth plant I didn't say I owned it. It was taken from me along with some other precious things. But I have a few surprises for PetroSynth Corporation."

"What are you, some kind of geriatric vigilante?"

"It's not about revenge, Patrick, it's about returning order, about fixing something that went wrong. I created this mess through my lack of foresight. I have to fix it. That little ball of energy I dropped in your car, well that, my friend, is really going to screw them! Especially when I start giving them away for free." Ancient chuckled. "So what's your big bloody secret then?" asked the old man.

"The world is going to end," Patrick said seriously.

"Oh, shit," Ancient replied, a grave look of disappointment coming over his face. "When?"

"Soon. Really fucking soon."

TWENTY-SEVEN

Angel straightened her back and looked away from the calculations she had been working on for hours. Her hand sore from writing, her eyes focused but strained. Having everything come to her so easily in the past, it was now quite surprising that she found these computations challenging and time consuming. She couldn't remember ever having to stop and think about mathematical equations before. Solutions had always appeared in her mind the same way vision and sound were received and processed. It was as if she had an unnamed invisible receptor, working like the eyes or the ears but collecting answers instead of sight and sound. It wasn't working at the usual pace now. Was this what it was like for normal human beings who couldn't think as fast as she did, who couldn't feel answers or perceive solutions? Of course the average person would be struggling to grasp the basic abstracts of what she was working on. The intrinsic complexity of the concepts were overpowering her receptors. The answers were like bright lights shining in her eyes. All she needed was time for her pupils to adjust, time for them to fall into place.

Angel ignored her mother's knock on the door and returned her attention to the task before her. She was pioneering a new realm of quantum physics; she didn't have time for idle conversations. Her mother pushed the door open slightly. "Angel, dinner's ready!" her mother said.

"I'm working. I'll be down later."

"Okay, dear, you can reheat it when you're ready."

"Thanks, Mum." Angel said without lifting her head from her work.

The door closed as Angel moved from the slow medium of notepaper to the swiftness of the computer keyboard. She typed furiously as the ideas began to crystallise, the answers presenting themselves in rapid succession, the big picture still evading her. Never mind, just focus on each problem as it occurs, like pieces in a larger puzzle. She couldn't solve this in an instant; its mass was large and expanding, a set of components that needed to work together. Resolution was only going to be found by tackling one piece at a time.

TWENTY-EIGHT

As Costas walked into the warm night onto the Athenian tarmac he felt the familiar vibration of his mobile phone oscillating in his inside jacket pocket. The sound of the PetroSynth fuelled engine almost drowning out the caller. He walked to one side and pushed the phone firmly to his ear.

"Mr Paradisos, this is Mrs Fong, I was hoping you'd be able to tell me how you are progressing?"

"Hello Mrs Fong." Costas immediately pictured her firm athletic body. It was not procedure to talk to a suspect about an ongoing case, but a few things occurred to him in that short moment between recognising who was on the phone and making a reply. Firstly she could be calling because she found him extremely attractive. Despite the recent loss of her husband or indeed as a direct result of the loss of her husband, she was now transferring some feelings or was in need of a strong male in her life. Clearly he would be a candidate for that role given the mutual attraction he had detected at their first meeting. Secondly it was suspicious that she would want to know what was going on so soon after the commencement of the investigation. Perhaps she wants to know that she is in the clear. He'd said he would keep her informed but she hadn't waited for him to contact her. Yes it could only be attraction or suspicion. Better to let her think she's off the hook for the moment.

"I've had some success Mrs Fong, but I must go to the island of Rhodes."

Warm pockets of fuel-heated air blew across his face but left his slicked black hair undisturbed. The mild, almost pleasant, burnt citrus smell of PetroSynth filled is nostrils.

"Rhodes, really?"

"Yes, I think I will find the answers there. I have some very hot leads. Very hot!" He said now remembering young Eko's body.

"Please call me the moment you know anything Mr Paradisos. I'm keen to have this business cleared quickly and those responsible brought to justice."

"Of course Mrs Fong, as does the Athenian Police Department."

"I know you won't let me down, Mr Paradisos."

"Please call me Costas."

"Certainly, Costas. Thank you for keeping me informed, goodbye."

Costas boarded the plane, placed his phone in his brief case and made himself comfortable. The flight would allow him a short respite, perhaps even a few moments to sleep. But when he closed his eyes Eko was waiting. A flash of memory – gently holding her thin form in his large hands, one hand moved to support the back of her head and held it gently as their lips met. Softly at first, tentative, then open mouthed with forceful tongues and hardened lips. His free hand moved down her body, slowly exploring its contours, its shape almost invisible to the eye. His fingers crept across her inner thigh, lightly stroking her silken skin, but moving purposefully towards her crotch. His finger sat softly at her moist, thinly fleshed aperture before penetrating slowly. He felt her body move against his and writhe at the control of his fingers. He could smell the sweet scent of her excitement as if perceived by every pore of his skin.

A tap on the shoulder brought Costas back and he opened his eyes to an attractive stewardess.

"We've arrived in Rhodes, Sir."

"Already!" He said with surprise. "Thank you." He lifted his jacket from his lap and noticed the small wet spot on his trousers.

Costas walked from the plane, expertly covering his wet patch with his jacket folded over his arm and held at the correct height. Had he been dreaming about Eko or was it a memory? Had he experienced more with Eko than he could fully recall, that little pill causing him memory loss? What a memory to lose! Surely if he'd ended up in bed with Eko his brain would have found a way to save it. No chemical could destroy that experience, he simply needed to find a way to access it.

He checked into his hotel and changed out of his soiled suit pants and sticky boxer shorts. With no clear leads he found himself walking along the ancient city walls, unsure if even his reliable nose could get him out of this dead end situation. It was feeling like a fruitless trail.

He moved through the streets of the medieval town going from shop to shop, looking for anything that matched the charm of the god Helios he'd found hanging from his navel a few nights before. A slim lead, but that was the nature of Eko and there was little else to go on.

Finding nothing but tourist souvenirs he moved on to the museum at the Palace of the Masters. Perhaps here he would find some information amongst its exhibits. Wandering its dimly lit corridors and rooms he found some pieces representing Helios but they were radically different to the one he held in his palm. What little was written to explain these exhibits failed to assist him.

He moved out of the Palace and saw the gates to the city walls were open. The seven-century old walls impressed him with their grandeur and durability and for a moment he allowed himself to feel like a tourist. It was a pleasant warm evening and a nice change from the built-up hustle and bustle of Athens. A walk in the night air would help clear his mind, would help him think of a new approach to the whole case.

He strolled along the city walls, his attention drawn to the well lit medieval town then across the dry moat to the new city with its high-rise resort towers. The thought of giving up the pursuit of Eko crossed his mind. There must be better leads he could find if he tried harder in Athens. Mr Fong was a powerful man and Eko could only benefit from him while he was alive. And that call from Mrs Fong definitely required follow up, especially if his instincts about attraction were correct.

Costas walked up onto a raised platform that looked out over the deep arid moat. While it was flooded with bright arch lamps he wondered how it might look during the day, in natural light. He pushed his way through a group of tourists and stood at the edge. He wedged himself into a cutaway section of the parapet. With both hands holding either side of the gap, he looked down and it occurred to him that he was wasting his time. This lead was as dried up and dead as the dusty remnants of the ancient moat below. He should get back to Athens as soon as possible. Eko was nothing more than a ruse to keep him off the scent. He tried to move away from the opening in the wall but a shabby little man wearing a crumpled seersucker suit was blocking his way. Costas turned and looked over the view once more, hoping the little man would go away. Before he knew what was happening he felt his feet being lifted out from under him and he toppled over the edge.

The little shabby man made his way quickly through the crowd of tourists as Costas desperately clawed and grabbed trying to stop his downward slide. His hands took hold of a protruding stone and his feet shuffled and slid until finally finding footholds in the broken surface. The growing kerfuffle of onlookers jostled and swelled before a hand reached down and pulled him to safety. Costas saw the seersucker suit making its way through the crowd and quickly pursued. The little man turned briefly and saw that Costas was on his tail. His brisk walk turned into a steady run, then as Costas gained ground the short man shifted into full speed. His little legs moved rapidly over the old stones of the Venetian wall, his small body weaving easily through the crowd.

They ran off the city walls and into the old town, the little man weaving in and out of tourist groups, racing down the narrow streets and ducking round corners. Costas kept right behind him, just short of catching him. Close, but not close enough to risk a tackle. If he missed he'd lose him altogether and his belly was hurting like hell. The last thing he wanted was the wound to split open.

They ran out of the old town, through one of the many ornate gates, both dodging and weaving a continuous stream of PetroSynth Mopeds that sped past. As they ran along the harbour front the little man increased the distance between them. Costas couldn't believe the speed with which those short, seer-suckered legs were moving; three or four times the rate of his own. Just as Costas started to made some ground the shabby little man jumped on the back of a parked moped. He tapped the shoulder of the young man at the controls and the pair were off, leaving only a faint smell of burning PetroSynth.

Costas slowed himself down and then stopped. His waist bent and his hands held onto the top of his legs as he gasped for air. The pain from his navel quickly forced him up as he saw the little seer-suckered bastard and his accomplice disappear behind the city walls. Breathing heavily, he sat himself on the nearest bench and closed his eyes. When he opened them he could not help but notice a building. He slowly rose to his feet in amazement, still breathing heavily. The top section of the building in front of him had a triangular frame. There were several sculptures within that frame, the centrepiece however, stood out clearly as if it were being illuminated by a giant spotlight. At least that is how it appeared to Costas, but in reality it was the golden dawn rays of the sun that highlighted the images. It was the sun god Helios and its radiant beams shone down on Costas, the sculpture being a perfect match for the charm he still had pressed in his palm. He felt a hand rest lightly on his shoulder. He turned quickly and took hold of it firmly.

"Eko!" he said.

"What took you so long?" she replied.

TWENTY-NINE

Professor Gardener sprayed a few jets of minty breath freshener into his mouth and excitedly opened the door to his office. His phone buzzed and he pulled it from his coat pocket. Closing the door behind him he read the reminder notification of his meeting with Kirby. He'd been waiting all evening for the moment she would acquiesce and tossed the phone on his desk now that moment was at hand.

Another few jets of mint to be sure, though he preferred to have a savoury taste lingering on his palate. Best not offend Kirby's sensibilities. Once he'd won her over he could move on to the next stage, corrupting her into the glories of foetid cheeses, spiced meats and mustard coated offal. Together they would explore the pleasures that savoury delights could bring to a union.

For now he'd concentrate on the first stage of his operation. He opened the built-in wardrobe and examined his reflection in the mirror on the inside door. He had to hand it to himself, giving Kirby the Helios document before the station wide briefing and ensuing communication lock-down was, by his own reckoning, a dangerous yet ingenious course of action. Soon it would deliver the deliciously desirable young woman into his arms. No longer would he be considered the social misfit with bad breath and flaky skin. His image, indeed his entire social standing would be ameliorated by her acceptance of him. And he would be her saviour, her deliverer from death and destruction. Helios was indeed dangerous information to know, a document that had seen the demise of many, but reading it would convince Kirby of the need to escape. She would see the sense of it all, she would gladly take his hand and join him for a life of universal exploration.

Looking in the mirror, he adjusted his tie, flicked his thinning fringe to one side and brushed the white flakes from his shoulders. She would be arriving soon for their meeting. It was all falling into place.

But what if she remained unconvinced? What was plan B? The all-consuming desire to possess her had become a major distraction. Had he thought it all through? He closed his eyes and breathed deeply, his heart pounding, the blood flow giving him confidence.

His eyes opened and he stared at his reflection. This wasn't the first challenge he'd overcome. There must have been some skill and expertise employed to gain his current standing within PetroSynth. Somewhere beneath the surface, beneath the flaky skin, the wafting collection of odours that emanated from his person, was a strong and powerful man, a man to be reckoned with, a man of great capabilities, unrivalled intelligence, passions and intense love. Misunderstood by his socially connected wife – what did she know with her constant refrains, her false claims that it was her influence, her rich and powerful family and their networks that had opened doors for him. What did it matter; a door opening is useless unless you know what to do when you walk through it. He'd known what to do, most of the time. He would not fail with Kirby, just as he'd not failed with his career. She would submit, she would be his, completely.

Gardener glanced at his watch. There was still time before Kirby was due for their meeting.

'Computer, run Kirby simulation Beta'. A holographic Kirby walked into the room wrapped in a white robe, looking dishevelled, as though she'd spent the day copulating. Gardener smiled at the nuance of the program. He could have made it so she appeared in the middle of the room, but it was comforting to have her walk through the door as though she had done many times.

"Good evening, you look amazing," Gardener said as he began to remove his clothes.

"Good evening my dearest," replied the holographic Kirby.

"Come and sit on my lap. You know you love to," Gardener instructed and the digital Kirby complied. He loved that she didn't occupy real space. He became surrounded by her, his pale naked body consumed by her luscious holographic projection, his mind filling the gaps between what was real and what was digital. Without prompting, holographic Kirby got to her knees and despite the professor's faux protests began kissing his pasty white thighs, moving closer to his groin.

The door buzzed.

'One moment! End program!" Digital Kirby disappeared and the professor quickly dressed. He stole a rapid glance in the mirror before shutting the wardrobe and then opening the office door.

"Professor Gardener," Kirby said as she entered the room. The door closed behind her and she stood firmly at the end of his desk. Gardener, falsely sensing an imminent victory over Kirby, didn't register the determination and strength in her tone or stance and he casually returned to his chair.

"Yes, Kirby. What is it?" He said confidently, certain that soon he would be exploring the glories of what lay concealed under her lab coat.

"I need to go back to Earth urgently, Professor."

"Back to Earth?" he said with clear disappointment.

"Some personal issues I need to resolve," Kirby said, giving away little of her desperation to leave.

"Have you read the report I gave you?"

"No, I haven't had time. Not with all the extra activity."

"This is a very bad time, Kirby. We have been put on full alert. We are working round the clock. The first colonists will be arriving in a matter of days and we'll be digitising on a mass scale. I can't see that we can do that without you."

"Well you'll have to, Professor. I must return on the next shuttle."

"Kirby, if you are returning because of something you have read in that document I must warn you to consider your actions seriously. You could get us both killed."

"Professor, I'm not interested in your love notes or your official bloody secrets. I want this life in space as much as you do, but I need to resolve something on Earth before I leave. Surely you can understand that?"

"We will all get a chance to go back to Earth before any ships leave this station. You'll have time to say goodbye to friends and loved ones. But right now I need you here."

"Fine. But forget about ever approaching me on a personal level again. I will make anything you say or do public. Oh, and I read your little report and your sickening love note made me vomit all over it. Choke on that you red-nosed garlic-breathing pimple!" Kirby slammed her fist on to the door release and walked out before the professor had a chance to say a word.

The professor sat for a few moments, unprepared for this moment of uncertainty. Pieces of his failed plan falling rapidly about him, imploding, drawing him in, tearing his life into unrecognisable shreds. Expectations heartlessly dashed. Kirby walking away fully clothed, his position on the station and career jeopardised, his own life in peril. Self-loathing and contempt frothed in his throat like irrepressible bile.

The names she'd called him were nothing compared to what he thought of himself. He was a garlic-breathing pimple, he was a lecherous leering slime, he had flaky skin and dandruff and an unnatural obsession for younger women and salami sandwiches, sometimes apart but preferably together. His wife loathed him and the contempt from his colleagues and subordinates was palpable. Finally it was time to face the reality of his personality, of his condition, his predicament. But the pain was too deep, the reality too severe, too horrifying and ugly. He tried to look inward but his mind wouldn't let him. There was only one road to salvation and his ego was determined to take it. Faced with the alternative of a personality meltdown what choice did he have? The word floated in his mind and pushed the foaming bile of reality back from the surface. Containment.

He pressed a button on his communications console.

"Security!" he said with all the misdirected anger of self-denial. "I need to report a breach."

THIRTY

"I think I've found the problem?"The old man said as he pulled his hand out from the inner workings of the car. He held a slimy oval object up to the light for Patrick to see. "A Kangaroo eyeball caught in your fan belt. It should work fine now."

Patrick turned the key and the engine started perfectly. He shifted into reverse and the car eased out of the shed.

"Fantastic," Patrick said.

"Looks like you're on your way," said the old man.

Patrick turned off the engine and got out of the car. He joined Ancient as the old man was wiping his hands clean of engine grease and kangaroo cells.

"You know I really am going nowhere."

"I know. Why don't you just go home? You have one, don't you?" the old man asked.

"That whole thing about the world ending, I didn't actually tell you how," Patrick said.

"Does it matter?"The old man shrugged.

"Of course it matters. If enough people knew then maybe it could be prevented."

"Seems to me that everything must end sometime, nothing is constant. Well, change is constant, but what makes you think this isn't Earth's 'sometime'?"

"Because I don't want to die just now."

"You've got yourself a healthy selfish motivation there, human, honest – but definitely selfish."

"Ancient, my wife has been floating around in space for the last twelve months working on a top secret project to send humanity into the galaxy, to find new planets where we can establish human colonies. She must have known that the grand plan to send humanity to the far corners of the universe was actually only an escape route for the rich and famous. I've seen the documents, Ancient. There never was any genuine attempt to fix carbon emissions. Okay, so the PetroSynth plant neutralises carbon but PetroSynth Corporation's own carbon output has risen, as if they had some god-given right to pollute because of their magic wonder plant. And carbon is only one problem; what about all the other toxic shit that humanity pours into the air we breathe and the water we drink twenty-four bloody seven. The Earth is one big melanoma factory. But if you have enough money then you can piss off out of here and leave the rest of us to die. You can sleep peacefully, if you call being vapourised, your genetic code broken down to ones and zeros and stored on a hard drive as sleep. Hardly restful to be dormant in data storage, is it? Just plain selfish bullshit! Put your life on hold while the plebs live and breed on your spaceship, gathering information, looking after plant life and searching for a new home. And then when a nice new world is all set up you can come back to life and exploit the crap out of it. Not only do you get to exploit one generation you get to exploit their descendants. I can't believe Kirby wanted me to go with her, to be a crew member, to have children who would grow up to slavishly work for the survival of the rich, the connected and the moderately talented celebrities who happen to have more money than morals!"

"It's still the survival of humanity," Ancient said.

"Genetically they're human, but I'm not convinced about their souls," said Patrick.

"What's so special about the human soul?"

"We're the only living creatures on this planet that have conscious thought. We ask questions and have an understanding of our own mortality and some of us strive to be better," Patrick said.

"So because the human mind is filled with questions and some answers that makes them the only conscious beings?"

"Yes," Patrick replied firmly.

"What if all other living creatures apart from humanity are born with an understanding of universal truths. Seems to me they tend to live their lives in sync with nature rather than in opposition to it. They don't destroy to the capacity and scale that people do. Perhaps humanity is wasting its time trying to find answers to questions that every other living being already knows instinctively?" The old man smiled.

"That's bullshit," Patrick said.

"So says your human brain, which is all you have to work with, I know."

"Look, all I'm saying is that these bastards shouldn't be allowed to run off while the rest of us die. All their money and resources could be used to solve our problems; instead it creates them," Patrick said.

"But what will they have to spend their money on? How can they be considered rich once they leave all their assets here on Earth? Surely it's the Earth that has made them rich. Personally I say let them go. We should have sent them off years ago. I'm sure the entire senior executive of PetroSynth will be on board."

"Well of course. It's their bloody project, Governments can't afford this crap."

"They might find they are in store for a very rude awakening after their digital slumber..."

A loud beeping sound interrupted Ancient. Both men turned towards the sound coming from the house. "I'll be back in a minute," Ancient said as he walked off and disappeared into the house.

Patrick leaned against his car with the starlit night filling his gaze, contemplating humanity's future in the dark unknown. It felt better having talked to someone, but sharing the knowledge didn't stop the futility of it gnawing away at his questioning human mind. The separation from Kirby was taking its toll. Twelve months they'd wasted, their relationship continuing over the vacuum of space between them, through satellite communications and irregular space shuttle mail runs. Now that vacuum seemed emptier than ever, having absorbed every speck of their connection. Anyone at Kirby's level must have known what was going on, but until he actually asked her plainly, how could he be certain Had she been fooled along with the rest of the human race, along with himself? He'd not given her much of a chance to speak. Their last conversation overflowing with accusations, all output, no input. It wasn't the first time he'd let fly only to find later he'd been a little rash. He made no claim to being the perfect communicator. Fuck, he was no better than the rich corporate sharks of PetroSynth, selfishly fleeing Earth without giving anyone any warning of what they knew, but just like them he'd not given Kirby a chance.

The old man reappeared from the house and walked towards Patrick with a strange determination in his stride, his soft features now looking harsh and angular.

"It's more desperate than I thought!" he said.

"What is?" asked Patrick.

"We must leave immediately. We'll take your car. It's more comfortable."

"I need to make a phone call," said Patrick.

"Later, when we're on the road," Ancient said as he climbed into the passenger seat.

Patrick leant into the window and looked irritably at the old man.

"But where are we going?"

"Does it matter? I'll explain on the way, just get in now and drive." The old man waved his hand impatiently and then leant over and opened the door pushing it into Patrick. Patrick reluctantly got behind the wheel, turned the key and listened to the soft hum of the engine.

"Well?" the old man barked, "you said you wanted to live, save the planet? Let's get a move on, or would you rather stay and be a dead man going nowhere?"

Patrick shifted the car into gear and pulled out of the shed. He didn't know where the old man was taking him or where this would lead. It didn't seem to matter. Ancient's sense of purpose was infectious and the alternative of continuing his flight into the unknown was no longer appealing. He'd been out on the open road looking for some kind of answer, some way of dealing with the information he carried. Now he wanted to be somewhere, he wanted to be in the company of people, perhaps even do something to help. He didn't know why but staying with Ancient felt like the only course of action to take.

THIRTY-ONE

The incessant knocking at her bedroom door finally pulled Angel to action. She hit save and shut the laptop, climbed between the sheets of her unmade bed and wriggled around a little.

"What is it, Mum?" Angel said as she jumped out of the bed again, messed up her hair and quickly pulled her dressing gown on over her clothes.

"You didn't come out for dinner yesterday. Are you alright?"

Angel opened the door and gave her best fabricated yawn. As expected her mother peered into the room looking first at the bed to see if it had been slept in. Did her mother truly suspect her of having a boy hidden in her room? A thought confirmed by Linda's glance at the unopened window.

"I'm going to do some work on a physics problem. It's very exciting. Do you want me to explain it?" Angel gave another small yawn, confident her mother would soon be scared off by the idea of having to listen to an abstract physics construct. She had enough trouble wondering how she'd given birth to a child so gifted, let alone actually contemplating any spatial ideas herself.

"Maybe later, darling. Just wanted to see that you were alright."

"I'm fine. I'll eat something later, I promise."

Angel closed the door as her mother's head slowly retracted and then she quickly returned her attention to the laptop.

As her fingers began to fly once more over the keyboard her brain swirling with mathematical calculations, Angel began to hear a mild humming. She stopped typing and cocked her head slightly and tried to focus on the sound. She looked down at her hands and lifted one off the keyboard.

She held it up to the window and the twilight rays of the sun illuminated its surface. She lifted her other hand and traced the glowing edges of her fingers. Pinching a small amount of her skin between her thumb and her forefinger, the hum increased. She brought her hand closer to her face and her piercing blue eyes examined the minuscule pores of her skin. The humming increased again and Angel dropped her hands to the keyboard once more. A moment went by as she looked out the window and into the warm rays of light that filtered through the semi-open blinds. They receded quickly into darkness as the evening began.

And with the movement of the sun, taking its warm rays of illumination, leaving only the artificial light created by human invention, Angel's fingers recommenced their delicate orchestration of creation. She played the computer keyboard as a virtuoso would a grand piano, breathing sighs of wonder at what she was creating. Not knowing where it would take her, not knowing where it would take everyone. Could the sea of antecedents have foreseen what their genetic code would lead to? To Angel, the history of her own coming into being was all part of the wonder of what was erupting from her mind, what was flowing through her brain, pouring through her mind, dripping from her fingers. The technology before her hardly able to keep up with the speed of her creation, its only function now to record as much as possible, to document, to preserve.

The humming increased with every moment. Every idea extrapolated, every thought exploited, every notion she followed amplified the incessant noise. But it didn't distract Angel, it only drove her forward confirming her genius. Each increase in its pitch convinced her she was heading in the right direction, like the applause of an appreciative audience. A small fear emerged. What if she got something wrong? Would the noise lessen? She couldn't stop to test the theory. She could only keep going, committed to what was flowing, allowing any doubt to be drowned by the all-consuming tsunami of creation.

THIRTY-TWO

A strange metallic taste filled Costas' mouth as he woke in his hotel on the island of Rhodes. He swallowed the bitter saliva but the taste remained. He sat up sharply in bed and felt the mild pain of the wound on his navel again. It had been healing well until he gave chase to that shabby little prick in the crumpled seersucker suit. And then Eko, had he seen Eko? His eyes shifted hopefully to the space in the bed next to him. He found only disappointment amongst the pillows and ruffled bedclothes. The headache was back, the same one he'd had the morning after his first encounter with Eko in her Athenian apartment.

Sluggishly he moved out of bed and propped himself against the bathroom vanity. He examined his face in the mirror. His eyes puffy and tired, his thick black stubble brittle to the touch. The metallic taste persisted and he opened his mouth to investigate. His eyes sharpened as he saw a metal stud sitting in his tongue, piercing it about a centimetre back from the tip.

Swearing at his own reflection, his swollen tongue distorted his pronunciation, only causing him to swear more. He retracted his tongue and closed his mouth.

"Thuck, that thucking little thuck," he yelled and brought his fist down firmly on the marble surface of the vanity.

He turned on the water and put the plug in the basin. The steam rose from the hot water and warmed his face. There was little he could do now except find another body piercing surgery and have the offending stud removed.

Costas splashed his face, hoping the hot water would trigger his memory, his mind blank from the moment he'd taken hold of Eko's wrist. For a moment he thought he could recall her being in his hotel room. Was the image of her undressing slowly before him a fantasy or a memory? Had his hands gently caressed her shoulder, his lips pressed against her smooth firm neck? Had his tongue excitedly teased the goose bumped skin of her breast and hardened nipple? Try as he might, his mind could not provide an answer. All he could remember clearly was that moment down by the harbour, holding that delicate hand in his own firm grasp and feeling as though he'd just discovered the Holy Grail. And now it was gone.

He opened his mouth again and examined the stud in his tongue. Angrily he wiped the mirror clear of steam. He held out his tongue and looked underneath. There was a clip on the back of the stud, not unlike an earring. Costas gripped it in his fingers and pulled it from the stem, quickly removing the stud from his tongue. A few drops of blood dripped into the pool of warm water, rapidly dissipated from bright crimson to soft pink.

He moved into the other room and stood by the window bringing the stud into the sunlight to examine it better. There on the outer edge was a small engraving. It looked like houses, Greek houses. There was no mistaking this one, Costas thought.

"Santorini," he said to himself with satisfaction and he ran the stud under his nose for confirmation. His eyes rolled back and eyelids fluttered.

"I'll see you Eko, in Santorini!"

THIRTY-THREE

The various technologies employed to emulate Earth-like conditions all came to naught when Kirby lay in bed. She could feel the space station moving in its orbit about her home planet with a giddy intensity, as though she were stuck on a giant ride in an amusement park. Once that feeling had taken hold she found it impossible to shake. The blood rushing to her head, the overwhelming feeling she was about to fall on to the floor only to suddenly be flung in another direction, her feet rising, her head falling back, her bed the centre of a giant spinning wheel.

It was bad enough, Kirby thought, when she'd deliberately stayed in her quarters, waiting endlessly for Patrick to contact her, but now it was intolerable, being confined there by Professor Gardener. Forbidden to work on the very project that had taken her off the planet in the first place.

Kirby's head spun, the recent past forging with future plans. Just how long would Gardener keep up this security business. It was an interesting romantic technique. She'd underestimated how dangerous he'd become. The change in confidence a result of eating fewer salami sandwiches and smelling a lot less like a chunk of rotted garlic. The minty freshness of his breath had put some conviction into his stride and straightness into his posture. By her simple frankness she'd created a confident cockatrice that was proudly parading its features and standing ready to strike from its coiled reptilian body. It was now clear to Kirby that it was nothing less than her duty to cut him down.

He'd brazenly intruded her quarters ahead of Security and reclaimed the Helios document. He couldn't be sure if Kirby had read it. He would have found it in the bin under her desk; along with his love note and a glob of her spittle. Best let him continue to have doubts about her reading his precious top secret report. Of course she'd read it and it changed everything for her. She no longer wanted to be on the station, feeling as affronted as Patrick had been by the facts she'd now digested. She'd been used, lied to, her knowledge, skill and time extracted from her under false pretences. And bloody Patrick, how dare he think she could've had prior knowledge of the clandestine PetroSynth motives? How dare he suspect her of colluding? She would deal with Patrick and his lack of faith, but for the moment she needed to concentrate on getting off this man-made chunk of metal orbiting the Earth.

Gardener and his amorous advances were the prime obstacles. Violence occurred as her first solution – extreme violence, blood spurting out of his neck from a wound she could inflict using some kind of ad-hoc weapon. There must be something in her quarters that could be fashioned into an implement for Professor Garner's demise. She could break a glass and use a shard, or a pen, a nice sharp Biro plunged into his jugular, a few jagged rips and he'd be on the floor, his pathetic soul separating from his pathetic body.

The contemplation of murder registered with Kirby as being a side effect of the long confinement.

She dropped the Biro that she had been nervously clicking and came to a calm, solitary conclusion. She had to play him for the fool he was and then perhaps she could obtain freedom to move, freedom to do damage.

The doors to her quarters opened and Professor Gardener swaggered in. Now that he could enter her rooms with the authority of his security override she expected he might try to catch her getting changed, to steal a glimpse of a firm, supple breast or her tender shapely back.

"You wanted to see me, Kirby?" asked the professor with cool minty charm.

"Yes, I've been thinking about your offer."

"You wouldn't try and trick me now would you Kirby?" he said.

"No, of course not, Professor. I want my chance to live on one of the colonising ships and I can see that having a partner of your credentials would be a rewarding experience."

"But you told me..."

"I know what I said, but I have been thinking a great deal since our altercation in your office and well, I have to admire you for your persistence." Kirby could not believe her own words, inwardly retching as she kept up the deception.

"I would take it as a great show of your honest intent if you were willing to consummate our arrangement?"

The mere thought of him touching her sent shivers of reproach flying through her entire physical system. She almost disgorged the contents of her stomach there and then into his leering lecherous face. She could practically see the bile clotting his grey hair, running down his cheeks and casing his obtuse red nose.

"Professor, I am still a married woman, and you are a married man. That means something to me. I will need to extract myself from that situation before I can enter another. I have principles," she said, taking the high moral ground as her safety net.

"I see," the professor said, disappointment running through to all his extremities, especially the distended swollen organ bulging in his trousers. "Perhaps just a kiss then. That wouldn't be too bad, now would it? As sign of good faith and then we can see how things develop."

"A kiss?" she said.

"Just a kiss."

"Okay. Just a kiss."

Professor Gardener lent forward with a victorious grin, closed his eyes and puckered up his lips, keeping his mouth slightly open in anticipation of welcoming Kirby's warm tongue. She didn't know where to look. Perhaps best to follow and close her eyes. She lent forward and tentatively placed her lips against the professor's. Swiftly, his arms encircled her and propelled her body forcefully into him. Kirby felt the wind blast from her lungs and her mouth instinctively opened to allow the air to fly out. She gasped for more air but instead got the professor's hot tongue. It slithered around in her mouth like a serpent in desperate search of prey. She had no choice but to breathe in and could taste the professor's mint spiced breath, the underlying guttural tang of his salami sandwich still detectable and it took all her will to prevent herself from vomiting down his gullet.

Kirby pushed herself away from the professor's arms and his tongue slid out of her mouth. She forced a smile on her face and the professor beamed from ear to ear.

"I'm glad you've finally come round, my dear Kirby," he said licking his lips.

"Well, it was only a matter of time," she replied holding in her distaste.

"I'll call off security and we will discuss our future plans tomorrow. You can return to work. Frankly we need you down there as soon as possible. I've advised staff you were ill."

"Thank you, Professor."

"Please, when we're alone you can call me Cyril."

"Okay, Cyril," she replied.

Professor Gardener opened the door victoriously and indicated for the security team to follow him. As soon as the door closed Kirby raced to her bathroom and spat violently into the basin. She grabbed her toothbrush and squeezed an extra thick strip of paste onto the bristles and quickly began to scrub out her mouth.

She looked into the mirror and spat out any remaining cells of Professor Cyril Gardener's saliva that might be in her mouth.

"Sorry, Patrick. That was worse for me, than it ever could be for you."

THIRTY-FOUR

"You know humans have been sending probes and other craft off into the far reaches for almost a century now, all projecting an image of an inquisitive peace-loving, cultured, egalitarian species, when the reality is that humans are violent destructive creatures, killing all including themselves, thoughtlessly consuming resources, poisoning the very air they breathe and the food they eat. Recklessly corrupting the vital food chain and ecology that created and supports them. The ultimate in biting the hand that feeds, experts at ingratitude and ignorance." Ancient took a breath and shifted in his seat.

"I get the picture," Patrick said, his hand steady on the wheel, his focus on the road ahead illuminated by his high beams.

"Do you? Then you are amongst the very few that do. Imagine for a moment, what it would be like if you were not born and bred of this world, that you existed in a different place and time, perhaps you even had a completely different physical means of perceiving your surroundings, different laws governing your existence. Your non-human consciousness hears a noise, a tiny squeak from beyond your sphere of knowing. The squeak continues and steadily increases in volume. Then objects arrive. The objects seem to contradict the onslaught of sound and images that are now constantly bombarding you. You are not human, remember, you are something other, you don't have a human brain that sorts and categorises information, you don't hear these sounds on the radio, you don't watch these pictures on a TV screen. They wash over you like water, they hit you like wind, they drench you like a storm, they permeate your being and you don't know how to turn them off. You can't turn them off because your non-human form would die if it blocked its receptors. You have to let the good in with the bad; you have no choice but to listen and see and to feel every bit of information being hurled at you. Your only option is to move out of range, but the noise just keeps coming. It travels faster than you can ever imagine.

"How does any of this help us now, old man?"

"Exactly the response I'd expect, disappointing, but exact. To that being, Patrick, does rich or poor matter, does good or evil matter, do social unrest, political machinations, sex and love and the glorious realm of artistic expression even register?"

"Your hypothetical, hyper-being would probably go mad," Patrick said remaining on the lookout for unexpected kangaroos.

"Finally, empathy. Yes they may well go mad. But they would no more understand you and your reptilian brains than you understand them."

"What have lizards got to do with it?"

"A few million years of evolution has made some significant differences but there are some violent similarities, Patrick. Humanity has forgotten that its origins lie in the same murky pools of sludge where all life on this planet started. From single celled organisms to multi-celled, from sea creatures to reptilian land creatures, then to birds, primates and so on. The human brain carries all parts of that evolutionary process including the reptilian. It is the aggressive, instinctively violent part of humanity." Ancient ended his lecture and looked out the window.

'Well this cold-blooded lizard, bird, primate conglomerate would like to know where the fuck he is going? I mean I feel for these fictional beings you've concocted. Really I do? But I am real and I am right here! Am I not?"

"Debatable." The old man pulled out a piece of paper from his top pocket and looked at a few numbers in black ink. Patrick glanced over and thought it looked like three sets of longitude and latitude coordinates.

"Just keep going this way for now," the old man answered as he folded the piece of paper and put it back in his pocket. Patrick shrugged and put his foot down on the accelerator. The car really flew now after the old man's tune-up and Patrick didn't mind cruising through the night down the open highway.

THIRTY-FIVE

Angel sat at the kitchen table eating as quietly as she could. Her ears twitched like a cat's as she tuned in to the constant humming sound that was getting louder and louder. She dropped her spoon and got to her feet. She moved to the fridge and placed her hands on its cool stainless steel surface. No that wasn't it. She shifted to the microwave oven, the toaster, the coffee maker. Nothing. She pulled out the step ladder and pressed her ear to the air-conditioner. None of them the source of the persistent hum. She stood at the top of the basement stairs and turned on the ancient fluorescent lights. The incandescent tubes flickered and buzzed to life but they vibrated at a different pitch.

Angel returned to her bowl, picked up her spoon, but held her focus on the sound.

"I'm glad you are finally eating," her mother said as she walked in.

"Shush Mum, I'm listening." Angel replied irritably.

"I'm sorry to have expressed an interest in my daughter's state of health," Angel's mother continued. Angel gave her mother a disapproving look and the older woman got to her feet and mouthed silently that she understood Angel's reproach.

"Can't you hear that, Mum?" Angel asked.

"Hear what, darling?"

"That humming. Can't you hear a hum?"

Angel's mother stood still a moment as she too tried to home in on the mystery sound."

"No, can't say that I hear anything like a hum. But now you are worrying me."

"Well I can hear it, and it's getting louder all the time."

"Perhaps I should call the doctor?"

"Mum, you always want to call the doctor. I'm fine. I'll be in my room." Angel stood and left the room, leaving the half eaten meal on the table but carrying the mysterious humming noise with her.

Back in her room she fell on her bed and closed her eyes. She allowed the noise to envelope her. It surrounded and permeated, it moved around, it moved over, it moved through her. Her eyes opened sharply and she jolted bolt upright. It was suddenly very very clear. The sound was not external at all, the hum was in her head, completely, totally and undeniably contained within the confines of her brain. Her ears were not perceiving it; her mind was.

Unlike her mother, Angel wasn't going to jump to conclusions. She didn't need a doctor, she wasn't going mad. It wasn't the sudden onset of schizophrenia simply because the sound was not a sound. The sound was in fact a signal, a signal being received by her brain and not her ears. This did not deflect from the obvious that it was still a signal and that it had a source and that it was getting louder, well not louder but stronger. It was getting stronger all the time. Yes it was a signal being transmitted to her mind, telling her something, telling her something in a very annoying way. Now realising, more or less, what was happening, Angel sprang to action.

Back in the kitchen she pulled the cling wrap and aluminium foil from the draw. Her mother stood by and watched Angel wrap the crown of her head in the clear film and then cover it with foil. The sound abated.

'That's done the trick. See I didn't need a doctor.'

As Angel returned to her room, her work less interrupted by the noise, she replayed the last few moments in her head.

She imagined her mother racing to the phone to arrange some kind of medical opinion on her behaviour. But Angel couldn't concern herself with that now. One thing the noise made clear, before she shut it out, was that time was short. Something was coming and when it arrived she would have to be ready.

THIRTY-SIX

Costas lifted his glass of beer to his broad dark lips and sipped tentatively. He swallowed quickly, afraid the amber liquid might pass through the hole that was slowly healing in his tongue. He placed his glass back on the table and looked out at the view from the *Sun Rise Bar*. The white-washed houses with blue roofs and doorways of Santorini's caldera were unmistakably where that stud left in his tongue was meant to lead him. He'd not hesitated to check into the Hotel Atlantis. Why not? His expense account permitted him quality accommodation. It was good to relax now and watch the sunrise. Each mouthful of beer washed down his failure to find any obvious landmarks or clues to discovering Eko.

Santorini was an odd name, Costas thought. It sounded too Italian to be a Greek Island. He presumed it was named after Saint Irini, having seen a number of tavernas and guest-houses with the namesake. Then he remembered the Greek name was originally Thira. Some, he recalled, even suspected that the island was originally that of Atlantis, long before the volcanic eruption that tore it into fragments.

Costas breathed in the calm atmosphere of the *Sun Rise Bar*. It was good to relax, after a restless day's sleep, avoiding the heat, and the fruitless wanderings of the evening. Being still was what he needed. Perhaps if he remained in one place long enough what he was looking for would find him.

As the first flickering of the orange sun appeared from below the horizon, a wave of doubt washed over Costas. Was just following Eko for his own gratification. Would she really lead him to the killer or killers of Wilfred Fong? Was she just playing with him because she had little to do now that her sugar daddy was gone? Or did he follow because it was her he wanted to find? Did he even care about who killed Wilfred Fong? He felt he did at the beginning, but then even that was clouded with the memory of the widow Fong and her athletic body. Was everything he did motivated by one sexual urge after another? The clarity of his life's decisions were becoming foggier as the light began to fill the day.

As if too close to a truth about himself, his mind quickly switched back to the facts, the facts as his mind presented them. Mrs Fong would certainly not be pleased with his results so far. The only thing to go on were two pieces of jewellery he'd found wedged in his body, an elusive nymph named Eko and a shabby little prick in a seersucker suit who'd tried to push him off the city walls at Rhodes. Not quite the hard cold facts Costas should have accumulated by this stage of the investigation. This was feeling more and more like a waste of time and Eko was proving to be more of a Siren than a Nymph, leading him astray, diverting him from his path rather than helping him towards the solution, entreating him to lash himself against the ragged rocks and find a watery grave.

It took a few moments for Costas to realise that the annoying beeping noise he was hearing was his own mobile phone. He downed the remainder of his beer and gave the waiter a wave to bring him his bill before pressing the answer button.

"Hello!" He answered.

"Costas? This is Mrs Fong."

"Ah Mrs Fong. How are you?"

"I'm fine, Costas, I just wondered how things were progressing?"

The waiter placed the account on the table and Costas opened the folded piece of paper and looked surprised as he read the account. Not only did it detail how much he owed in Euros but there was a little drawing of an erupting volcano and a time; 10am written underneath.

"I am very close, Mrs Fong. I may even have had a run in with your husband's killer."

"Really?"

"Yes, the little bast... the little guy tried to push me off the city wall in Rhodes. So someone's feeling the heat of my investigation."

"I see, and are you alright?"

"Oh, don't worry, Mrs Fong. It would take more than a turd, I mean more than a guy in a cheap crumpled suit to do me in. I'm in Santorini now."

"Following a hot lead?"

"Absolutely volcanic, Mrs Fong," Costas said as his finger glided across the drawing. "I'll have the killer in a few days, rest assured."

"I have every confidence in your skills, Costas."

"Thank you Mrs Fong," Costas replied, not sure if he shared her conviction.

Costas' feet moved over the volcanic gravel as he made his way up towards the rim of the crater of Santorini's volcanic island. His shoes buried deep into the black and red stony path with every step. Small pebbles leapt in and nestled themselves between his socks and the soles of his shoes and he could feel a growing deposit collecting in the cuffs of his trousers. He carried on regardless, aiming to arrive early for his rendezvous.

At first he wasn't sure if he'd misinterpreted the mildly cryptic instructions and perhaps should have been looking for Eko in one of the many "Volcano" Tavernas on the caldera. The sulphurous vapours filled and irritated his nostrils as he followed the path. It was a novelty to be walking in the daylight and nowhere near as hot as he had imagined, despite the extra protective clothing he wore. Even through the pungent humid air that seeped from the cracks in the terrain, he could still smell Eko. She had walked this path, there was no mistaking it.

Costas sniffed a little to confirm Eko's scent and then moved on, still following the rocky track. He reached the summit and stood at the edge of the volcanic crater. For a moment he forgot his purpose as he considered what a pathetic tourist attraction this was. How disappointed he would have been to climb all this way to see a few wafting sulphur vapours and a big hole in the ground, not like the violently erupting volcanoes he'd seen on television. The boatloads of aging tourists he'd seen returning on his arrival, moving swiftly before the day became too warm, would surely be sorry they had risked heart failure, strokes and ruptured aneurysms for this unspectacular 'attraction'. Perhaps it looked better at night, when its inadequacies could be hidden in the dark and the vista included the lights of the town. Perhaps watching the sun rise on sulphur fumes was worth it.

Costas looked up from the crater and saw that the track led on further to a small peak. Standing at the top of the path was a solitary figure. Costas inhaled and knew it was Eko. He moved quickly again as Eko disappeared over the hill.

Eko sat motionless atop a stone that marked the summit of the volcanic island.

Costas sat next to the young woman, unsure what would happen next. This is all he had ever been able to remember of their meetings and now he was determined to make indelible mental notes of what would transpire.

Eko took his hand in hers and moved close to him. She pressed her young lips against his and gently kissed him. Costas did not respond though his whole body ached to.

"Aren't you happy to see me?" Eko asked.

"I don't know. Every time I see you I wake up the next night with a killer hangover, a piece of metal piercing my body somewhere and no memory of the last twenty-four hours."

"Again?" she said.

"What do you mean, 'again'? You're the one doing this to me. You're the one leading me from place to place, leaving me little metallic clues."

"I've been following you!" she replied.

"I don't remember anything?"

"The orgasm drug, it must still be affecting you. Giving you post coital memory loss."

"So every time we have possibly the most incredible sex of my life I wake up with no memory of it. Fucking terrific."

"It won't last forever. And it was definitely the most incredible sex of your life."

"So how come I keep waking up alone. Why are you following me, why don't you just travel with me?"

"The day after I met you in Athens I received a letter from Daddy Fong that he'd posted the day he died. He told me someone was trying to kill him and that if anything happened then I should lay low but that I must get to Thira. I thought if I followed you then I would be okay. But someone tried to kill me in Rhodes and I thought it would be safer to be with you and not just following you. I've told you this before but you don't remember. We had a wonderful night together but then you disappeared. You said you would meet me but you never showed. I tracked your mobile phone to Santorini. You gave me your GPS so I couldn't lose you."

"So you know who killed Mr Fong?"

"No."

"Then you know who is leading me from place to place?"

"No, but I can help you."

"I'm sure you can, but all I want to know is what the fuck am I doing in Santorini?"

"Do you know what the other name for Santorini is?"

"Of course it's Thira."

"Well they've led you to Thira, but it's the wrong Thira."

"I suppose you know the right Thira?"

"Yes, and we need to get there."

"Well, where is it?"

Eko tilted her head and looked up into the sky. Costas' head followed Eko's, uncertain what he was supposed to be seeing. He looked down again and examined Eko's crisp beautiful features, trust in her feeling elusive. His nose told him she wasn't lying, his desire fogging any chance of clarity.

"Up there," Eko said.

"Up there?"

"Yes," she whispered as she clasped his hand tightly, her fingers stroking his with reassurance.

THIRTY-SEVEN

Freed now from the captivity of her quarters but not from the processes of her mind, like all humans Kirby had no option but to perceive the world via her very human brain. Its synapses, its electrical impulses, its very structure filtering information that her physical body captured through the senses and making it into something human, altering it by the very act of receiving it. That was the human brain and Kirby knew of no other way to look at the world. In fact she'd never stopped to think about it before, but there it was. Even the phrase 'look at the world' suddenly seemed outrageously narrow. Here she was, in a human made space station, actually looking at the world. And by that very act her 'world view' was different to that of everyone else's on the planet. A 'world view', a 'human view' of what came before the eyes, of what registered in the olfactory senses, of what brushed against the skin, of what tantalised the tongue, of what sang into the ears, all filtered into the small idea of there being only the world, the human world. How tiny, how human. Anything outside the human experience was somehow not valid, not real. If the human brain didn't see it, didn't understand it, didn't de-construct it, didn't pull it to pieces to build its own copy, then that 'thing' was slapped with a 'no' in front of it and given the very human label of being a 'no-thing', becoming 'nothing'.

Kirby's eyes widened and she shook her head to clear it. It was increasingly difficult to concentrate on the immediate tasks before her, of which there were now a multitude. Stop human brain, stop and focus. From security risk to love interest. Was it only Professor Gardener who now watched over her? Would the recent course of events be raising a few eyebrows higher up the food chain? Those who wield the power couldn't all be as incompetent as Gardener. He couldn't go unnoticed and unsupervised. His knowledge and skill in his field of expertise would only go so far in protecting him. Yes he knew a great deal. Kirby reluctantly accepted that she herself had initially marvelled at his concepts. But now those ideas paled into insignificance. They recoiled, as did her own skin, when the thought of the man's actual and real physical presence entered her mind. Everything was overshadowed by his fundamental grossness. Human brain or not, that repulsion would be real to any form of perception.

But now she was back at work and using her own extensive knowledge and experience, skills that actually got things done. Kirby was no stranger to making herself indispensable. Gardener might have had some grand ideas, but it was Kirby who came up with systems to make them actually work. They needed her, for now anyway. But what did Kirby need? All she thought she needed was the work before her. Why did it now feel as if it wasn't enough? She'd wanted this, to be heading up this team, making this project a reality and yet it didn't match the expectation. Here it was, all laid out, everything she'd worked to achieve and for some unknown reason all she could think about was sabotage. Was it herself she wanted to sabotage or Gardener, or was it PetroSynth, the high and mighty global force for good that was so ready to sell its soul and leave behind the remnants of a human race that had no power, no money, no value?

She could drop a bug in the system and slow the whole process down, but with Gardener watching her so closely it would have to be something very sophisticated, undetectable. Simply not enough time. The first wave of human subjects would be arriving in a matter of days, and despite them being rich and famous people they were still human. Kirby couldn't knowingly put their lives in danger. If she could get the professor to agree to be a test subject, she could digitise his sad collection of neurons, move his data to a separate storage device and smash the shit out of it. It wouldn't feel like murder, not really, it would feel like a wonderful release of aggression. Who was she kidding? It would still be the end of existence for a living being at her hands. Her life and work was all about saving and preserving life, not destroying it, even if it offended her and her very human sensibilities.

There had to be a better way than murder to cease the professor's lurid advances. It was easier to have security on her and be confined to quarters than being the subject of the professor's lecherous gaze. His watchful eye hardly straying from her, not out of distrust but out of pure lust and it was getting a little obvious. Members of the team pretending to step over his tongue as his mouth lay gaping open, his eyes transfixed on Kirby's body. Her shape was completely hidden by her straight white lab coat, but that didn't stop the professor looking like one of Pavlov's salivating dogs.

As the work began piling up around her, Kirby realised that she could not leave the station. Her only course of action was to try and contact Patrick. Hopefully by now he had turned his fucking phone on and she could get his GPS signal.

Like a dark shadow in the corner of her eye Kirby could feel Gardner approaching. She turned and gave him her best fake smile. He took it as genuine warmth as he'd only ever been on the receiving end of Kirby's venom. This would be delicate, but if Kirby could get through that revolting kiss, then she could get through almost anything, except perhaps another kiss or, worse still, more intimate contact.

"How are you today, my dear?"

"Please, Professor, I don't wish the others to be jealous of our situation. Could you please continue to address me in a professional manner?"

"Of course I understand, I'll keep myself in check."

"I need to call Earth," Kirby said.

"Kirby, you know all personal communications have been barred until launch."

"I know Professor, but I need to contact my husband to discuss terms for a divorce."

"Can't you write to him? I've already sent a letter to my wife."

"No, I need to speak to him personally. I won't do it any other way."

"I'll see what I can do."

"It will have to be a secure channel, Professor."

"Why?"

"Otherwise someone may know we made a personal call."

"Of course. You are not just a pretty face."

"Thank you, Professor. So you'll fix it up?"

"Yes. I have access of course. You can make your call after this shift."

"Thank you."

"That is quite alright my dear, I mean Kirby."

The professor walked confidently back to his office, pleased that he was one step closer to tearing Kirby's lab coat from her body and diving into a passionate tryst.

THIRTY-EIGHT

Patrick pulled the car over. It felt strange to be in a suburban area again after driving so long on the open road. He'd stopped reading street signs some time ago and now relied on Ancient's occasional instruction on which path to take. The appearance of neatly collected houses had crept up on Patrick. That odd feeling of knowing he'd been at the wheel of a car, been responsible for steering it, yet he couldn't remember any details of the journey. He was on the highway one moment and now, as if by some sorcery, some slight of hand, some mechanism beyond his understanding that could fold space and time, he was suddenly parked in a quiet neighbourhood street.

Patrick unplugged his mobile from the re-charger and stepped out of the car.

"We don't have time to stop, Patrick. We must keep moving," Ancient insisted.

"I need to call my wife," he replied.

"You won't get through!" Ancient said.

"How do you know?"

"Just trust me, we can't waste any time. You'll see your wife soon enough."

"This is the first decent signal I've had in days," Patrick said, ignoring Ancient's protestations. He dialled the number of the communications relay centre.

"David? Yeah, it's Patrick."

"Where the fuck have you been?" accused the voice on the other end.

"It's a long story. I need to speak to Kirby. Can you put me through to Thira?"

"They are on some kind of lock-down."

"Just try will you?"

"Okay, but you should know, you are in some major crap here."

"HR is the least of my worries. Can you put me through to Kirby, please."

The phone rang and rang but there was no answer. He was surprised her voice mail didn't pick up. Patrick cut off the call and redialled.

"David, it's me again. Something's up with the voice mail. Can you get a message to Kirby that I called. She can reach me on my mobile."

"Will do what I can," said David.

"Thanks." Patrick hung up and got back into the car.

"Can we stop wasting time now?" Ancient asked.

"Sure." Patrick put his foot down and they set off again. The old man pulled out his piece of paper with the numbers on it, reading it like a street map. They took a left, then a right, through roundabouts, give-way signs, school zones, over pedestrian crossings. It felt like aimless cruising, going in circles, but Patrick could feel the old man's desire to reach his destination. It kept them moving, pushed them forward.

"Stop," Ancient yelled.

Patrick slammed on the brakes and the car skidded to a stop.

"This is it."

"This is what?" asked Patrick.

"Our first stop." The old man looked at his watch. "Good, despite your delays, we are still on time."

Patrick parked and then moved to get out of the car. The old man caught his shoulder and brought him back down into his seat.

"Wait!" Ancient said.

"What for?" asked Patrick.

"This has to be handled delicately, Patrick. At this moment that means waiting."

"We rushed here so we could wait?"

"That's correct. You're picking things up much faster now."

Patrick shuffled in his seat and moved to turn off the engine.

"Leave it running," said Ancient, "it's not like you're wasting fuel or creating emissions."

Despite the old man's cranky demeanour Patrick decided to see this through. He sensed an underlying feeling that whatever the old man did, he did deliberately. He might seem irritable, but it was not completely convincing. It was somehow an act, a projection of what he felt was needed to get the best response from Patrick. The old man was far more in control than he would ever be prepared to admit, like a wise teacher giving his students what they needed rather than what they wanted. Patrick had little in the way of other options and a forced kind of trust in the old man, an acceptance of the situation and of Ancient's ways of behaving settled over Patrick. Waiting seemed easy now. Anything seemed easy.

THIRTY-NINE

"Save file!" Angel instructed to her computer.

"Saving now," it replied.

Angel sat back and looked triumphantly at the screen. She didn't need to save the file, she could remember it in all its detailed mathematical glory. Still it was easier to save it than retype it.

She took the foil and plastic wrap from her head and scrunched it into a ball. The hum returned immediately. With her calculations finished she could concentrate on finding its source. It was louder now and the steady increase she'd detected earlier in the tone had plateaued.

Angel stopped scanning for a moment and took a memory stick from her drawer.

"Backup to wireless drive," she ordered.

"Backing up," the computer replied.

Angel cradled the memory stick in her hand as she walked through the house again, her ears like satellite dishes, moving to tune in the sound. She rechecked each electrical appliance, the hot water system and even her fish tank. The sound was coming from none of them and definitely not being audibly perceived.

As Angel moved past the front door the sound spiked. She moved away again and it dropped. Walking back and forth in front of the door, the sound would peak and then recede. She threw open the front door and the sound sharply rose. She walked out into the garden and again it got stronger. She moved up the driveway towards the street, the hum increasing with every step. She reached the road and saw a car parked across the street. A dark haired man in his early thirties was sitting behind the wheel and next to him, in the passenger side, was an octogenarian whose eyes seemed startlingly familiar. The old man lifted his hand and the younger man responded by turning off the car's engine.

The humming stopped and everything around Angel seemed to melt away – the house, the garden, the driveway. The only thing that remained was the old man's eyes and a strange feeling of recognition.

The old man waved his hand again and the young man turned on the engine. The humming started immediately. Angel walked slowly over to the car and stood at its bonnet. The early evening glow of twilight washed over the street, shimmering in unearthly orange and blue tones as the old man got out of the car and lifted the hood. He jiggled something in the engine and the humming stopped.

"That shouldn't bother you any more, Angel." he said.

"Thank you. Who are you?" Angel asked.

"You've been doing some very interesting work. Is it complete?" Ancient replied ignoring her question.

"Yes, I've just finished it. You want to see it?"

"I'm afraid there is little time. Can you bring it with you."

"And where would I go with you exactly?" Angel said, a little incredulous, her thumb stroking the precious memory stick in her palm.

"Well, Angel, the sky's not quite the limit."

The old man smiled warmly and rested his hand on Angel's shoulder, and at that instant she knew where she'd seen him. His face had been younger, much younger but there was no mistaking the touch of that skin or the look of those eyes. Those eyes had made all space and time melt away at her fifteenth birthday, the touch of that skin so similar to her own. That face, those eyes and that skin, had vanished as quickly as they had arrived, but now they stood clearly before of her. She remembered all that he'd whispered into her ear that day and she'd followed his instructions clearly. Gained vast knowledge, resisted working for government or private enterprise. She'd used her time for the development of scientific and mathematical thought. In his touch she could feel the moment to put all that she'd learned into some form of action had arrived, and she was ready.

The old man removed his hand from Angel's shoulder and she shivered slightly at the disconnection.

"We have no time to waste, Angel."

"I'm ready. Well actually, there's one small problem," she said.

Ancient and Patrick found themselves sitting around the kitchen table with Angel's parents looking quizzically at them. Ancient had managed to scrub up okay after retrieving a half decent shirt and some pants from the boot of the car. Patrick hid calmly behind his sunglasses and left the situation to the old man and his charms. Angel had quickly packed an overnight bag with essentials and she stroked it nervously with her feet as Ancient spoke confidently to Richard and Linda.

"As you would well be aware your daughter's talents have not gone unnoticed by PetroSynth Corporation. It's not the first time we've made overtures to you and Angel regarding employment. Naturally given her age you were reluctant to see her move too quickly. However we now find ourselves in great need of her abilities and the bottom line is we are prepared to compensate handsomely for her time and skill, if, of course, Angel is prepared to take up the position." Ancient took a sip of water.

Patrick thought it strange that Richard and Linda seemed so quiet but it didn't seem appropriate that he raise concerns about the girl driving off into the evening with an odd old man and his driver, if they were not going to raise those concerns themselves.

Richard looked warmly at his daughter and placed his hand on hers. "Is this what you really want? I've spent my life working for PetroSynth and found it rewarding but always thought you would want more?"

"This is what I want, Dad. It's fully funded, I'll have autonomy, the latest resources at my finger tips. But I may not see you for a while. You understand they want me for high level secure projects?"

Richard put his arm around Linda's shoulder reassuringly and they both nodded their acknowledgment.

Ancient opened the back door of the car and Angel quickly climbed in. Ancient took his seat in the front next to Patrick at the wheel.

Looking expectantly between Ancient and the open road, Patrick came to rest his eyes on a distant object ahead. It was a red postbox, its bright colour and simplicity drew his attention. He envied its normality, its primary function being so clear and without distraction in purpose by thought or emotion. So it was inanimate, but it still existed and it was useful.

Ancient rested his hand gently on Patrick's shoulder and gave his deltoid a friendly squeeze and then a nice manly pat.

"Off we go, before they change their minds," the old man said, with just the right combination of request and command. Obligingly, Patrick put the car in gear and started off down the road, quite unsure where this was all going to lead him, yet strangely unable to work his vocal chords in order to voice any complaint. Not unlike the postbox, he now had a single purpose and that was to drive. A single purpose he could easily fulfil without thought or emotion, a state of mind that felt calming to embody.

Angel waved from the back of the car to her bewildered parents. "I'm doing this for them you know," she declared.

"We are doing this for everyone," Ancient replied.

"What are we doing exactly?" asked Patrick.

"At this moment, driving," replied the old man, knowing that's all Patrick could cope with hearing. "Just driving."

Ancient's reassuring hand patted Patrick's shoulder once more and he felt calm and in control of his immediate future, even if the world's long term prospects were not hopeful. Right at this moment he had a purpose, right at this moment he existed.

PART THREE

FORTY

Tracing the threads of his life Patrick wondered how they'd been woven into such a complex pattern, that all he knew, all he felt, said and did, the archive of action and inaction could be traced back to that moment when he and Kirby first kissed. That kiss set him on course for where he now found himself, a journey he'd willingly taken despite no knowledge of the destination at the time of departure. It wasn't so much where they were headed; it was more the fact they were heading there together. And where was she now? If all he knew were to come to a sudden stop, if his world were to end then at that moment he wanted to be holding Kirby's hand. Not out of fear, not out of loneliness but out of love, out of an inexplicable understanding that they belonged. Their bodies knew it, their emotions knew it, but somehow they'd allowed their intellect, their passion for achievements and their desires for other experience to create a physical separation. Now it was an emotional separation. How was it that he'd allowed this to happen? How had he been so careless with the one thing he treasured above all else? In that one moment of understanding, the massive distance between them seemed to double, triple, quadruple, compounding on its empty self to become larger and larger by the second, pulling Kirby further and further away from his touch, ever thinning the connection between them.

Self-defense kicked in and Patrick shifted his mind to something else – those eyes, that girl's eyes. Her eyes drew him in, with their crisp whiteness and deep blue irises. The pupils were like pin-pricks during the day, but at night he'd noticed they would swell to cover the entire pool of colour.

They became as black as the night itself. It was hard to keep his mind on the road, his own eyes wanting only to look into her eyes. He sensed that he could lose himself in those eyes, as once he had in Kirby's. Not in the same, mutually adoring way. Angel was a still a child to him, but to be lost in those eyes was a desire he was being drawn to. There, in her eyes, he would no longer need to worry about all he thought he knew, what nightmares he imagined might transpire. It was only her eyes that drew his attention. Despite the idea of a disapproving Kirby, Patrick forced his stare away from the young woman's eyes to examine her other features. Her face was well defined and balanced, harmonious even. Her demeanour relaxed and comforting and her skin had a curious luminescence. His gaze flicked back to her eyes. Occasionally she caught him looking and smiled, as though she were used to be people staring at her for long periods of time while they were trying to operate a motor vehicle.

He consciously acknowledged he was not overly attracted to her physically, except for those bright alluring eyes. She had a natural beauty, he should desire her, but Patrick was also mindful of her age. She could not be more than seventeen. What would a connection with her be other than physical? It may well have pleasurable outcomes, but where would it leave him. The frowning image of Kirby relaxed and Patrick smiled to himself, remembering their closeness. If Kirby were in the car now he knew who would be holding his attention. The smile soon faded as reality crept back under his skin and into the forefront of his conscious mind. She was orbiting Earth in the darkness of space, while he blindly scrambled across its surface, both moving, both pulling in directions that opened the distance between them.

Patrick returned his focus to the road; they were once again on the freeway. It looked familiar but something was disorientating, different. He couldn't keep his eyes from flicking back to his passengers. He'd not taken much notice of the old man's features before, just that his face was wrinkled and creased and that he had a strange paleness to his skin for someone who had spent so much time out in the heat of the day. But it now seemed as if his facial features were changing slightly. His eyes were becoming more and more like the young woman's in the back seat. Or had they always been that way? Patrick looked from the girl in his rear-vision mirror to the old man in the front seat, trying to clarify details of his comparison.

"Does this car have a computer?" Ancient asked and Patrick took the opportunity to engage his eyes. It wasn't easy and the road quickly drew back his attention. All this staring and driving was taking its toll. He really needed to keep his eyes away from that rear-vision mirror. As much as it was pulling him, he was determined to keep his focus forward.

"Of course," Patrick replied, compliant but annoyed at an interruption coming just at the point he'd decided to keep his focus solely on driving. Leaning forward, he tapped lightly on the passenger side of the dashboard. A small keyboard and screen moved out and stopped in front of the old man.

"Voice activated?" Ancient asked.

"Yes," Patrick replied defensively. "State of the art!"

Ancient flashed Patrick an incredulous look and then turned to the young girl in the back of the car. She leant forward, excited to be included in the conversation.

"Angel, may I have your memory stick?" he asked.

Angel handed over the stick, pleased her hard work was soon to be acknowledged.

The old man examined Angel's files, moving through the data quickly, faster than Patrick thought possible to read.

"Very impressive," he said. "I'm sure this is going to do very well."

"You can follow it?" Angel asked.

"I couldn't have written it, but I can understand it. You're an absolute genius, Angel."

"What is it?" asked Patrick.

"Something to help us readjust some of those world truths you so love to cling to."

"Look it's all very nice to go for a ride in the country with you and your grand-daughter here, but I want to know where we are going and what the hell you are planning? Because if this is leading us nowhere then I have a few ideas of my own."

"Like what, Patrick? Tell the world that the carbon crisis never really ended and that life on this planet is doomed if we don't start legislation to fix the problem?"

"Yes, that's exactly right. That's what I'd do."

"The energy that goes into getting any internationally agreed legislation is not worth the carbon offset. There is more going on than carbon driven climate change."

"What are you talking about? I personally intercepted a document detailing the evacuation plan for those who can afford it. All it talked about was bloody carbon levels and irreversible climate change." Patrick pulled open his glove box and searched through some papers as he swerved over the road. His hand finally came to rest on a bundle of untidy papers and he threw them into Ancient's lap. "Here's the bloody transcript."

"It's a cover up, Patrick. First they convince the world it's something they are fixing, then they convince those with wealth it's something they can't. The first creates calm for the masses, the second drives the escape. And the truth my young friend, is far worse."

"What could be worse than global warming?"

"The sun is dying!" Angel said from the back.

"What?" Patrick said into his revision mirror.

"The ozone is fine, even the increase in carbon is negligible. They really have been working on that problem, the sun however, has gone prematurely into its death throws. In about a million years it will explode and that will be it for the solar system."

"Well what's the rush then? We've got plenty of time." Patrick said.

"It should take four billion years to reach that point not one million. Each year it gets hotter. In fact, at the current rate of change every hour counts. According to my calculations, within the next 12 months all life on Earth will be gone. Nothing will be able to live on this precious rock of yours."

Patrick slammed on the breaks and skidded to a stop.

"You knew about this when I told you what I had discovered!" Patrick accused Ancient.

"Yes, I did." The old man nodded. "Now we must get a move on, Patrick."

"Then why the fuck didn't you tell me?" Patrick yelled.

"I didn't want to alarm you. Can we get going? Remember every moment counts now," the old man said.

"Alarm me! You didn't want to alarm me. Well I'm not alarmed, see I'm totally fucking calm – see, deep breath. No, okay I'm not calm. I'm totally fucking pissed off and I'm not going anywhere until you tell me what we are going to do!"

"We are going to fix the sun, Patrick."

"Fix the sun? Like it's a broken tap? You, me and Angel eyes here are not just going to save the world, but we are going to save the solar system?"

"That's correct," Ancient replied.

"Great, perfect, sounds wonderful, let's go save the solar system and then we can all go back to my place and have a BBQ. How does that sound, we'll kick back and laugh about old times and maybe even talk about the future in some strange way that does not include our immediate demise." Patrick's head started hitting the wheel in disbelief.

"Patrick, I know this is difficult, but I need you to focus and let go of this hysteria."

"Hysteria, yes of course. So inappropriate of me to be hysterical at a time like this. What was I thinking? How selfish. Let me just pull it all together and we'll be on our merry way, holding hands and skipping down the golden path to salvation of the solar system. Naturally we'll discover some wonderful insights into our true selves along the way so we can all be better human beings. Really learn to live in the now and with any luck we'll develop a deep love for humanity and respect for all life on the planet. We'll reject hedonistic consumerism and develop an ability to realise what's truly important in life. Oh, and let's not forget that it's the beauty on the inside that really fucking counts!" Patrick took a breath, his hands still gripping tightly onto the steering wheel, its rigid state holding him up.

"Well, if you insist," the old man replied, raising an eyebrow.

"Oh yes, I most definitely insist. I mean what would be the point of saving everything if we didn't actually reflect on what the fuck we were saving, Ancient? I just have one minor question, if it's not too much trouble?"

"Yes Patrick, what is it?" The old man's passive reply drilled into Patrick's head.

"Where do we actually go? Are we to be forever in the middle of fucking nowhere?" Patrick asked.

"You know it better than I do. We are going to Space Station Thira!"

Patrick sat for a minute. He began to ingest the hysteria. His shoulders shrugged, his neck clicked, his gut tightened. It was so ludicrously past anything normal now. The craziness of it all was feeding his brain, giving him energy and focus. The random spurting of words, the cry of wasted invective was turning in on itself as he realised he could actually be of some help.

"I've been missing for a few days, but I am the Technical Chief of Communications at the launch base. Clearly I'm a drone who is not meant to know the big picture but I can probably get you on to the base. I'll tell them I was on rec leave or something, that HR lost my leave forms. It's a big bureaucracy; they are always messing up forms and losing emails."

"Patrick, you are raving a little,"

"Yes, of course. Look I can get you in, but after that, you are on your own."

If the sun was truly dying then there was nothing anyone else could do about it. Going to the media would just cause panic and no amount of legislation or popular opinion was going to force it to go back to normal. Democratic people power was a fundamental human right able to affect great change, but last time he checked it couldn't actually alter the physical universe. His enigmatic passengers may be the only hope he had. The words floated for a moment. The only hope he had, the only hope to save everything, the only hope to see Kirby again…Kirby, the woman he had been running from and now the woman whose arms he wanted more than anything to be in.

As the moment came to a close it was almost as if his odd passengers had witnessed his thought processes as much as they had witnessed his rants. They sat calmly and observed as Patrick consolidated his ideas into actions. There was no more talk as Patrick slammed the car back into gear and sped off down the road. Now the image of the Launch Base was fixed in his mind, he had no need for the old man's co-ordinates, or even less need for his emotional manipulative antics. The Base was the very place where he'd started this journey; for that reason alone he disliked the idea of going back. It was now impossible to fight. Everything was clicking into place and it was all too neat to be random. His life had been turned upside down, the chaos had taken hold of his dull routine and shaken it beyond recognition; still, it was making sense. His role, his purpose now, was not hard, not demanding. All he had to do was accept it, accept that the landscape had changed, accept that whatever he'd generated as a plan for himself was fast being thrown out the window. Patrick himself was essentially the same, everything around him was not. He could help. Not only was he useful but he was now necessary, an essential component in the grand plan, be it his plan or the plan of some wrinkled old man who appeared hell bent on removing the foundations of his existence just to manipulate him into giving him a ride. Could it be an accident that he found that bloody document, that it disturbed him to the point of desertion, that the desertion led to an old man who could actually do something about the knowledge that had driven him crazy in the first place?

Patrick shifted the car into fifth and they sped towards their destination with new focus and determination, his eyes on the road, his mind on the task at hand and his heart still floating round the globe with his precious Kirby. That feeling, his love for Kirby, his desire to be with her, was proving unshakable and it fed him now like a raw, powerful source of energy that only grew stronger the more it was used.

"That's how it works, Patrick. The more you use it the stronger it gets." Ancient gave the younger man a tap on the shoulder and then there was silence between them all. Silence of speech and silence of mind as Patrick moved them all in the direction they needed to go.

FORTY-ONE

Costas watched as the deep blue Aegean Sea crumpled and folded under the force of the ship's hull. In the twilight he pondered incredulously at his own failings and considered whether or not it would be a good idea to join the frothy breaking water as it passed under the large passenger liner. The realities that Eko had whispered to him in their time together since meeting at the volcano were more astounding than his own inability to have uncovered them. It would be so easy to just slip over the edge of the boat; all his troubles, concerns, self doubt, the cocky façade that carried him through life would pleasantly fade as his body sank and became a fleck of insignificance in that endless blue brine.

Costas turned his back on the water before the sirens of the deep sang too sweetly to be ignored, and his eyes came to rest on Eko. How beautiful she was. Too exquisite to trust, too divine to scorn, she basked in the last rays of the late afternoon sun, lying on a sun lounge under a UV filter. He desired nothing more than to join her, to lie next to her, to feel her body arch and writhe under his. But that couldn't happen, not for some time, not until these stupid drugs were out of his system. He couldn't risk losing her again and the thought he might wake up with some part of his body adorned with a new piercing lingered with apprehension. For now all he could do was admire her, at least until he found out who was giving him those little silver messages to help him along and who, conversely, was trying to kill him.

Now, on top of everything else he was burdened with the knowledge contained in Eko's letter from the late Wilfred Fong. He'd heard talk for years that a space station was being built, that there were plans for humanity to venture to other worlds, but he'd always considered it a popular myth and taken little notice. If the station existed and was somehow a safe haven for Eko then he would have to try and find a way of getting her there. Eko seemed quite sure that Daddy Fong would have made provisions for her and now that he was dead, she could simply take Costas with her. Could he simply trust that, trust her? A darker thought crept in, that he might have to wait centuries before he could have another sexual encounter with Eko, one that he would be able to recall fully. The idea burned unlike any frustration he'd known, but still he kept it contained. That he might end up flying through space and helping to colonise new worlds was even more incomprehensible. Whether that was the outcome or not, unlike the broken waters beneath him, it was crystal clear the answers he sought lay literally out of this world. Answers perhaps beyond detection by his comparable professional abilities? Even his ever-reliable ultra sensitive olfactory sense could not be trusted. The cold uncertainty was an unwelcome feeling. How quickly it had replaced his usual, though somewhat deluded, self-confidence. He could only be sure of one thing; that Eko would lead him to Wilfred Fong's killer and that was still his responsibility, his charge, his mission. Regardless of how much Eko and her tantalising presence swayed him, he must keep that objective in focus.

Costas leant down and kissed Eko on the forehead, allowing himself this minor pleasure.

"Don't get excited, now," she teased. "You don't want to forget who I am."

"I can't believe I took that pill!" he said.

"It was worth it, believe me it was worth it," she said, running her finger down his chest. Costas took hold of her hand, craving to kiss her. He held himself steady no one but himself and Eko aware of the extreme will power he was exerting, standing firm against the greatest biological desire his system had experienced.

"We must be careful when we get to Crete, I don't want anything to happen to you," Costas said.

"Daddy Fong told me in his letter that I could get to Thira from the old NATO base near Hania. I thought it was a strange way to get to Santorini until I remembered the stories of the space station and realised he meant quite a different place. Shuttles must go to Thira from there. We have to get on one of those shuttles, Costas. I'm sure my name is on a list somewhere. Daddy Fong would've taken care of that."

"Can I see that letter?" asked Costas.

"It's personal," she replied firmly.

"There may be something in it that I need to know."

"I've told you all you need to know from the letter. You'll just have to trust me."

Costas moved back from Eko uneasily. He didn't like to trust anyone except himself. Even that had led him astray a few times. Was it leading him astray now? Trusting Eko was simply asking for trouble. At least it was trouble he could expect, but trouble nonetheless he could see no way of avoiding.

He stroked her face again gently.

"Of course I trust you, Eko." The lie slipped easily from his lips as he put his hand into his jacket pocket and moved back to the rail. It was safer, he thought, to take his chances with the allure of the ocean than to play with the lustful flame that was his desire for Eko. A fire that burned so fervently that all the waters of the blue Aegean before him could not dampen it. There was little choice, for the moment he must try and trust her and hope his instincts would prevent his heart or his cock leading him to an early demise with his body and soul languishing against the jagged watery rocks of a destruction entirely of his own making.

FORTY-TWO

"Don't you think you could have talked to me a bit more? I mean you just flew off the handle and didn't give me a chance to speak." Kirby stopped pacing and waited for Patrick to reply. He knew he was being slow to answer but he was so taken up with watching her that it was hard to get his mind to focus on putting words together. Being in her presence was a sensory over-load. All he wanted to do was take her in his arms and tell her how sorry he was. He knew Kirby well enough to understand that a full explanation could not be by-passed. She would need an answer before they could move on to physical forgiveness.

"I know, I should have let you talk," he replied.

"How could you think I would know something like that and not tell you? How could you think I would do that to you?"

"I suppose I knew you didn't know the whole truth. No one knew. Not even I knew what was really happening until Ancient and Angel told me."

"So why, why did you do that to me?" Kirby moved closer and put her hands over Patrick's as she stood in front of him. He found it hard to look her in the eye but knew he had to. He turned and faced her.

"I wanted my life to be here on Earth, where I was born, where I belong, where people belong. I overreacted because it was an escape for me from the fear of leaving the surface of my planet. You wanted that life so much. I love you Kirby, but I was scared."

Kirby lifted her hands, gently resting one on his shoulder and with the other she lovingly traced her fingers down the side of his face. Like a feline, he moved his head into her caress, relishing the moment of peace between them; soaking in the affection, feeling comforted, feeling forgiven and loved. The hand on her shoulder dug into his muscle and she began to shake him vigorously and before he could hold on to her she was gone and Angel was facing him. She was in the front of the car leaning into the back where he was sleeping, her hand agitating him to consciousness.

"Ancient asked me to wake you. He said it's almost time to go. He'll be out in a minute." Angel's soft tones registered as Patrick roused himself back to reality and prepared himself for more driving. In the space between wake and sleep he was unsure if it had been Angel's eyes that had conveyed her words to him or her lips. He remembered the sound, he understood the meaning, but had her lips moved?

Patrick sat himself up and rubbed his eyes groggily and looked out the window. They had stopped in a PetroSynth truck stop somewhere on the highway. He presumed the old man was taking a leak. Patrick returned his sunglasses to his face and looked out at the afternoon glare.

"How long have you known about the sun?" Patrick asked

"A few days," Angel replied.

"And the old man? You know him?"

"I'm not too sure. I think he visited me a few years ago, on my birthday."

"Then how do you know he can help?" Patrick asked.

"I just know he can. I know this is what I have to do. What about you? Why are you here?" She looked at Patrick intently for the first time and he withdrew slightly from the intensity of her bright eyes.

"I have no idea why I'm here. Nothing would surprise me. Perhaps the old man had something to do with me discovering the information I did. Perhaps he needs me to help him like he needs you. So far all I've been doing is driving, but that won't last."

"How much further is the launch site?"

"Another day."

"You shouldn't feel so bad about your wife. She's only doing her job."

"What do you know about my wife?" Patrick said, alarmed that this young woman could get into his head as easily as the old man.

"You were talking in your sleep. Does she know where you are?"

"No, but I think she will soon enough. Here comes the old man."

Lifting his sunglasses to his forehead, Patrick stretched his arms out and rested his hand on the wheel as Ancient got into the back of the car.

"You can sit up front for a while, Angel," he said. "I could use a bit of a sleep myself." The old man lay down on the back seat as Angel settled into the front and buckled in.

"Are you okay to drive, Patrick?"

"Yes fine, I'm well practiced at driving days on end. I'll let you know if I start hallucinating."

"I thought you already had."

"Stay out of my head old man! Actually that goes for both of you."

Ancient shrugged and lay down in the back of the car as Patrick started the engine. He dropped his sunglasses over his eyes and took off down the highway. Uneasiness filled him as he shifted through the gears. His dream of Kirby left him cold and uncertain. How could he say those things to her in reality? It was hard enough in a dream. Where would he find the fortitude to lay bare his soul like that, to admit to her face the very real truth behind his actions, a truth he'd only just realised? And now that it had come to the fore of his conscious mind it was growing, bigger by the minute. He simply didn't want to live away from Earth; the endless empty vacuum of space filled him with a cold fear that chilled him to the core of his being.

The thoughts swirled round his head, compounding and pressing in, imploding like a giant black hole in his psyche, relentlessly sucking in all the light and energy of his spirit. It was hard enough being an insignificant little creature on the face of a small planet; how small would he feel being faced with space infinitum? Knowing he would die long before the journey ended and that centuries of his descendants would be born to a life that had no understanding of Earth; his life's very origin, their origin. There was something comforting in having the surface of the Earth to cling to in the face of an expanding, boundless universe. He didn't want to go, and Kirby did, she wanted it more than anything, perhaps more than she wanted him. Knowing the true reason he'd taken flight only made it harder to return.

If he were alone now he would turn the car around and speed off in the other direction, back into the void of nowhere. Escaping the fear of one void by driving endlessly off into another. But he had passengers now. How had that happened? How had he collected an old man and a young girl who were intent on getting to where he had run away from. Why the fuck was this happening? Why was Kirby gracefully orbiting the globe without a care in the world or a care out of this world. Her head full of a future so beyond experience. And here he was, chaotically moving on the surface of the planet she floated around, wrestling with decisions that had to be made, situations that required resolution and emotions that needed to be felt; all flowing from her desire for the unknown. 'The Unknown' he thought, is quite possibly what the solar system may soon become, if Angel and Ancient were correct. He hated that feeling most of all; that they were right, that these two oddities were somehow patched into knowledge that he didn't intrinsically possess. An old man and a young girl; what was so special about them? Why was he excluded from their sense of knowing?

Patrick's hands clenched tightly to the steering wheel, with those who controlled the fate of the world sleeping soundly in his car. All he had to do was make one wrong turn, his hands to slip slightly, to lose control, to micro sleep, to swerve and crash. Did it matter if they lived or died? Were they all heading for oblivion regardless?

FORTY-THREE

Hania's ancient Venetian harbour bustled beneath Eko as she stood on the balcony of the hotel and pressed herself against the wrought iron rail. A multitude of tourists paraded past in the warm night air and she could hear hundreds more dining at the plethora of restaurants that lined the foreshore. She turned excitedly to Costas who walked out to join her. He moved close, enjoying the temptation that Eko embodied. No longer fighting it with resistance, but assailing it with awareness. The cacophony of sounds from below washed over him, the smell and feel of Eko so close, the night air warm and inviting, all combining to make a moment, a string of moments that were complete in themselves. There was nothing to do but breathe and accept all that was going on around him. He saw in Eko's eyes that she was sharing in this simple pleasure of soaking up the moment. Then his mind moved and reluctantly he drew in the future.

"I'm going to rent a car and check out the old NATO base. I'd like to see what we are up against."

"I thought we might eat on the harbour front?" Eko said.

"We can do that when I get back. Just lay low for now."

"I want to come with you. I don't want to stay here on my own," she pleaded. The young woman before him seemed suddenly no more than a child and he readily gave in.

"Okay, but do as I tell you and stay quiet. We may have to pretend we are lovers if anyone stops us."

"What's to pretend?" she replied.

"Once we get out of town you can drive. I'll need to take some pictures." Costas picked up his briefcase and tapped it reassuringly. "Let's go."

They drove slowly past the base as Costas pointed his infrared miniature camera at the site, both keeping their eyes on the road as the images fed straight into the computer. His confidence growing, he would soon have what he needed to get them on the base, to keep her safe. Maybe, just maybe this tangent would lead to Wilfred Fong's killer.

As the moments passed, as the camera clicked and images downloaded, Eko and her safety were becoming more and more important to him. If he was truthful with himself, it was more, something stronger. He wanted her to be with him. If that meant being projected through space for centuries in some kind of stasis then he would do it. What would it matter to him? It would only feel like moments. One minute it would be 2067 the next, who knows, 2267 or perhaps 3067. What did it matter as long as they were together?

"Pull over here," Costas said once they were clear of the base.

He flipped open his brief case and tapped away at the keyboard rotating images and extrapolating a 3D perspective.

"This is good," he said. "I can see the layout clearly. These hangers here could easily contain a shuttle. We just need to find out when they are going to lift off. Perhaps I can check this out with a contact."

"You have a NATO contact?" Eko asked.

"It is my job to have contacts everywhere."

"I see."

"I'll call him from an internet kiosk in Hania."

"Very safe," she said mockingly.

"Yes it is. We must be careful Eko. You can't just walk up to the front gate and ask to be let in. We will have to find some way to get onto the base. They must receive deliveries of some kind."

"You don't understand Costas. Daddy Fong told me about this place. They are expecting me. I can go in at any time and claim my seat."

"Just trust me on this Eko, that's not a safe option. If you want me to help, then do as I say."

Eko looked irritated by his unnecessary show of masculinity and sulked quietly as they drove back to the harbour.

Costas was a little dizzy when he woke. It had been a long night, most of which he'd not slept. Eko had quietly slumbered in his arms, her body, covered only in a T-shirt and underpants, had pressed against him as he'd rested his arms on her warm, soft-skinned hips. He'd curled his body to avoid repeatedly stabbing her with his erection. He could not remember a more tortuous night, his hands longing to wander, his mouth craving to kiss and his cock yearning for the warmth of Eko's sweet scented wetness. Somehow he'd kept his hands still, his mouth closed and his engorged cock at bay. Eventually he accepted the situation, relinquished expectations of physical interchange and accepted her body's warmth, her very presence in his bed as pleasure enough. At that moment, as he had breathed in her fragrance, soaked in her essence he'd fallen into a deep sleep.

Now awake, he rolled over onto his back and slowly processed the information being relayed by his optic nerves to his brain. He considered the situation and decided that he should be surprised. Surprised that he'd fallen asleep, surprised that Eko was no longer in his arms and nowhere to be seen, but perhaps most surprised that Wilfred Fong sat in the chair at the end of his bed, calmly looking at him as if it were the most natural thing in the world that he should be there.

"Get dressed," he said.

"I guess this means I'm off your murder case?" Costas said putting on his shirt.

"Not exactly, but I do need to sidetrack you," Wilfred said.

"Why do I fear that this has something to do with Thira?"

"Because you're getting better at your job."

"Thank you." Costas raised an eyebrow, unsure how to take the comment as his hands worked slowly on the remainder of the buttons on his shirt. By the time the shirt was on and he'd shaken and pulled it into shape over his torso, he'd decided anything a dead man had to say was best taken with an open mind.

FORTY-FOUR

Patrick's gut tightened as he slipped his arm into the navy blue cotton shirt of his uniform. Each button wrenched his stomach ever tighter. Tucking his shirt into his trousers and clipping his ID onto his collar almost sent a deluge of faeces into his shorts and a gush of vomit into his mouth. He leant against the car and held both sphincters firmly closed.

The old man rested his hand on Patrick's shoulder.

"It's not that bad, is it?" Ancient asked.

"I know I can get back into the base, there's no problem with that, and I think I can get you into the grounds. It's just that I..."

"I know you don't want to go back in there Patrick. I know they've lied to you, they've abused your humanity, perhaps even affronted your ego, but it will be a help to have you back in your position."

"So you don't want me to go with you, into space? I'm staying on the ground?"

"Who said anything about going into space. There's no need to do that. Is there Angel?" Ancient looked to Angel for confirmation.

"None at all," she reassured.

"In that case let's go," Patrick said, quickly reassured by the idea that he could stay firmly planted on the ground, right where he belonged.

"Does space flight really bother you that much?" Angel asked once they were back in the car.

"Maybe it's the flying, maybe its just that I'm a human being and I know my place," he answered.

"I didn't think any human beings knew their place," Ancient said. "They're always taking over everything."

"Yeah, well this one doesn't want anything except to live happily ever after on his own little world. Is there anything wrong with that?"

"Not at all Patrick, but I thought it was you who said that the key to humanity's claim to consciousness was the ability to ask questions. And surely travel to other worlds is part of humanity's quest for knowledge. Human beings have always been migratory. The oceans of the world were once just as frightening and unknown as the universe is," Ancient said.

"There's a big difference to me between getting in a boat and getting into a space shuttle. Part of the wonder of consciousness is that we can all ask different questions, that we don't have to sheepishly follow anything, not even our own nature. So although some human beings want to know what other life there might be out there in the universe, I would answer with the question, 'Why do I need to know?' Patrick said, the conversation clearing his earlier anxiety.

"I see your point Patrick but you are up against more than you can imagine."

Before Patrick could answer Angel had sat up on her seat and was pointing out the window.

"There's the base," she said.

Patrick turned off the main road and headed towards the gate.

"Now just keep calm and let me do the talking. Okay?" Patrick said. The old man and the young woman nodded in agreement.

Patrick drove cautiously up to the gates of the base and stopped at the guardhouse. The guard looked into the car and saw Angel and the old man. Patrick lifted his ID for inspection.

"We're on High Alert, Sir. Who are your passengers?" The young guard asked.

"Their car broke down and I picked them up along the way. Perhaps they could just make a call from my office and then I'll give them a lift back to their car. You know mobile reception sucks out here."

"I'm sorry, Sir, they can call from here. That's the best I can do."

"Excuse me young man, but is this where these might be of some use? One for me, one for my granddaughter." Ancient handed over two highly reflective metallic gold rectangles the size of credit cards.

Confusion and bewilderment took hold of Patrick, as the guard took the cards into the station house.

"What the fuck are they?" Patrick said as he stretched his neck to see the guard slot the cards one at a time into some type of reader attached to his computer.

"Tickets," Ancient replied, "to Space Station Thira and beyond."

"You're a fucking trillionaire aren't you?" Patrick accused.

"Well, yes, and I have a few connections."

"If this was just some ploy to stop me from telling the truth, it won't work. You should have topped me and left me in a ditch to cook in the sun. I'll be on the phone as soon as I get inside."

"Relax, Patrick. This is a means to an end. It's not so easy to tell you the truth you know. You're so sensitive about these things."

"Sensitive," he said through gritted teeth.

Suddenly the guard was at his window and Patrick had to force a smile.

"Sir, apparently you're down as missing!"

"What? I've been on leave. HR must have lost my forms," Patrick said.

"Okay, well you better see them about it as soon as you are inside."

"Thanks, I will. I better make sure they paid my rec leave."

"You've got to watch them, Sir."

"You certainly do."

"You can take the VIPs to the visitors' orientation centre."

"Thank you, I didn't know we had one?" Patrick said.

"Just completed sir. Behind hanger 8."

"Great."

Patrick flicked a switch to close all the windows, and waited to hear the sound of the perfect air-tight seal before turning on his passengers.

"VI fucking Ps now. Has anything you've told me been true?" Patrick yelled as they drove through the compound.

"My wealth, Patrick, has some advantages. It's my doorway to information and how I came to learn what PetroSynth has planned. Like it or not you'll have to trust me when I tell you the best course of action was to appear to go along with it. I've heard of some who were less fortunate when they indicated their opposition. Sometimes the best way to effect change is to work from within the machine and not by banging on the walls outside the factory."

"Look, I've had it with this little adventure, your perspectives on reality and your filtered justifications. I've got my job to do, now that I'm here, and let me tell you that's a lot easier to take suddenly than any more time with you."

"You can drop us at the visitor's centre. If we need you any more Patrick, I'll let you know."

"Great, do that, I'm at your beck and call. Seriously, I'll drop whatever I'm doing and come running. Well, what are you going to do anyway? Are you going to Thira?"

"Does it matter? I thought you didn't want to know things that were outside of your immediate concern? You've been very helpful and I don't want to burden you further. The best thing you can do now is return to your job and perhaps contact your wife. I think she may have some news for you."

"Thanks, I think I can take care of my marriage on my own." As soon as the words escaped Patrick's mouth he knew it was an opening for Ancient to slide in with a comment. If he'd been anyone but himself he would've found it impossible to resist. Clearly he'd not handled things well with Kirby. If he had he wouldn't be where he was at that moment. Returning from an unauthorised leave of absence after a failure to communicate effectively with the one person he was most connected to in the world, a world that would soon reflect the state of his fucked-up marriage.

Ancient and Patrick exchanged a look and in that moment there was a sudden breakdown of Patrick's defences. Ancient sidestepped the obvious retort and simply smiled. His eyes communicating that they both knew where the truth lay on this subject. Ancient leant across and embraced Patrick. The warmth and comfort surprised him and it took all his reserves, all his years of awkward male emotional denial, to hold fast and not give in to tears.

"Good luck and thank you my boy," Ancient said as he released him. Patrick sat still for a moment as his new-found companions got out of the car. He powered down the window and leant out.

"I really do hope you can fix this. Stay safe, both of you." With that Patrick shifted the car into gear and drove off towards his office.

"I hope he gets over his fear of space travel in time. We may still need him," Angel said.

"He will," Ancient replied, "he has to."

Patrick parked and looked into the rear view mirror. He could still see Ancient and Angel and watched as the two disappeared into the visitors' centre along with another group who had just arrived in a PetroSynth stretch limo.

"Fuck, fuck, fuck," was all Patrick could manage to say as he steeled himself for the return to ground zero. The very place from where he'd taken flight, the very clothes he'd worn, back to the very routine, the workstation, almost back to the feeling of that moment he'd turned and walked away from it all.

He took a deep breath, allowed a final 'Fuck it' of defiance to escape his lips. He checked himself once more in the mirror, adjusted his tie, shifted his sunglasses and got out of the car with new-found purpose and resolve; a momentarily steadfast resolve, for it was undermined by the clear knowledge that it may break and shatter into a thousand pieces the instant it were tested. As certain as the midday sun would burn the living who wander in its rays, Patrick's resolve would be tested, as all resolves made by human minds inevitably are.

FORTY-FIVE

"Would you like to tell me exactly what has been going on or would you prefer I told you?" Costas said as he sat on the edge of his bed.

"Go ahead," Wilfred said.

"Obviously you faked your death when you realised that someone was trying to kill you, your wife perhaps? You couldn't face leaving Eko, the bond between you was too strong, something I clearly understand from first hand experience. She is quite compelling. No doubt you expected some minor development between her and me so as to ensure I would keep her safe, also the reason you left me clues. But you didn't figure on her falling for me, so you've risen from the grave to claim her back and here we are, two relatively older men, heart-struck by the same young woman. Is this going to be a case of old bull versus slightly less old bull?" Costas looked to Wilfred for confirmation.

"Not bad, Costas, given all the data as it must have been presented to you I can see you could come to little other conclusion. When all this business is done I'm sure I could use a man like you."

"Thank you," he replied.

"You're not remotely close however, but I think you know that. I am as good as dead my friend because of vanity. I'm a foolish vain old man to think she could have truly loved me."

"You are not that old."

"But foolish and vain I am. We had grand plans, Eko and I. We were going to change the world from the anonymity of death. Together we would live, remote and unknown and from our cocoon we would feed what terrible truths we knew about the fate of humanity into the mainstream. People would be inspired; they would rise up and take action against those in power who had betrayed them.

"I went first, hatching an expensive, elaborate, yet ultimately successful plan to make it appear I'd ended my days in blood-ied segments on the tracks of PetroSynth's Athenian Metro. A fully fleshed 3D organic replica complete with conscious thought was pushed before the train that day. I wonder what went through his mind before he died? He was me after all. Only hours old but to him it seemed as if he'd lived a lifetime. He had no idea of my plans with Eko, his memories tailored to suit our purpose.

Eko was to follow me; instead she took all that I entrusted her with, not just the files but my heart, my very soul. But can I blame her? Look at me. Why did I ever think she would actually love me?"

"Enough with the self loathing. Where do you think she is now?"

"I had her followed. She has been detained by PetroSynth security. She attempted to get on to the base this morning. She must have told them what she knows or possibly she discovered and activated the ticket PetroSynth gave all its executives. They have either killed her or she has been allowed to join the launch. My guess is someone will soon snatch her up, as you did."

"I'm not so sure I was the one snatching. Why don't you go to the press now, or the police?"

"I would love to, Costas, but to the world I'm dead. The afterlife I created has income but no power. I'm locked out of access to all my data and the copy entrusted to my dear Eko is unlikely to be available to me now. I'd be killed in moments, properly this time, PetroSynth would see to that, long before

I could access evidence. It would be convenient to blame the siren for her sweet song, however I must accept responsibility for my own failings in this matter. I have left myself with very little room to move. I could have hidden it online somewhere, but PetroSynth are too clever for that. I had to let them think they had reclaimed what I had. Eko was my key and now she has absconded."

"So we must get your key back," Costas said, the hope of seeing Eko again driving his enthusiasm. Despite having been dumped by her, regardless of her leaving him to perish along with a dying planet, he still wanted her. There was no fighting it, even if it were only the chemical commingling of their pheromones that drove him. If the siren sang sweetly to Wilfred Fong then the tune was doubly alluring to Costas.

"You must get onto the base. I'm dead and can do little, trapped by my own faulty scheme and vanity."

"And unhealthy self-loathing. I'll need a false PetroSynth ID. It won't be easy."

"There is another way. "

"Do I have to jump in front of a train?"

"Only metaphorically."

FORTY-SIX

Patrick approached his workstation, weaving through the labyrinth of co-workers, ignoring the *good evenings* and the *how are yous*. A strong bitterness rose from his stomach and filled his mouth with an unrelenting acrid taste. Being back where he started burned under his skin, the test of his resolve coming much earlier than he'd expected. He sat at his desk and closed his eyes, hoping with all the desire he could muster that he was dreaming, that Ancient or Angel with those endless pools of possibility for eyes, would appear and shake him by the shoulder, shake him awake, shake him to his senses, shake him out of this nightmare, out of this parallel existence where he kept looping back into places and emotions he'd tried to escape.

Patrick opened his eyes, his desk still in front of him, no miraculous end to the present nightmare. Notes filled his vision, a mound of little yellow stickers, overlapping, interweaving, all yelling out for him to contact Kirby. He hit a button on his communication console.

"I want a channel to Thira. I want to speak to my wife immediately."

"Is this personal, Sir?"

"Of course it's fucking personal. I need to speak to my wife!"

"I'm afraid all communications to Thira are restricted to official business, Sir."

"Then it's a fucking official communication," Patrick seethed.

"You've already told me its personal, I can't do that, Sir, it's against the Code of Conduct. And sir, could you please refrain from using profanity."

The guy was right, there was no cause to be abusive. He hadn't created Patrick's situation, he was just in the firing line. Patrick took a deep breath, centred his thoughts, intending to continue with calm and dignity.

"Listen fuck-head, I'm the Chief Communications Officer! Put me through."

"You'll have to speak to the base commander, Sir. In fact he's asked for you several times this week, but especially in the last 24 hours. Have you been sick, Sir?"

"No, I was on leave."

"There's no leave recorded, it's not on the roster."

"Well I'm responsible for communications not HR. Can you put me through to Commander Adams?"

"Certainly, Sir. And I need to inform you that I'll be making an official complaint about this conversation."

"Fine, complain, you'll still be a fuck-head and I'll still be Chief Communications Officer." As the words slipped from his lips he regretted them, loathed himself for debasing another human being from a place of anger and frustration. A fruitless, pointless abuse that had leaped from his lips with primal charge and lacked any of the independent thought and control he so valued and expected from others. But what the fuck could he do about it?

"Adams!" the Commander answered gruffly.

"It's Patrick, in communications, Sir."

"Where the fuck have you been?"

"On leave."

"I didn't approve any leave. We're in full swing here, people can't go on leave. What is this – a fucking holiday camp?"

"Well it was approved months ago, Sir."

"Fucking HR. Fuck the 30 hour week, fuck annual leave, and maternity leave, parental leave, sick leave, special leave, short leave, I've got a sick animal leave and especially fuck stress leave. What's with this fucking company?"

"I don't know, Sir." Patrick replied, feeling fairly certain complaints about his own abusive conversation would fall on deaf ears.

"Look Patrick, fuck the leave, I need you on Thira."

"What?"

"My top communications man on the station has space sickness. Stupid prick trained for months and he's as useless as tits on a bull. I need you up there. You're the best I've got. Anyway there's an application here from you and your wife to be crew on one of the exit ships. So I'm giving it a big fucking rubber stamp."

"What?"

"I'm fast tracking it because we need you on Thira. You know we look favourably on married couples with varying technical skills. You'll work on the station until the last exit ship is ready to leave, then you and Kirby will be on it."

"I can't."

"What do you mean you can't? Of course you fucking can!"

"I'm not an astronaut. I'll get space sick, like the last guy."

"You don't have to be a fucking astronaut, and I'm ordering you not to get fucking space sick. Do you hear me? Everything is acclimatised and sterilised and fucking environmentalised. You'll be fine and you'll be on the next shuttle. It leaves in 12 hours. Report to the waiting lounge immediately. Adams out."

Patrick sat at his desk, looking blankly ahead, the stack of yellow notes becoming blurry as he tried to process. Finally Kirby would get what she wanted. Had she orchestrated this into being? Certainly she'd made the application without his knowledge. She must have, but then how could it be submitted without his approval? Begrudgingly, he could admit to himself, there was every chance his occasional slip into passive listening may be responsible for both the materialising of the event and his complete lack of awareness of it. It wouldn't be the first time Kirby had abused his bad habit of not listening but still agreeing. This was looking like the greatest abuse of it. If Kirby chose her moment well enough, when he was distracted, enjoying a well brewed coffee, reading the newspaper, lying in a post-coital stupor or engaged at the climactic moment of the latest first person shooter, Patrick may well have agreed to whatever it was she was saying.

Looking back he'd found himself receiving new furniture he hated, or at dinner with friends he didn't really like or on a holiday in a location not of his choosing, simply because he'd said, 'yes' to Kirby when he was otherwise occupied. Like a tired and worn out parent, Patrick had fallen into a dangerous practice of saying 'yes' when passive listening. A behaviour he clearly had to work on, as soon as these more pressing issues were resolved.

Patrick's mind wandered to the man he was replacing. If she'd managed his absent-minded agreement, could she have gone as far as putting the head of communications on Thira out of action? Had she become that desperate? He would know soon enough. And if the old man and Angel failed to do whatever it was they were planning then at least it was a safe place to be. Earth was looking less and less appealing by the minute.

Patrick swallowed; the bitterness in his mouth was now a solid lump of fear, mixed up with a large measure of self-doubt and loathing. So much for his resolve, now well and truly eroded. Disbelief consuming his free will. He and Kirby would finally be in space together, the Earth left behind with the rest of humanity to die. What a rotting mound of betrayal he suddenly found himself standing on, a rancid mountain of bile that looked out over the crumbling remains of all he felt and believed. With no way out and nowhere to go, Patrick finally surrendered to the inevitable forces at work bringing him to this moment. He acknowledged their show of power in the face of his supposed self determination. He felt a little broken, a little numb in the white light of the reality that lay ahead of him. A reality not of his making, but what could that little speck of a life called Patrick really expect? And with that acceptance Patrick allowed the numbness to permeate throughout his body, throughout his being, through to the spinal cord of his very spirit.

"Fuck it!" he said, trying again to kick-start his resolve, as he got to his feet. He turned his back on the note-cluttered workstation not giving a second thought to that shitty little space he was leaving behind, or the shitty little life he clearly had no control over.

"I fucking give in," he yelled, not caring who around him heard, hoping only the heavens took note, but feeling quite certain they were deaf to his feeble cries.

FORTY-SEVEN

Costas lifted his heavy eyelids and immediately recognised that throbbing, mother of all headaches. His eyes wearily scanned the hotel room as objects came gradually into focus. His bags in the corner, his clothes strewn on a chair, but something wasn't right, something wasn't as it had been. He moved his head a little but it was too fast too soon. The pain shot from the frontal lobe deep into his brain before moving to the back of his head. He sniffed a little, relying on his ever-faithful sense of smell. He was still in Hania, but there was something else in the air, or more precisely on the sheets. Costas examined the pillow on the other side of the bed. The aroma was clear, unmistakable. He only had to smell someone once for it to be an indelible record.

The information he was receiving from his ultra keen olfactory sense was not aligned to his memory of recent events. An altogether unexpected female aroma in a different bed, in a different hotel room than the one he last remembered being in. He'd liked that room, the one from his recent past, not just because he'd spent time there with Eko, but the outlook was pleasant. It had sweet smells and rustic finishes. This room was a little sterile. Sure the sheets were clean, apart from the lingering stains of sex and the room somewhat larger. Actually it was a suite, an elaborate and stylish one. A very different class of hotel, much more up-market than the room where young Eko had abandoned him and where he had a vague memory of witnessing Wilfred Fong's return to the world of the living.

The smell of sex now became the dominant fragrance, the key to clearing the misty fog in his mind where his memories were playing hide and seek.

As he breathed in the remnant pheromones the memories started to come; the feel of a firm body pressed against his own, the touch of her breast, the salty tang of her juices. It wasn't Eko – older, athletic, dominant and altogether more pungent. His hand ran across his chest and traced the scratch marks of fingernails. He could almost see it now; violent movements on the bed, falling on the floor, more a wrestling match than love making. Mouths biting instead of kissing, hands pulling hair instead of gently stroking, pelvises moving ferociously, devouring rather than exchanging.

Though he could not see a face in his memory his nose told him all he needed to know. He heard the water running in the shower; she was still in the suite. He lifted himself from the bed and as he reached for his clothes he saw something written on the back of his hand, immediately recognising his own handwriting. 'Briefcase' it read.

Costas got out of bed and picked up his Briefcase. He entered the password onto the digital display and the case opened. An envelope sat neatly on top of his other possessions, with 'Read me – quickly' scrawled again in his own hand. Costas tore open the envelope and read.

'This is me writing to me. Make sure you are alone when you read this'.

Costas could still hear the shower running and so read on.

'If you have no memory of the last 24 hours then you have, in part, succeeded in your plan. The drugs you took with Eko may still be having some effect. You have seduced Mrs Fong in order to convince her to take you with her to Space Station Thira. Eko has disap-

peared and may be on the old NATO base or on the space station itself. You are now working with Wilfred Fong to expose PetroSynth and their plan to abandon Earth. Wear your micro camera at all times and record everything. Forget about Eko. She dumped you as soon as she was finished with you.'

p.s Wilfred Fong wants you to forget Eko. We both know you can't.

Costas closed his briefcase as Mrs Fong entered the room. He dropped it to the floor and lay back in bed. Mrs Fong slunk across the room and moved in under his arm.

"It's a good thing that you're in Hania," he said, speaking softly to reassure his victim as his arm gently caressed her shoulder.

"Tell me Costas, did you find my husband's killer?"

Costas moved closer determined to speak even more softly, drawing Mrs Fong closer to him. She would have to breathe in the aroma of his manhood, his pheromones would do the rest.

"I have uncovered a considerable amount, Mrs Fong. I am close, very close," his hand moved down to her towel and began to unravel it, exposing her firm athletic figure. Suddenly his mind flashed with thoughts of Eko, the best thing he'd uncovered was her body, or was it his feelings for her? The two were blurred, enmeshed in his thoughts. Even with the sight of Mrs Fong's exciting form and the smell of her fresh body, the heat gently rising from her skin, the image of Eko still occupied his mind.

"Will you make an arrest soon?" She looked straight into his eyes and he felt the chill of mistrust between them.

"That remains to be seen," he replied.

"Oh," Mrs Fong sighed with disappointment.

"I know everything, Mrs Fong."

"How wonderful it must be to be so omniscient."

Costas leaned closer and whispered in Mrs Fong's ear. He took her hand and gently caressed its surface.

"Your husband was murdered because of certain information. I now know that information."

"Really, then I hope the knowledge doesn't affect you as badly as it did my husband."

"You're a very attractive woman." He gently kissed her ear and she relaxed into the bed ready to hear more. "And I know I can make you happy."

"Well yes, in some ways you can." Her hand moved up and rested on the nape of his neck. She pushed him into her throat and his mouth opened and licked and sucked her sweet-smelling skin. Costas returned his mouth to her ear.

"I want you to take me to Thira with you."

Mrs Fong suddenly pushed him away and sat upright on the bed. Costas readjusted himself but remained close.

"I see you do know quite a bit then, don't you. Do you think I killed my husband?"

"No, I don't."

"Why so sure?"

"I have a nose for these things. Even if you did, it's of no consequence to our future. So what do you say?"

"It's true you are a good specimen, and there are not too many of those amongst 'them in the know'. Most of the boys' club are well and truly past their shelf life. But of course it's money that counts in this enterprise. Not physical prowess."

"Of course you may take me for a further test drive," he said returning his mouth to her ear.

"I had every intention of doing that anyway."

As Costas moved his hand forcefully between Mrs Fong's legs he couldn't stop the image of Eko returning to his mind. He wrestled with the body that now lay under him and penetrated deep into the warm wetness of her cunt, allowing it to swallow the pain of being left behind. Mrs Fong tugged at his hair and scratched his skin. He thrust aggressively in retaliation, trying to kill that part of him that would not let Eko go.

FORTY-EIGHT

Patrick took a bite of his sirloin and allowed the tender meat to slowly break apart under the methodical grind of his jaw. His silver plated cutlery danced around the baby Asian greens before he bunched some up with his knife, piercing the collection of fresh leaves with the tines of his fork.

The meal was a welcome distraction from the inevitable space journey that would soon rip him from his mother earth. This entire part of the base was a distraction; a section he'd not been permitted to set foot in until now. Plush and opulent as one would expect it to be in order to cater for the wealthiest amongst Earth's citizens before they jetted off and abandoned the masses. The only advantage Patrick could see in private enterprise driving this operation was that everything was first class. Why bother with an economy section when the economy class was being left behind to die?

The dining lounge was practically empty as Patrick had hoped it would be in the late afternoon. He harboured little desire to mingle with other passengers, though they would filter in soon enough, once the sun was shining on the other side of the world where it could do no harm to them directly. He was happy to enjoy what their money provided. One entire wall of the cavernous room was a giant screen, projecting images of the earth, early satellites, the original international space station and even its secret big sister base, Thira.

The pictures triggered Patrick's thoughts and he began to connect the dots. PetroSynth, spending a fraction of its squillions of dollars, expanding and exploiting the international space station, hiding the construction of Thira behind its high profile space tourism operation run from the smaller station.

It must have made them a packet with their non-polluting renewable fuel powering the operation. Average millionaires getting their day in space and paying a premium for it. Patrick laughed to himself at the simplicity of it. Billionaires being exploited by trillionaires, paying for a party they would never be invited to. Forget the economy class, the middle rich were also being taken for a ride.

With the images of space exploration he questioned his own naivety. Why had he been so surprised, so distraught to learn their intention was to escape, to do nothing other than save themselves? Now he was getting prepped and ready to become one of the lucky ones, one of the survivors, a pseudo pioneer, part of the collective to take the human race into the universe. As if they somehow existed outside it while contained on their floating rock in its bubble of air, not truly part of the universe until they penetrated it, corrupted it with their presence, their influence.

His table jolted suddenly, along with the noise of chairs moving. His thoughts vanished as he looked over to see Ancient and Angel joining him at the table.

"Are these seats free?" the old man asked.

"No, I think you've already paid through the nose for them."

"Indeed you are quite correct." The old man and Angel sat, their strange eyes keeping others away.

"What are you doing here?" Angel asked.

"What do you think? I've been called up and there's nothing I can do about it."

"That's excellent news!" the old man said.

"Yes, I can hardly contain myself. And why do I suddenly feel you knew this would happen?" Patrick replied.

"We have some free time on the station before we are scheduled to be placed into digital stasis. We may need your help," Ancient said.

"Look, I'll do what I can, but only because I'll want to get my feet back on Earth as soon as I bloody well can. But if you get converted to zeros and ones there is nothing I can do."

"We'll have enough time," Angel replied.

"I hope so."

Patrick returned to his meal and ate quietly. He didn't want to say more. He didn't want to tell them how much he was depending on them, though he figured they would some-how extract the thought from his brain given any window of opportunity. This strange pair with their penetrating eyes and intrusive minds weren't just saving the Earth or the Solar System, they were going to save him. Save him from an Earth-less life in the endless void of space. And after that life his remains would be jettisoned into the vacuum, perpetually floating, never having a chance of decaying back into the soil, into the ground from where his molecules came. How would he survive without land to walk on or oceans to swim in or real air to breathe? It was an inhuman life and the coldness of it continued to chill him. His gut tightened sharply as they were called to board the shuttle.

FORTY-NINE

Costas shifted uneasily in his seat and glanced at Virginia Fong sitting on the other side of the limousine before returning to look through the tinted windows. The old NATO base came into view and his mind filled with images of his recent reconnaissance. A different car, a different companion. How could a recent occurrence feel like an old memory? But it did feel old, worn and fuzzy around the edges like a photograph pawed over for many years. The virtual landscape of the base he'd pieced together would soon be real enough.

"We'll be at the European launch site soon," Virgina said, retrieving two gold passes from her purse and resting them in her lap.

"Yes, next stop 'Space Port Thira," Costas replied.

The limo stopped at the gates and a PetroSynth security guard opened Virginia's door.

"No private cars past this point Madam. You'll need to transfer to a PetroSynth transport."

"Of course," she replied.

Virginia handed over her passes as their belongings were transferred. She approached the driver's window of her limo and it lowered. At the wheel sat the shabby little man in the seersucker suit.

"That little prick tried to kill me," Costas said. He moved forward ready to rip the little bastard through the open window. Virgina's hand pushed Costas back and he allowed himself to be contained.

Virginia pressed some cash into the man's hand as Costas sneered. The little man's grin widened as the tinted window rose, his eyes staring Costas down until they disappeared from view.

Virginia took Costas' hand and brought her lips close to his ear.

"I'll miss Elonzo. He was a good employee. Of course he knows nothing and owns nothing so he'll just have to die like the rest of them," she said as the limo reversed, turned and headed off down the road.

Not letting go of his hand, Virginia led Costas into the transport. As they moved through the base she kept hold of him and moved in close. Her gentle kiss on his cheek felt surprisingly affectionate.

"Circumstances have made me a hard person, Costas. I am a survivor."

"And Wilfred Fong was soft."

"I gave him plenty of chances, Costas. I even bought him a little girl friend. I thought if he fell in love he might not follow his stupid ideals and tell the whole world what PetroSynth was doing."

"Eko," Costas said.

"You met her then?"

"Yes, I thought she was a suspect for a time."

"No, she's just one of my employees. She did a very good job but Wilfred was a stubborn, principled man and he left me and PetroSynth no choice in the end," she said.

"What about Eko?" Costas asked.

"Oddly enough she turned up here last night. Security detained her. The base commander was most upset with me as she was throwing my name about and telling people she knew everything. She could get herself killed like that."

"So what will happen to her?"

"They will either decide to put her into the program or she'll be removed from concern."

"That's a very nice way of saying she'll be pushed under a train or over a wall. You could pay her passage."

"Why are you so concerned about my dead husband's mistress?"

"I'm not particularly, I just hate to think of someone so innocent dying."

"Eko! Innocent, Costas. I'm surprised a man of your experience could be fooled by such an act."

"Perhaps it's just that she's so young."

"Well at least she'll never have to face the horror of having to lose her charm through the degradation of growing old."

The transport stopped and they were guided into the visitor's centre, Virginia keeping one arm linked to Costas.

He looked around, not giving away his inward impatience, hoping to find a sign that Eko was not already dead, her body lying lifeless, twisted and broken in a ditch somewhere, while he endured the luxurious surrounds, enveloped by his helplessness to do a thing about it.

They moved into the flight briefing room and as Costas took his seat he caught the mild remnants of Eko's aroma. It was the faintest indication she was alive but he readily accepted the idea she had been in this very room, had gone through this very process. She would be waiting for him. He just needed to stay calm and follow his instincts.

They took their first class seats in the shuttle and it seemed as though they were there for hours, waiting for the final announcement to strap themselves in. With each minute Costas could feel himself getting closer to Eko, each moment of inactivity feeding his impatience.

When the final call came Virginia took his hand again. He was surprised by her sudden vulnerability and realised why it was so easy for him to seduce her. This was not an easy thing to do. To give up everything and head out on an unknown journey. She could have her husband killed, she could lie and cheat to save her skin, she could leave the world forever to save her life but like any human she still needed someone to hold her hand and tell her everything would be okay. As the shuttle's engines started up he gently, reassuringly squeezed her hand and then whispered softly in her ear: "Everything will be alright," and then once more, even more softly, to himself as he wondered if he would ever see Eko's beautiful face again.

FIFTY

Patrick's knuckles whitened as his fingers dug deep into the first class leather armrest of his shuttle seat. A crew-member walked by and placed a comforting hand on his shoulder. He knew the girl from a party. She was a friend of Kirby's and she smiled at him warmly. He couldn't remember her name and hoped he did not have to try. He focused his will completely on holding in the contents of his guts. Too long thinking about anything else and he would lose his slender grip.

"Patrick?" she said.

"Hi," he replied, still unable to remember her name.

"I didn't know you had joined the program?"

"Kirby's idea really. I'm not too keen on space flight."

"Well, there's nothing to worry about, a bit shaky on lift-off but then it's smooth sailing."

"I wish it was sailing."

"Just relax."

"Thanks," Patrick replied and the girl left him in peace. He loosened his hold on the arm of his seat and wiped the sweat from his brow. It had been over an hour since they were told to take their seats. Patrick looked around the craft again and saw the aging faces of the PetroSynth executives. A bizarre mix of people; old men with young wives and older women with younger men. Had everyone dumped their partners for someone younger and traded up? Ancient and Angel looked calm and relaxed a few seats back, completely undeterred by the situation. How could he possibly have any faith in them doing anything to save him? They looked out of sync with reality. He pushed back the growing doubt; was there really any hope if it rested with them?

The shuttle began to move and he felt the blood pumping at his temples, the panic intensifying with every movement, Patrick's hands grasping his armrests as tightly as possible. It was quiet for a moment apart from Patrick's own breathing. He closed his eyes and tried to calm himself, thinking about how clever humanity was for creating this machine he sat in. The sound of the engines coursed through him and he pictured the tons of PetroSynth burning furiously away. His gut twisted into all new kinds of knots, he held his anal sphincter tighter than ever before. He could marvel at the ingenuity of humanity but he cursed his own species too. He cursed them for ever thinking of building space craft, for ever wanting to discover the universe. He hated every single one of history's great thinkers. Why hadn't they just kept their fucking ideas to themselves? No, they had to go and tell other people and get them all excited and now as a result he was in a space shuttle that would soon jet through the atmosphere, that would soon break through that precious layer of air that cocooned his home and gave him life, taking him somewhere he didn't belong.

The shuttle picked up speed as it moved along the runway. Patrick didn't need to look out the window; he could feel the distance between himself and the ground as the shuttle shifted from land to air. This was like no ordinary flight. The craft picked up more and more speed as it quickly gained altitude, tearing through the Earth's atmosphere as it moved further and further out.

Curiosity took hold and Patrick was compelled to look out the window. As the air became thinner and thinner, the light-blue atmosphere giving way to the darkness of space, a sudden sensation raced through his body leaving a bitter feeling of severance, as though he were a new born baby exiting the womb. His cord was cut. The Earth was behind him and the infinite blackness lay ahead.

A dim light appeared through his window, only a tiny speck at first, but it was growing quickly and its rapid increase was the only measure of speed Patrick had at his disposal. Space Station Thira contained his wife Kirby and now undoubtedly held his own future. The reality of the situation was as unavoidable as the unreality of it. Patrick closed his eyes, but it was no good. It was all too much. The days and days on the road, the old man, the young girl, their eyes, the sun, PetroSynth, those evil corporate bastards that ran PetroSynth, those ineffectual government officials that let those evil bastards from PetroSynth run everything, including the demise of the planet. His earth, his Mother Earth! And Kirby, Kirby, Kirby. Why was she doing this to him?

Patrick leant forward, took out the space sick bag and emptied his guts in several involuntary convulsions.

Ancient got out of his seat and moved quickly to Patrick's side. He leant in the aisle, placed his hand on the younger man's back and gently patted, saying nothing, until Patrick fell back. The old man gave Patrick another comforting pat on the shoulder and took the bag, passing it to the girl Patrick had met one time at a party.

Patrick no longer existed. He was no longer a human being of planet Earth. He floated in and out of what was now his existence and all that he knew about himself suddenly seemed open to interpretation and reorganisation.

'Gentle there,' said Ancient. 'There's no rush now.' And strangely Patrick knew what the old man meant. He could take his time, he could pull himself together now anyway he wanted. Keeping his eyes closed, Patrick fell consciously unconscious and willingly remained that way until the craft had completed its journey.

PART FOUR

FIFTY-ONE

Seeing his enemies up close like this was deeply disconcerting. Patrick wasn't in the least prepared and until this moment he wouldn't have imagined he'd be sitting at this table. He looked down at his hands and noticed they were neatly manicured, soft and supple. His shirt cuffs were starched and tightly pinned together with cuff-links bearing the PetroSynth corporate insignia. An immaculate Armani suit coat covered his shirtsleeve. He dropped his hands to his lap and they moved across the top of his thighs, discovering the same fine material covering his legs. He couldn't remember the last time he'd worn a suit, perhaps at his wedding? Certainly never for work, that was all uniformed, cheap and dull fabrics, boring and annoyingly durable. This was not his suit, these were not his cuff-links and more disturbingly these were not his hands.

Not wishing to cause suspicion to those around the table, Patrick discreetly moved a hand to his face to find a neatly trimmed beard instead of his usual three night stubble.

Alarm growing, he shuffled in his seat, straightened his back and felt the weight of his body. An unfamiliar distribution of fat and muscle, stockier than his lean construction, heavy set, firm in the arms but a soft paunch threatening to hang over his belt. This simply was not him. Yet here he was, and all around him the men and women he most hated in the world, the international board of directors of the PetroSynth Corporation, the multinational to end all multinationals. The one company that had taken more than just the money from everyone's pockets, but had taken their governments too, taken control of economies, of all shapes and sizes and manipulated world events accordingly, executing its corporate charter of feeding its coffers by fuelling consumer desire. He suddenly realised he was sneering, his contempt for the loathsome beings around him escaping unrestrained. Fearing discovery, self-preservation kicked in and he quickly relaxed his borrowed face into an unreadable expression, narrowing the likelihood they would turn on him like the pack of vicious beasts he knew them to be beneath their thin veil of corporate polish and manicured façades.

Some at the table, giants of PetroSynth, he knew from their high profiles, their transparent charity work and faux community building, some from their reported political influence communicated through fifteen second video news bites that always popped up on the web before you could watch what you actually wanted, or what they'd led you to believe you wanted. But there were others here he'd never seen before: the unknown faces of the evil corporate empire that had humbly started with a plant that could save the world from its thirst for dirty power. A simple single plant, engineered to burn cleanly, to replicate quickly and to grow where other plants couldn't. These were the men and women with true power over the workings of human existence in the late twenty first century. Yet strangely, though he had never seen some of these faces before, Patrick knew who they were. With this borrowed body he also had a borrowed consciousness. This mind he occupied was acute, and there were profiles and opinions that Patrick could intrinsically follow. He understood where they belonged in the hierarchy, he possessed well observed and keenly formulated ideas on what each individual's position and perspective may be on various issues. Without knowing how, he understood their moral and spiritual standing or lack thereof, across a number of complex propositions.

The CEO called the meeting to order and Patrick flicked his wrists, adjusting his cuffs, interlocking his fingers and placing his hands on the table in front of him. Unsure why he was there but nonetheless clear that he belonged. It was only then that he saw the document that had started everything for him. The same papers he'd discovered by accident in the back of his manager's filing cabinet, though this copy was pristine, neatly bound and looking as if it had just been freshly produced. Not like the ragged, coffee stained version he'd discovered. But that was a different Patrick, who wasn't the person sitting at this table. That was a man horrified by the information that had unwillingly entered his consciousness. Who he was in this moment was unclear, but it was someone who cared little for how a person like Patrick may or may not react to the contents of the document before him.

Patrick had little trouble following the discussion, the assumed knowledge underpinning the debate was all available to him. Some he'd learned before driving off into the unknown, some from his time spent with Ancient, but there was more available to him now, more than he could recall ever having discovered for himself. The sun had accelerated in its life span and was continuing to burn at an advanced rate. In years rather than millennia the earth and indeed the solar system would be uninhabitable by humanity. Efforts by PetroSynth Corporation to halt or in anyway alter the sun's unpredictable activity had failed. If all agreed, a path the CEO forcefully suggested, then all company finances would be channelled into the only viable alternative. Developments into digital stasis would be the prime focus with the aim of storing all high ranking PetroSynth personnel, their families and other essential human beings; scientists, trades persons, models, award winning actors and other creative types, great thinkers whose ideas they agreed with and naturally anyone they wanted to fuck. A human being equated to approximately 8.5 gigabytes of data, to be stored and reanimated once a suitable new planet had been discovered. To maximise the potential success of the plan four spacecraft would be built, each with a living crew of one hundred who would repopulate as required via traditional means and each carrying a complete copy of all digitised passengers along with the appropriate organic material required for human reconstitution. Space exploration, the search for new worlds, would be the general cover story. Something to keep the scientists happy as they worked towards a completely different goal.

Patrick looked around the table and knew there would be two questions raised. The first would be from Annalise Farvis, French CEO. The second, he knew, would be from Wilfred Fong, the Greek CEO.

"What would happen if all four spacecraft discover suitable planets and all four sets of human beings were reconstituted? Where, may I ask, does the human soul fit in your scenario?" raised Annalise.

"While every effort will be made to maintain contact between spacecraft with the aim of having only one set of data banks eventually utilised, the group collectively agrees that there is no conclusive evidence, including our own experience and existence, that pointed to the existence of a soul, we are most likely a random collection of electrical impulses as opposed to a continuing consciousness. Therefore all four data banks could be theoretically utilized at the same time without any consequence other than the perpetuation of the species. Each individual person, once reconstituted would be independent from any other based on the same data and once reconstituted would go on to form unique memories from that moment. We feel our own consciousness would align with one of the reconstituted beings based on his or her own data and that would most likely be the first to be 'awoken', for no other reason other than that seems logical. Subsequent reconstitutions would just have to look after themselves and if they didn't possess the original consciousness then at least they would be human with, of course, the added advantage of being based on a superior data set. Naturally tests will be carried out to ensure the safety of the system but there may not be time to conduct a spiritual trial. Efforts will be made to conduct a full human trial including the reconstitution of a single human being from four sets of data, however that would only occur if time permits once primate tests conclude the process to be safe." The CEO smiled pointedly at Annalise, his eyes telling her to accept all he'd said. His eyes shooting down any challenge. She moved to speak, Patrick expecting a further argument.

"Thank you," she replied and sheepishly fell into line.

To Patrick's ears it was confirmation of the deluded and intensely selfish nature of those around him. Exactly the kind of answer he'd expected to hear. He wanted to jump to his feet and interject, proclaim the presence of the CEO's consciousness might actually make that particular being less human, the first remade on his data perhaps the most unfortunate one with the other three possibly standing a chance at some kind of alternative. Patrick wasn't able to control the power of speech, only the power of movement and thought, even the very idea of forming his mouth into a shape to direct speech felt blocked. There was no choice, other than to watch on.

Before Wilfred Fong could make his inevitable contribution Patrick was both surprised and then mildly bored by the unexpected contribution from mid-western American software trillionaire, Miles Foley. "Could we just change the terminology from 'Reconstituted' to 'Resurrected'? I just don't want to sound like I'm orange juice travelling through space."

"Absolutely not," chimed in the Vatican representative Monsignor Gardello.

"Well, you would say that, but I don't even understand why the fuck you are at this meeting," said Foley.

"Foley, we are here because we have an established control of a large section of the masses, and you know that. Plus we still have a lot of money, don't forget. It hasn't all been paid out in compensation cases. If you don't want widespread panic then you need people to have faith that what is happening is part of a divine scheme. At the very least we offer the best distraction available, while you carry out your plans in secret. To your original request, giving a religious connotation to the scientific process of the digital stasis of human beings is inappropriate and completely unacceptable."

"We've been down this road," the CEO interceded, "there will be no change to the terminology. It's a process for preservation, not salvation, for God's sake."

Foley scowled, Gardello smiled and Wilfred Fong leant forward.

'But what about those left behind?' Patrick heard Wilfred Fong finally ask, as he knew he inevitably would.

The CEO made it clear. There was to be no further talk of those left behind. The risk of widespread panic must be avoided at all costs. Society must continue to function to ensure a successful transition of all essential beings into stasis.

Anyone not able to comply with the company ruling would be terminated from his or her position without entitlements, nor would their families be included in the departure process. It was clear to Patrick and all those at the meeting that being 'Terminated' was not merely in reference to job function but would also include the cessation of one's bodily functions.

Wilfred Fong fell silent. There was no point going further unless he was on a path of self-destruction.

Patrick's overwhelming desire to support Fong, to get to his feet and champion the majority of the human race destined to be abandoned, left to perish on a dying Earth, in a dying solar system, was denied him when he woke suddenly, still strapped in his shuttle seat. The shuttle jolted sharply as it docked with the station and his mind floated between what was real and what was not.

The repugnant collective of the International Board of PetroSynth Corporation swirled and spun round in his head like a vile unsavoury soup. His mind poisoned by their corrupt existence filling him with a bitter distaste for humanity and in turn for himself, being undeniably part of that animal classification. The dream stained his thoughts with a bitterness as real as any memory. As it took shape, drifted in and out of his mind the way dreams do when you first wake, Patrick realised there was more in those thoughts than he could or should remember. Names he did not know, faces he'd not seen before, information and details beyond the re-constructive abilities of his subconscious. Was it merely a dream, a creation of his mind resulting from the unprecedented shock of space flight? He turned to see Ancient and Angel getting out of their seats and the old man shot him a glance. In those knowing eyes Patrick saw the possibility that he was the victim of another mind game. Ancient was not just taking unwelcome readings of his thoughts, but planting ideas, images, perhaps even memories that were not of his own experience.

Patrick shook it off as he walked through the air lock, unsure if Kirby would be there to greet him, his attempts at pre-launch contact no doubt blocked by the communications officer he'd berated. A simple effective revenge after not finding a supporting shoulder in the base commander who would have surely abused him further when he made his report against Patrick.

He looked around again, keeping Ancient and Angel on his radar as they came through the air lock passage.

"That wasn't too traumatic, was it?" Angel asked.

"As always I'm not sure what you are referring to," he replied.

"I'm sure I don't know what you mean, Patrick," said Ancient.

"Yeah right, listen you can find me at my wife's quarters if you need me, but for fuck's sake stay out of my head." Patrick handed him a piece of paper with Kirby's details on it.

"Thank you. We better go to our lodgings too. It is very important we don't do anything out of the ordinary. For the time being that is. Low profile," Ancient said and he and Angel followed the group of passengers to a reception desk.

Now that the initial terror of his separation from the Earth was over Patrick relaxed a little. The space station's high buttressed ceilings with reinforced steel and transparent panels reminded him of a grand cathedral, the unexpected openness helping him to breathe, to adjust. He'd imagined the station would feel closed in, more like a crammed orbiting airport. Naturally no planes, just four enormous spacecraft docked onto the outer rim.

He wandered by an observation lounge and found the pull of the view too great. His body fell effortlessly into one of the several reclining lounge chairs positioned perfectly in front of a giant window. He looked in wonder at sights he'd hoped he would never have to see. The moon not as close as he thought it would be, but to see it without the hindrance of the Earth's atmosphere gave the object a crisp sharp edge. The station not only orbited Earth but rotated on its own axis to maintain an approximation of Earth's gravitation. Patrick felt a little light-headed and decided it was due to the gravitational controls being less than perfect. To Patrick, anything different from Earth was less than perfect. He recalled the pre-flight briefing and knew the sensation would soon pass. The station continued in its rotation and the Moon passed out of view. As Earth came into sight Patrick breathed a sigh of regret. He felt so distant from it, separated and strangely cold, as if living on that piece of floating rock was never part of him or might never be again. Its fragility never more apparent to him, the vast distance he'd travelled through the atmosphere now looking so very, very small.

Earth, too, soon moved out of view and Patrick found himself staring into the dark reaches of the unknown. A mild panic ran through his bones and despite the excellent climatic controls, he shivered in his seat. Feeling like an infinitesimal speck of nothing, he picked up his bag and resumed his search for Kirby's quarters, determined to make her pay somehow for putting him through this.

Patrick followed the numbers, counting down to his wife's quarters. A few more doors and he would be there, a few more moments and he would see Kirby.

Crouching at her door was a middle-aged man in a lab coat with a bulbous red nose and flaky skin. He pushed a note under the door and Patrick stopped behind him waiting for him to get to his feet.

"Hello," Patrick said. The man jumped up.

"Can I help you?" the man in the lab coat said. A wave of mint laced garlic breath washed over Patrick and he took a step back to avoid fainting.

"Yes, you're in my doorway," Patrick said as he steadied himself on the wall in response to the pungent odour of the man before him.

"You must be mistaken, these are Kirby Stevens' quarters."

"Then I'm in the right place," Patrick replied.

"Who are you?" the lab coat asked with another wave of garlic breath, the conversation becoming harder to take than the shuttle flight.

"Would you mind just stepping back a little. Personal space! I'm Patrick, Kirby's husband," Patrick replied.

"Well she's on a shift now. You'll have to come back later."

"I don't think so." Patrick pressed the key-pad and punched in a code.

"I've been assigned to share my wife's quarters," Patrick said as the doors opened. He walked inside and heard the crumpling of paper under his feet. He lent down and scooped up the note that had just been slid under the door.

"This is for my wife, I take it?"

"Ah, yes," Gardener said nervously. "Perhaps I should give it to her personally." His hand reached forward to take the note from Patrick but he quickly tucked it into his pocket.

"I'll pass it on. No trouble." Patrick pressed a button on the wall and waved happily to the distraught, contorted face of Professor Gardener.

Patrick dropped his bags to the floor, bounced onto the bed, pulled the note from his pocket and began to read.

FIFTY-TWO

Sleep was not coming easily. It hadn't since arriving on the station. His shoulder pinned to the bed under the weight of Virginia's unconscious body, Costas could feel her unrestrained drool as it ran from her mouth, over his chest and under his arm. His body was tired, his mind fatigued from her near constant engagement. Virginia had been relentless in her determination to have as much fun as she could before it was time to 'sleep' for a few hundred years or so, before her body was broken down into its purest organic compounds and her consciousness, if there were such a thing, was stored as a digital signature. She was making up for lost time, time she had not actually lost yet, time she had only just discovered.

Sex with Virginia Fong was combative; an aggressive wrestling-match that had circulated his blood sufficiently to remove any remaining effects of that little pill Eko had tempted him to take. He felt grateful for not discovering further unwanted body piercings, but the aching emptiness that followed their lustful union left him shaky. His cock raw, and his feelings more so. He longed for tenderness, for gentle caresses, for lingering foreplay, for deep passionate kisses.

He tuned into Virginia's gentle breathing. It was strangely calming and the only thing holding him back from an emotional fracture. It was not as though he'd spent his life alone and this liaison with Virginia, aggressive and lacking in tenderness, was more normal to him than the loss of emotional control, loss of rational thought, loss of dignity, well-being, ego and self preservation – indeed all that flowed from him like a burst water main the moment Eko arrived into his world. There had never been anything like Eko, and he doubted there would be again. In all the thrusting and scratching with Virginia, the nibbling and gnawing, the hair pulling, the arse smacking, the tossing and tumbling, the deep hard fucking, the pain-numbing, penetrating fucking, holding her like a doll with his hands on her hips and pulling her back and forth, up and down on his cock. No sign or hint of building towards a climax, just fucking, fucking and fucking with that sweet face coming into to his mind, gorgeous Eko, divine Eko occupying his every thought, while Virginia's hard body kept riding him with no end. Virginia with her face flushed with colour, her eyes void from so much fucking. Her body responding to his thrusting, her pelvis pushing back on him, her fingers digging into his flesh, her teeth biting, her nails scratching, but her mind elsewhere, caught in a sex induced stupor. He could see nothing in those black pools, just the reflection of his own misplaced desires. His body was moving, his hardness penetrating deep into her wet, taut cunt, that fit little cunt, his body pressed hard against her athletic figure, but it was not Virginia he was seeing under him at all; it was only Eko.

Nothing felt right now, how could it without Eko? She'd betrayed him, led him on, led him astray, led him down the garden path, drugged him, quite possibly not even have slept with him. She'd dumped him in a hotel in Crete and left him to die on Earth with the rest of humanity, attempting to save her own skin, her own precious, beautiful skin. No, nothing would ever be the same again, now that he knew he loved Eko in that most dangerous, unconditional, addictive, self-destructive and all-consuming way.

Costas gently lifted Virginia's sleeping head from his shoulder and slid out of bed. He dressed quietly in the dark, anxious not to rouse his slumbering opponent. She stirred momentarily but didn't wake. He crept slowly around the bed and opened the door, moving quickly into the bright light of the corridor, the doors to Virginia's quarters closing behind him. He looked left then right, sniffed a little and followed his nose down the passageway.

FIFTY-THREE

Kirby's thoughts drifted as she sat at her desk in the lab, her pen tapping out an unknown rhythm, a distracted melody providing a soundtrack to her random musings. Ideas and images floating and commingling, both connected and freely forming, nothing solid staying in her mind. A myriad of possible futures existing in her thoughts alongside the past and present. A long day, historic even. The first wave of affluent space explorers digitised and safely stored in data banks on the Fong server. Amusement at Gardener swanning around, officially the team leader, but Kirby enjoyed the self-satisfying knowledge that without her, little would have been achieved. What Gardener actually did with his time, other than parade around, was a mystery to her and her colleagues. He'd had some brilliant ideas in his time. He could claim the foundation of the very system, evolving 3D printing from producing simple organic forms into replicating the complexity of an entire human body, attaching an individual's digitally stored profile to new organic material; brilliant, but managing people, working on a time line, scaling the technology to work on multiple subjects, these were not his skills. They were her achievements. Where he'd failed she'd succeeded. It was annoying but fair to give him credit for the brilliant ideas he'd had but that's all they would have been if she'd not found ways of making them work, connecting the dots, streamlining, giving elegance to the crude raw material that she'd encountered when first joining the program. He was good at consuming the station's supply of small goods and no one could take that away from him.

Of course all the test subjects had survived their reconstitution, their digital sequence attached seamlessly to the organic rebuild. She'd been tireless in her efforts to make it work. Had the individual's personality been intact after the process? It appeared so. Would the project have stopped if after being reborn the primate subjects had coughed up their insides and lay on the floor of their laboratory cages, a mass of decaying molecules? No, the project would have gone ahead. Test subjects meant little to those with money enough to build such an elaborate escape hatch. As long as it worked in the end, it didn't matter what it took to get there.

Kirby wouldn't allow it to fail. She had to hand it to her employers; it was a stroke of genius to bring her on to the team, her personality profile working to her advantage as much as her technical skill. Somewhere in the data banks, in the IQ and personality testing of Kirby Stevens it rang out loud and clear; she would not allow a system to fail if that system held life in the balance.

This was a well-oiled machine; actually, Kirby thought, this was a well-PetroSynthed machine and it was she who had made it that way. It felt pointless to be looking for flaws in the system, akin to questioning her own professional integrity. There were none because she'd made it that way, yet still she needed to try and find something that would delay everything long enough for Patrick to resurface and for her to have an opportunity to yell at him for his disappearing act.

The staccato of the pen became more rapid, an action driven by her mind with no conscious awareness, a nervous habit expressing thoughts and feelings with no other means of release. What did she have left at her disposal to find Patrick, to expedite his return to the living? She realised how ridiculously desperate she was feeling, and who could blame her with salami-breath buzzing around like a persistent little bumblebee ready to suck the polliniferous secretions from her honeysuckle bloom at a moment's notice. The secured channel to the base Gardener had arranged would only have resulted in another message being left on Patrick's already note-cluttered desk.

Officer Lockie's stomach flu had been fortuitous. He would recover soon but his absence from duty would have them looking for Patrick to fill his shoes. If only she'd thought of it herself she could have taken him out of play longer. Lockie was a nice guy, easy to take advantage of, and he had a sweet tooth. A small but carefully measured dose of salmonella in his chocolate pudding would have done the trick, easy enough to acquire thanks to the healthy paranoia of the PetroSynth's board. HG Wells would be proud his stories still carried influence, a small secured room on every ship holding all known diseases, a safeguard against unknown hostile alien life, a justifiable resource. Humanity's deadliest threats to itself carried along for the journey, as though the species can only thrive if it lives under the constant threat of extinction. Desperate times, call for desperate measures they say. Kirby was a woman of thought, of science, she wouldn't be drawn any further into desperation. Calm, that's what was needed, not knee jerk reaction, not emotional responses, but calm, calculated, well thought out plans. If she were going to infect anyone it would be Gardener.

The tapping of Kirby's pencil against the desk slowed as the idea of removing Gardener and his lustful propositions from her world took shape. Could she stoop to that, could she knowingly harm another being? If Patrick were here she wouldn't need to be even thinking this way. His angry words replayed again in her head, 'Have a nice life. Have a nice life.' What a shit of a thing to say, 'Have a nice life.'

The pencil abruptly stopped moving and Kirby became aware for the first time that she'd been tapping it. Her fingers still wanted to move but the pencil was being held by another power. As she looked to investigate what quantum force was being applied to prevent the pencil from tapping the desk as rapidly as her brain was commanding, she picked up a familiar scent. She quickly released the pencil from her grip, got to her feet and took Patrick into her arms.

Kirby reluctantly released Patrick from her embrace. Neither wanted to let go of the other's hand.

"What are you doing here?" Kirby said.

"It seems my wife put in a joint application for us to be crew members on an exit ship. Not only that but a crew member on the station is mysteriously ill and the top brass believe I'm the best person for the job until my wife and I take up our never ending assignment on the last ship to leave."

"You're not angry?" Kirby asked.

Patrick considered the question. He truly thought he would be, truly thought once he was in the same room as Kirby he could let fly with all manner of abuse. How dare she put his name forward for something he clearly didn't want to do. How dare she scheme to get him to be with her. But strangely, as soon as he'd walked into the room and seen her tapping away nervously at the desk with her pencil, seen her long slender neck with her soft white skin, her hair tied back revealing the crisp outline of her profile, all anger had melted away. Once she was in his arms the alchemy was complete. His fears turned to joys, his self-imposed obstacles fell to the ground, his thoughts of the certainty of intrinsic human singularity dissipated before his mind's eye. Suddenly, only being with her mattered.

"I thought I would be, but I want to be with you Kirby, I don't know why but I don't care if that's in a remote part of the outback or flying through the endless blackness of space. Life is fleeting, I'm a minute speck of insignificant flotsam that will be forgotten by space and time as soon as I'm gone, but being with you, sharing this ridiculously rare experience with you, that makes sense."

"Can't you just say you love me, you shithead?" she replied.

"I'm working on it."

"I don't want recriminations, no emotional blackmail. You have to be here because you want this."

"I know."

"I didn't know those terrible things before, when you thought I did," she said.

"I know. I think I always knew. I just wanted an excuse to avoid this, avoid being dragged away from Earth. I thought that if I left its surface, perhaps part of me would die. The truth is that would only happen if you left me."

"I don't believe that."

"Neither do I, but it sounded good when I rehearsed it. The truth is I was simply scared, scared I wouldn't be myself if I didn't have the Earth under my feet."

"So we can take up the crew positions?" she asked.

"We have a small problem," Patrick said.

"What?"

Patrick reached into his suit pocket and pulled out Professor Gardener's note. He held the piece of paper in the air and looked at Kirby as if waiting for an explanation.

"What is it?" she asked.

"A garlic scented love note," Patrick replied.

"Oh shit," Kirby said, reaching to take the note. Patrick pushed her hand back, opened the note and began to read.

> *My Dearest Kirby,*
>
> *I've informed my wife of our situation and the divorce will be finalised tomorrow. Has your husband signed yet on the dotted line? I do so long to consummate our arrangement and to start our bright future together, a future written in the stars.*

Patrick looked at Kirby and waited silently for a response.

"It's a long story, Patrick."

"We've got the infinite reaches of space before us, so let's hear it."

"I needed to get him on side. He showed me some documents, research into the sun. I had no idea that this was all just PetroSynth's escape pod, that they planned to leave the world to die. You must know that. They have betrayed us as much as anyone, more so. We have been blindly working to help them, thinking we are doing something noble for humanity when we are aiding and abetting its worst elements. It makes me sick, Patrick."

"I know. Believe me I know. Anyway I saw and smelled the little drip and I could tell there was no way you'd let him lay a finger on you, let alone anything else."

Patrick took Kirby's warm body back into his arms.

"I have to report for duty now," he said as he reluctantly pulled himself away.

"I'll see you after your shift," Kirby said softly.

"I've been assigned to your quarters."

"Excellent. I'll break out the champagne."

"I've missed you Kirby. Why did I ever let you get out of my sight?"

"You're really dim sometimes," she replied.

"A total fucking idiot."

Professor Gardener walked into the room and saw the two embracing.

"Ah, excuse me Kirby, might I have a word. You're still on duty aren't you?"

"Yes Professor," Kirby replied.

"I'll see you later." Patrick began to walk out but slowed as he passed the Professor, careful not to get too close and hoping to stay down wind. "Oh, I delivered your letter. Safe and sound." Patrick said.

"Thank you," Professor Gardener said, pleased to see Patrick's body disappear through the door.

Professor Gardener moved quickly into Kirby's space and she backed away from the preceding wall of odour. The minty freshness was not holding up to the foetid guttural stench that seeped through his pores.

"What's he doing here?" he snarled.

"He didn't like the idea of divorce, so I'm sorry Professor, our arrangement is off."

"Kirby, don't play around with me. You've seen information that is dangerous to know. I can have security back on you if you like."

"Professor Gardener, I don't suppose your superiors would like to know who gave me that information?"

The Professor seethed with anger.

"This is not the end of the matter Kirby." He turned to leave the room but caught himself on the corner of the desk. He buckled with the pain that shot up from his groin and his hands instinctively moved to cup his throbbing genitals as he fell into a chair.

"Are you alright?" Kirby asked, trying to hold back her smile. With all the composure he could gather, Professor Gardener got to his feet, released his testicles from his own supportive grasp and walked to the door.

"You'll regret this Kirby," he said before finally leaving the room.

FIFTY-FOUR

Post-coital aches and pains usually invoked a sense of pride for Costas. He liked extending them, leaning into them, relishing in the cause. Like a tight muscle responding to a yoga stretch, it was hard to call it pain, more a sensation, a trigger that instantly recalled recent pleasures. The body always hurt in delicious ways after sex, muscles that otherwise lay dormant remembering the pleasure of their unexpected engagement. But it was different this time, the feeling of elongating the stiffness in his lower back or the tightness of his inner thigh only brought flashbacks of betrayal, humiliation, debasement. Virginia's punishment of his body ensured every turn he took, every step, every reach or movement echoed back to her. Pleasure for its own sake to be certain, but also an unmistakable cry to be remembered in a world of fleeting feelings.

He made his way down the corridor, easily navigating through the lax security, moving with intent and purpose. Where were the guards, the CCTV? The place was run like a health club not a top-secret space station. No one around during the day cycle, and if they were he hadn't seen them. He figured they were all focused on getting the arrivals from Earth processed. Virginia and he were scheduled to check out of their quarters soon themselves and report for something called Human Digital Compression. Not something he looked forward to with any relish, becoming a series of zeros and ones and later reconstituted like a pre-packed, freeze-dried TV dinner. Just add carbon and a few other base compounds, program the DNA from the captured Human Digital Compression and off you go. Fuck, what was he thinking to get himself caught up in this? What the fuck were they thinking when they came up with this stupid plan?

His hand tried every door handle he passed. Locked, move on, locked, move on. One gave way and he slipped inside. He found himself in a room of lockers, a large hamper in the corner with soiled uniforms. Quickly sifting through the discarded clothing he found a set acceptable enough to wear. His pants fell to the floor, the bending and moving reminding him again of Virginia and their coupling. As he pulled the uniform trousers on he felt the hard texture of his public hair, glued together in clumps by his own semen and Virginia Fong's fluids. Her scent strong and arousing, but not the scent of the woman he wanted.

Enough, Costas thought. He was a professional, unlike the fuck-knuckle in charge of security on this station. Sure, you needed one of those fancy gold cards Virginia had flashed at the gates of the launch site to get up here in the first place, but, if he was in charge of security it would not be so easy to move around the station as he was doing.

He found his way into a block of unattended offices, moving along the corridor and checking each office door as he went along, hoping to find one unlocked to avoid a forced entry. All he needed was a computer terminal, something that might be linked to the main data-base so he could check on the nagging notion that his instinct kept repeating.

After the third locked door Costas was ready to kick the next one in. Just as he moved to give his leg some room to kick he noticed a bright object at the end of the corridor. It wasn't the first time he'd noticed the super bright white light with a blue letter 'i' contained in a blue circle. In fact he'd seen them consistently since arriving on the station, with people standing under them looking up directions on the touch screen.

Costas moved quickly down the corridor and stopped at the information kiosk. Making his way through the maze of menus he finally came to the schedule for Human Data Compression. Following an alphabetical list he found his name, then Virginia's. They were scheduled to go into stasis in 30 hours and stored on the Fong Server. What a joke that was, Mrs Fong digitised and stored inside her husband's namesake alongside her new lover. Costas steadied himself, unsure if he could stand another few hours of exhausting lovemaking with the athletic Mrs Fong. Would the post-coital aches and pains, her bruising, pinching and nipple twisting, be felt by his new body when it was returned to form by this collective of Frankensteins with their organic 3D printing and genetic digital storage?

He returned his focus to the mission moving to 'E' in the Alphabetical list. As he ran his finger down the screen, he hoped, he wished, he almost prayed that he would find her name there. The names flashed passed his eyes and there it was; Eko. He ran his finger across to her status. She'd already been through HDC and was on the data banks. If only Wilfred were here, Costas thought, then the whole freak show of a family could be compressed and archived together.

Costas backed away from the information kiosk and contemplated his situation. He could wait a few centuries and find out the truth or he could try and find some way to bring her back. She may already be dead and all that Virginia had said was true. He should expect nothing but that his precious Eko was dead. And even if he could find a way to bring her back, what would she be like, her old body gone, turned into some kind of organic soup and recycled somehow on this stupid fucked-up piece of human ingenuity, that was nothing more than a temple to greed, power and selfishness. Costas caught his breath. He was in serious danger of becoming a radical. He was a moderate, a professional, but above all a self-centred individual, just like the silver-spoons who'd created all this shit. And what he wanted, what he craved, what would make him happy, was to have Eko. He couldn't wait centuries, he couldn't wait days or even an hour. With the seconds ticking by he moved back to the information kiosk, ran his finger down its screen and found directions to HDC processing. He hit print and the kiosk spat out a very helpful colour map with the directions clearly marked out for him. He scanned the map for a few moments then tucked it into his uniform.

"I'm coming, Eko," he whispered, and moved purposefully down the corridor.

FIFTY-FIVE

"There you are!" Ancient said as he sat himself down next to Patrick in the observation lounge. Patrick felt quite at ease with the idea of being in space and was enjoying looking at the Earth and the Moon as they moved by the large window. Even the endless star-covered vacuum was comforting to view. It was hard to pinpoint the exact moment he'd come to terms with being away from his precious Earth. He still breathed, he still ate, slept, his mind still thought. On the ground or up here in this false, man-made environment, he was still Patrick and it was relaxing being himself, regardless of what other factors appeared around him.

Ancient waited patiently for Patrick to speak, and the younger man picked up on the shared moment. He was even getting used to the idea of the old man's unwelcome intrusions into his consciousness. It was then that Patrick realised something. He could handle existing away from Earth, what he couldn't tolerate was the idea that Earth would cease to exist, and worse still that it might cease to exist when there was a chance to save it. While Ancient and Angel remained on the Station the chance for Earth's survival remained.

As Patrick looked at the old, time-withered face before him, he wondered why he felt so much confidence in Ancient. The deep creases around the mouth, the strongly etched crows feet, and the light grey patchy stubble that sprouted across his face. What was it in those eyes that had beckoned Patrick, that had coerced him into returning to face all he'd successfully run away from? Why did he believe the things that came out of the old man's mouth?

Ancient's eyes gleamed and held Patrick's mind steady for a few moments. He sensed it was there in those crisp blue pools that he saw the trust he so longed to feel. Was that all it was, that the old man's eyes were simply reflecting Patrick's hopes? There was something else in those eyes that he could see, and when the old man lightly tapped his forearm Patrick knew that Ancient needed his help.

"I'm afraid things haven't worked quite to plan, Patrick," Ancient said.

"What went wrong? Couldn't you do whatever it was you had to do?"

"Well we were close, Patrick, but we ran into a bit of a hitch. You see you know I told you that I created PetroSynth?"

"Yes."

"Well, I also formed the company, the original one that is, not the multinational beast it mutated into. Regardless, I'm seen by some to hold unique status with the company and an annoying religious order."

"Nothing would surprise me with you Ancient."

"Yes, well, some bright spark thought it might be good if I were one of the first to be placed into HDC. It would have been too suspicious if I caused any fuss. I had to go along with the idea."

"So when are you scheduled to be converted to ones and zeros, surely there's still time?"

"Well, you see the first round was yesterday."

"So you skipped it then. I don't understand the problem."

"The problem, Patrick, is that Angel and I have already been scanned, decompiled and saved on the server. We need you to reconstitute us."

"I see, of course you have become electrons in a data bank so naturally I'll have to come and hit the reconstitute button. I just have one question?"

"Of course."

"How the fuck are you here now if you no longer have a body and your DNA is now nothing more than an electrical imprint?"

The old man leant forward and began to shake Patrick vigorously by the shoulder. Patrick woke lying next to Kirby, the sweet smell of their sex lingering in the air. Patrick sat bolt upright and Kirby rolled over, disturbed by his movements.

"What time is it?" she asked.

"Time to get up, Kirby, I need your help."

"To do what?" she asked, a small smile appearing on her face, thinking a new round of love-making was soon to transpire.

"We have to reconstitute a couple of people from the Fong Server."

"We can't do that!" Kirby said.

"I need their help Kirby. There's no choice."

"Why can't you wake up in the middle of the day and want to have sex, like every other male. No, you need to put my job on the line."

"If you help me, Kirby, I'll go anywhere you want, but I need you to do this for me."

"You'll be happy. You won't make our life miserable, always complaining that you should never have left Earth?"

"Do this for me and I'll never leave you, even if you ask me to go, I won't. I'll annoy you till you die."

"I'm not going to bargain with you. Be here because you want to be. It's that simple."

"Then help me for no other reason than I'm asking, because I will do this anyway."

"How did I forget how annoying you were! It will show up on the system, but I guess I could make it look as if there were some concerns of data corruption. No one questions me on technical or safety matters. As long as we keep Garlic Gardener out of the way it could be okay. Get dressed. We're doing it before the end of day shift."

FIFTY-SIX

Costas tapped on the door and the technician looked up from his computer.

"I'm a bit lost, can you give me some directions."

The technician got to his feet, a little frustrated with another new crew-member confused by the space station's labyrinth of corridors.

"This area is secure. You need to go back down the corridor behind you and turn left," the tech said, through the glass doors.

Costas, pointed to his ear, indicating that he couldn't hear.

"For fuck's sake." The tech opened the door. "You go back down the corridor…" before he could say any more Costas had him in a headlock. He spun him round and the tech dropped to his knees. Costas gave him a quick jab to the back of the head, enough to render him unconscious.

Costas examined the controls of the HDC system, his face turning white with confusion. Easy enough to access the controls, but all these flashing lights and buttons. Where was the user-friendly interface with a nice big button that said, 'Reconstitute'? This was high tech state of the art, one wrong step and he could as easily kill or delete Eko as rebuild her.

He caught the slight waft of perfume, someone was coming. Looking around the room quickly, there was no choice but to dive under the desk.

FIFTY-SEVEN

Kirby's fingers moved quickly through the touch screen system of the mainframe. Patrick looked over her shoulder, his eyes following her swift movements but his brain failed to keep up with what she was doing.

"I've hacked the security system. Once we finish all data and CCTV records detailing our incursion will be replaced by a copy of the information from the same time last week. Best I can do on short notice, but it should cover our tracks. Okay, let's make sure we get the right people. Do you have their names?"

"Angel and Ancient," he replied.

"What? Is this a fairy tale. Do you have a surname?"

"No, that's all. The old guy called himself Ancient and the girl was called Angel."

"I'll have to do a visual search," Kirby replied. She pulled up the profile search and tapped in the parameters. 80 years plus, white, male. Faces began to flash across the screen as Kirby swiped.

"That's him," Patrick said, as he pointed to Ancient's face.

"The Founder?" Kirby said.

"Oh yeah, he invented PetroSynth," Patrick replied.

"You want me to revive the creator of PetroSynth, the man who's responsible for us all being here? The Founder, the man millions of kooky Khartuists pray to as their god incarnate?"

"Yes, and her, it says she's his granddaughter," Patrick pointed at the screen. "He asked for my help."

"Before he went under?"

"No, tonight, in a dream. He spoke to me in the observation lounge. Well I guess it wasn't the real observation lounge."

"Patrick, what the fuck are you talking about? Are you a fucking Khartuist now? This is beyond space sickness."

"Look, he's more than he seems. He led me back here Kirby, in person, before talking to me in my dream. You have to trust me, Kirby."

"Okay, look I'll do it. Just hang on a minute." Kirby swiped and tapped bringing the old man's data to full screen. The profile border began flashing in red.

"What's wrong?" Patrick said.

"Nothing, I've just made it look like his status is unstable so the system will force a reconstitution, the girl too."

"Thank you. You won't regret this," Patrick said.

"Why do I feel as if I already am?" Kirby initiated the revival program. "Okay. Now all we have to do is go in and get them." Kirby got to her feet and moved towards the revival chamber.

"Wait!"

Kirby and Patrick both turned at the strange voice they heard coming from the room. She looked around expecting to see the night shift technician but there was no one in the room.

"Who's there?" Kirby said.

Costas climbed out from under the desk. Instinctively he reached for his service revolver, his hand quickly discovering it wasn't there. Of course, back on Earth, along with everything else from his life.

"Who the fuck are you?" Patrick asked.

"Athenian Police."

"Athenian Police? Aren't you a little out of your jurisdiction?" Kirby replied.

"I'm not here in an official capacity."

"This is a secure area, you know. I could have you removed from the station."

"Look I've been under this desk long enough to know that what you just did you shouldn't have done, so if you do me a favour, we can all forget about it."

"If this is some weird sex thing, Pal, forget it," Patrick said.

"I want someone out of there."

"Great, let's have a fucking garden party," Kirby said as she sat back down at the computer.

FIFTY-EIGHT

Kirby surveyed her quarters. The room looked very small to her now that it contained four human beings she'd not previously known, and one human being that she'd been desperately trying to contact for more than a week. Two of these beings her husband had apparently been travelling with on Earth and had somehow asked him, in a dream, to come and save them. Not only that but the old guy was the founder of the PetroSynth Corporation and a missing religious icon. If this was all some wild ploy of Patrick's to get them thrown off the station it may well work. A polite request to leave seemed unlikely. However a future floating helplessly in the vacuum of space along with the human excrement, garbage and other waste products regularly jettisoned from the station was feeling more imminent.

Kirby had seen the old man and his granddaughter as they'd been processed through HDC. There was much made of The Founder and his granddaughter being the first people to be saved to the data banks. She'd not lingered in her observations of them other than the perfunctory scans related to HDC. They were merely the first in a long line of people she and her team had been required to process. Looking closely at them now there was something peculiar about their eyes, more so the granddaughter, who sat quietly on the edge of the bed. Those eyes drew her in and for a moment Kirby felt lost there, unable to look away. Is that what had kept Patrick interested as he drove across the outback? Kirby broke the stare and examined the young girl's shape. There was little to her plain but attractive structure. She was delicate and slight, more on the child side of adolescence than it first appeared.

Despite the pull of those angelic eyes, Kirby moved her gaze around the room. The Athenian policeman sat holding his young companion in the corner. She wasn't sure what their story was but they seemed happy to see each other.

"What's next folks? Any more revivals or are we all done. Perhaps a station coup if no one has any other plans," Kirby said.

"You were most kind to help us," Ancient replied.

"Yes, thank you Kirby," Angel spoke for the first time.

Kirby relaxed a little now that Ancient and Angel had confirmed that they did indeed want to be rescued.

"We need to launch a probe, into the sun," Ancient said.

"What?" Kirby replied.

"I've created, for want of a better explanation, a hydrogen-helium stabiliser. Once it comes into contact with the sun it will stabilise the hydrogen/helium conversion making it perpetual. The sun will never die. It will become the only constant in a universe of chaos and change."

"How's that even possible?" asked Costas.

"The source of the sun's energy is nuclear fusion, hydrogen nuclei at the core colliding at high speeds to make helium nuclei. My stabiliser re-educates atoms at a quantum level. They revert back into hydrogen and repeat their conversion to helium endlessly. The sun will remain as it is forever." Ancient holds his little ball of light in his hands.

"I took the liberty of stowing this in Patrick's belongings."

"Is that it?" Kirby asked.

"Yes."

"Won't the probe just burn up before it even gets close?" Patrick asked.

"That's where Angel comes in," Ancient replied.

All in the room focused on Angel, her eyes holding their attention captive.

"Well whatever it is you are going to do, I suggest you wait until the station goes into the day cycle. Security is obviously a little lax because so much else is going on. Patrick and I have to report for duty. It will look suspicious if we don't. The rest of you should stay here until Patrick and I get back. As to your revival, I've left a full copy of you in the data banks and erased our activities this evening. No one will know you are here."

Kirby turned to Costas, disrupting his absorption with Eko.

"Do you have a place you should be?"

"Yes, I suppose."

"Well, you'd better get back there. Your friend will be safe here as long as we all keep a low profile."

"A few words with her before I go?"

"That's fine," Kirby replied, enjoying her command of the situation.

"Angel and I will come up with some way of sorting this all out. There's no need for anyone else to get involved."

"We're already involved," Patrick said.

"I'd like to help." Costas added. "I don't want to stay up here if I can avoid it."

"Okay, then we meet back here in 8 hours," Kirby said firmly.

"Okay," they all agreed.

Angel and Ancient moved to the computer on Kirby's desk as Kirby and Patrick left the room to start their shifts. As they walked along the corridor Patrick took Kirby's arm, gently bringing them both to a stop.

"You know you're very sexy when you're in control."

"It kinda turns me on to boss you around."

"Why do you think I let you get away with it?" Patrick pulled her in close.

"Because you are a weak-arse dickhead."

"Thank you," he whispered as he embraced her, pulling her as close as he could, melding her body to his, feeling the form and contours of her shape, feeling her desire to be there as strong as his.

"You are amazing, you know that," he said.

"I know, but it's nice to hear it from you sometimes."

FIFTY-NINE

Costas leant in, kissing Eko gently on the forehead.

"You're not angry I had you reconstituted?"

Eko was slow to answer. The reconstitution was having a stronger effect on her than on the old man and his grand-daughter. It felt like waking from an operation, steadily regaining awareness after a deep anaesthesia. She was groggy, tired and starting to feel hungry.

"I'm happy to see you. What is reconstituted?" she asked.

"I want to know what happened to you. I woke up in Hania alone?"

"We got carried away, you know, you couldn't keep your hands from wandering and we ended up..."

"I don't remember that bit."

"The drugs."

"Yes."

"You were fast asleep in the morning and so I went for a walk, to get some breakfast. Someone grabbed me, shoved me in a car."

"Did you see who it was?"

"Some shabby looking guy in a seersucker suit. They drugged me and the next thing I know I was on a plane. I was hardly conscious. The time between the plane and being here is foggy. "

"Eko, do you know Mrs Fong?"

"I only know of her, I've never met her."

"That's all I wanted to hear."

"Tell me what they did to me? What's reconstituted?"

"You were scanned, digitised, your body broken down to its base atomic organic structure. You were stored as data on a hard drive and then your digital signature was reconstituted using the same base organic compounds," Angel explained.

"What the fuck? Well it makes you hungry".

"You must stay here where it's safe. Okay?" Costas interrupted.

"Sure, I just want to eat, then sleep. But also later I think I want to fuck. I guess this body is all new. It will be like the first time." She smiled and placed her hand gently between his legs. As much as he wanted it to stay there, the idea of the old man and young girl sitting on the lounge opposite them forced him to remove her hand. One of the hardest things he'd ever had to do in his life, but he made it through and shifted his focus to Ancient and Angel.

'Please, keep an eye on her. She tends to vanish. I'll be back as soon as I can get away."

Costas walked through the door and his nose twitched as it detected a strong sour smell in the air. Garlic, he thought, but extremely concentrated. He turned and walked towards his quarters where he knew Virginia was waiting for him, and hoped, possibly for the first time in his life, that he could find a way to avoid having sex.

Professor Gardener stuck his head round the corner again. The strange man who'd walked out of Kirby's quarters was gone. He walked to the door and placed his ear to it. He could hear something in there, some people talking. He punched in his security over-ride but the lock failed to open.

"Damn, cancelled. We'll see what the Commander has to say about this!"

Gardner stormed off down the passage. The door opened once he was out of sight and Eko's head emerged. She sniffed, uncertain what to make of the foul odour that lingered in the corridor.

SIXTY

Coastas watched intently as Virginia Fong, wrapped in a towel strode from the bathroom and stopped in front of the body-length mirror on the wall. Steam rose gently from her shoulders as she began to brush her long dark semi-wet hair, drops of water flicking to the floor with each stroke. Her body remained an appealing form to Costas. If it weren't for Eko, perhaps he would let things slide, perhaps he wouldn't do what his moral code told him to do, perhaps he would just forget everything and continue his sexual wrestling match with this highly compatible opponent.

"Where have you been?" she said, speaking to his reflection and maintaining a continuous motion of the brush through her hair.

"Just exploring. I've never been in space before, on a space station," he said, his hands firmly buried in his jacket pockets, his intent hidden.

She dropped her brush on the side-table and slithered serpent like towards him.

"I think we have time for one more round before we take our place in history." She dropped her towel, the sight of her naked body tempting Costas to give in, entreating his hands to cup her breasts, his mouth to tease the already hard nipples, but he held his ground, his hands staying steady where they were, his face betraying nothing of his intent. His cock swelled as the aroma of her fresh clean skin filled his senses.

"Virginia," he said looking into her eyes, trying to avoid her body.

She edged a little closer.

"I love the way you say my name. I always think you're going to say Vagina." She dropped onto his lap and felt the heat of his erection, her hand caressed the bulge raising his trousers. She pressed her lips against his and forced her tongue into his mouth. He responded, shooting his tongue back aggressively. This would be hard, he thought, very hard.

Costas took his hands from his jacket pockets, lifted her hand from his groin and quickly locked one side of the handcuffs onto Virginia's wrist. She smiled with excitement as he locked the other side of the handcuffs onto the chair.

"A kinky cop," she said. "How wonderful, but please don't hurt me, Officer," she said in mock concern.

"You are under arrest for conspiracy to murder Wilfred Fong, obstructing the course of justice and police investigations, possibly body-piercing without consent or license to practice and kidnapping."

Virginia's face changed and her desire turned to anger.

"This is not funny, Costas."

"It's not meant to be," he said as he slipped out from under her. He quickly moved out of her reach before she could bury her claws in his flesh.

"You have no proof."

"I have proof, Mrs Fong. Your husband left proof with his 'friend' Eko."

"She's a lying little whore, anyway she's out of your reach."

"No, she's very much back within my grasp and her proof is indisputable."

"Why are you doing this, you idiot? You could have had a future with me."

"Oh, I'm sure you would soon tire of me, Virginia."

"So now what? Do we both go back to Earth and die? I'm telling you they won't let you take me off this station. These are the people who wanted my husband dead. He was going to lift the lid on the whole deal. Do you think they're just going to let you walk out of here? They might not love me here but they understand me. I'm one of them, you arsehole."

"That you may be, but you could also be a very nice scapegoat to PetroSynth. They love their deflections. Anyway it's all being taken care of, Mrs Fong. We just have to wait."

"Wait! Like this," she said, displaying her naked body. Costas pulled a robe from the wardrobe and tossed it at his prisoner. She covered herself as best she could with one hand constrained by handcuffs.

"What about this," she said, lifting her exposed arm.

"That will have to wait too," Costas said. She sat in the chair glaring daggers of resentment.

"You're a fucking idiot, Costas."

"Maybe, but at least I'm warm blooded."

SIXTY-ONE

Angel pushed her chair back and shifted her eyes from the computer screen. The old man continued to peer intently at the information before him. He was slower, she thought, slower at grasping the ideas and concepts that had shot from her mind at lightening speed, but grasp them, eventually he did. Her surprise at the old man's ability to comprehend her work both frightened and pleased Angel. It wasn't arrogance, or an unrealistic sense of her own abilities that triggered her astonishment, it was simply that she'd never met another person capable of grasping the complexity of her ideas. There had only been one occasion in her seventeen years on the planet when that had happened.

"It was you, wasn't it?" she asked.

"What was me?"

"You looked younger, but it was only a few years a ago. You visited me on my birthday."

"Did I give you a present?" the old man replied. Angel knew he was taunting, answering her questions with more questions, playing with her the way he played with Patrick. Before she could discount his last comment as trivial the thought flashed through her brain that he had given her something. Those few moments when that voice had filled her ears; that touch had electrified her skin; she no longer felt alone. That voice had whispered many strange things to Angel; some only returned to her in dreams; others stayed in her mind, but nothing solid, except for one idea. That voice had told her to follow and trust the old man when he came. It would be important, the voice had whispered, it would be important.

"Perhaps," she answered.

"I guess some gifts are not as obvious as others."

"If it wasn't you, then how did you know how to find me?"

"I had good directions."

"From whom?" she asked like a persistent child.

Ancient moved away from the screen and placed his hand over hers. She felt an echo of that strange connection with his touch, so much weaker this time, but it was there.

"Let's get this done, then I'll tell you everything."

"You don't like to tell the whole truth, do you?" Angel accused.

"All people ever want is the truth," he said with frustration. "When are people going to learn that the truth isn't all it's cracked up to be? Truth, like Einstein's theory is relative."

"That's easy to say, when you know what the truth is."

"That is a good point, but it shouldn't sway our focus from our immediate task at hand."

"Which is a response to the truth?"

"That, Angel, it very much is."

Ancient returned to the screen and continued to read as Angel got to her feet and began to pace restlessly. She was ready for action. She didn't need any more time to review the data or look at the schematics, it was all memorised in her head and she was confident she could carry it off. She just needed to get going.

Angel looked around the small room and noticed Eko was no longer sitting on the bed. The bathroom door was open. She curiously poked her head in to find it empty.

"Ancient!" she said.

"What is it?" he replied, reluctant to look away from the screen.

"She's gone. The girl, Eko, she's gone."

SIXTY-TWO

Kirby watched the clock intently as she continued to supervise the multitude of VIPs being decommissioned of their human bodies. Once 3D scanned, DNA sequenced and the data safely stored on the Fong memorial computer server their organic material was liquefied. A rich source of nutrients, to be distributed through each of the ship's ecosystems. A human bio-fertiliser.

Who knew how long they would remain stored as data, waiting without consciousness until the discovery of a new world, when their bodies would be remade. Kirby could only imagine what their reconstituted selves would experience. Their new eyes would see light from other stars, their lungs would take in air from other worlds, their skin would feel warmth from suns other than the one that gave them life. Centuries of technicians would live and die while their code remained intact, a series of 1s and 0s on a hard drive. Then one day it would all change, a new planet and a new life. They would be brought back to life ready to live the remainder of their days comfortably on a new, stable world, their wealth and status intact. Perhaps by then they would be reborn stronger, their genetic code enhanced, their diseases, ailments, perhaps even their mortality, all adjustable in a new body.

The clock ticked on, the human soup sucked efficiently away as time brought Kirby towards her own uncertain future. She smelled Professor Gardener behind her and moved across the control room to avoid him. All he did was watch her. He no longer even pretended to work or have any interest in any part of the operation. He just watched her and tried to get close when he could.

Just this last group, Kirby thought, this last group of well-to-do space travellers to be scanned and stored and the shift would be over. Their human remains limp and lifeless, broken down before her eyes, no longer bodies, just a gooey mush sucked into the organic hold ready to be recycled.

"Good work, everyone," Kirby said into the microphone on the control panel. Her voice echoed through the chamber of the ship and she could hear her own nervous energy bouncing off the walls. "That's it for today. Tomorrow we move on to the final round."

Professor Gardener leant down next to Kirby and pressed his hand over her fingers on the PA button, keeping the channel open.

"Seven thirty start. Big night tomorrow people!" he said, releasing his hold on the PA and ignoring the audible groans of disapproval as everyone filed out. Kirby quickly got to her feet and made for the door.

"Are you free tonight, Kirby? I was hoping we might have a small chat," he asked.

"No, I'm sorry," she said sarcastically. "My husband and I have to catch up on the Kama Sutra, Number sixty-eight and you know what's just round the corner."

"Kirby, this is important and concerns your future."

"Listen, Professor Halitosis, my future doesn't include you in any way shape or form. Once I finish here, my husband and I are going on the PS Fairstar and I'm afraid it's an 18-35s cruise so you just miss out by a decade or so."

"Have it your way, Kirby, but I did try to give you, well, give us a chance."

"Professor, have you ever heard the one about the snowball and hell? Good night," Kirby said, quickly making her exit.

SIXTY-THREE

This was a very different kind of headache, Costas thought as he lifted himself from the floor. The drugs he'd taken with Eko had definitely worn off. He could remember with great detail all his encounters with Virginia Fong. If only it were so with Eko. Why couldn't he have those memories intact? The pain from the drugs was a dry, blistering ache that radiated from the centre of his brain. As Costas moved shakily to his feet his hand rubbed the back of his head finding the source of this new but familiar headache.

After so many years in service for the Athenian Police Force, he was no stranger to the occasional blow to the back of the head. But where this one had come from and who had delivered it was, at this moment, a mystery. His memory played hide and seek with him once more as he tried to recall his last few moments of consciousness. Virginia had been sitting, cuffed to the chair, trying to talk him round, offering him her wealth, her body, anything she could think of. Then bang, nothing else, just the carpet up close, then blackness.

He couldn't have been out long he guessed, or he would have been picked up by PetroSynth security guards in their retro disco space uniforms, with their flared trousers and psychedelic waist bands with the PetroSynth logo, the famous PetroSynth plant, featuring as a centre piece. It was not unlike a marijuana plant; the leaves less defined and inconsistent. Odd, he thought, that a genetically engineered plant wouldn't have been made more aesthetically balanced. More odd that he was wasting time de-constructing the visual elements of the PetroSynth logo. A few deep breaths as he tried to focus. 'Concentrate,' he said to himself. Time to move and move fast.

Why then was he going so slowly? Ah yes, he recalled again, someone had hit him on the back of the head.

Costas stumbled out of the room and moved with swift but erratic strides down the corridor, finding the need to steady himself against the wall every other step.

SIXTY-FOUR

Kirby tried to stay focused on what the old man was saying but her thoughts wouldn't be silenced. What was more ludicrous, the plan of action being laid out and discussed or the sudden reappearance of her husband and his unexpected entourage?

The old man's words forced Kirby's thoughts to splinter into tangents. She didn't hear the full construct of his sentences, only fragments of them registering in her mind. Part of his plan was to get onto one of the 'Exit Ships'.

'Exit Ships'. The very name now seemed so clear and obvious. How could she not have seen that the term used to describe the vessels built to launch humanity's exploration into the unknown was an indication of intent? Why weren't they given a nobler title, something to do with colonising, or expanding human existence? No they were 'Exit Ships', they were giant escape pods, the final and only way out for anyone who wanted to escape the impending demise of Earth and the collapse of the solar system. Anyone with the right money or connections.

Each craft was equipped with adequate quarters for up to one hundred crew, self-contained food and air production, a complete data record of the history of humanity, a complete data record of all individuals placed in HDC. And naturally powered by PetroSynth. The old man's words stopped distracting Kirby and she suddenly realised what she was getting herself into.

"The Exit Ships are more or less empty. Crew members don't take their place for another few days, but you can't just walk in," Kirby put forward.

"That's the only drawback at this stage," the old man conceded.

"It's not just a drawback; I'd call that a major obstacle," she replied.

"Well, if you want to look at it that way or we could look at it as an opportunity."

"Hey, thanks for re-framing it for me, I feel so much better about it now," Kirby rolled her eyes.

Patrick got to his feet and walked over to the communications console on Kirby's desk.

"I think I can get us in?" he said and pressed a few buttons.

"Security," a voice on speaker said.

"Yes, this is the Communications Chief."

"Patrick, I heard you were coming aboard. It's Collins here."

"Collins, how are you?" Patrick said, pleased to hear a familiar voice from ground base.

"I'm fine. What's up?"

"I need to run some communications checks on exit ship Endeavour. I need to get security access for me and a team for the next 24 hours," Patrick said, giving the others a questioning look.

"Hang on," Collins said.

"Okay," Patrick waited patiently, the others looking on with nervous anticipation.

"You've already got full access," Collins said.

"When were you guys planning on telling me?" Patrick replied.

"Well, we've been busy. Most of my staff are on crowd control."

"I see," replied Patrick.

"Listen, once you're in the ship with your team just make sure the airlock is closed and the main door is secured otherwise we get an alarm and officially have to respond, even if it's just a mistake, and I don't have the people to spare for that kind of crap at the moment."

"No problem, Collins. And thanks."

"Hey, let's have a drink once we get rid of all these civilians?"

"I'm afraid I'll be on the last ship, as crew," Patrick replied.

"I never thought you'd get this far let alone getting on a ship. Who suckered you in to that one?"

"My wife. Actually it was my own choice," Patrick replied, smiling at Kirby.

"I like being single; that's all I'm gonna say. Gotta run," said Collins.

Patrick pressed a button and terminated the conversation. "As if he has a choice. You've seen the guy, Kirby. I'm not exaggerating am I?" He smiled warmly and pulled his security card from his shirt pocket.

"Anyway, we're in," he said.

The door buzzed and Kirby moved to answer it.

"I hope that's not your friend with the fresh ring of confidence," Patrick said.

Kirby pressed her intercom button.

"Who is it?"

"Costas, open up quickly," Costas said.

The door flew open and Costas stumbled in, his hand still rubbing the back of his head. He quickly sat on the side of the bed.

"You're late," Patrick said.

"I got held up, or knocked down or something." He looked around the room and noticed Eko's absence. "Where's Eko?" he asked.

"Well, we thought she must have gone looking for you," Angel said.

"When, how long ago?" he asked.

"A few hours," Angel replied. "Is it important?"

"I think whatever you're planning to do you better do it soon. I don't think she can be trusted."

"I thought she was your girlfriend," Kirby said.

"It's quite possible she's betrayed me. More than once. She's not perfect, but I love her completely. I realise she's capable of anything. Your operation could be in jeopardy."

"She doesn't know what we are planning," said Angel.

"No, she doesn't," answered Ancient.

"Let's go," Kirby said, taking control of the situation, yet somehow terribly unsure of where it would lead.

SIXTY-FIVE

Angel looked too young and Ancient too old, but they still took the precaution of putting on the PetroSynth crew uniforms Patrick had acquired. Ancient felt particularly uncomfortable with the PetroSynth logo resting on the left side of his chest and wondered why the designer had decided that waistbands with the logo relentlessly repeated could in any way be considered attractive. That little plant he'd genetically engineered over sixty years before had haunted his thoughts ever since it was created. He walked at a calm pace, easily keeping up with his youthful companions despite his extended years, with that stupid little logo not only everywhere he looked put plastered all over him.

The team, lead confidently by Patrick and Kirby, arrived at the airlock. The entrance to the docked spacecraft was secured but unguarded. The size of the PS Endeavour took Patrick by surprise. Seeing the ship so close, he momentarily marvelled at its majesty before his general anger with PetroSynth returned. Refocused, he unclipped his security card and swiped it through the reader. Costas kept his eyes peeled and his nostrils flared in the corridor. He caught a small whiff of garlic but in a millisecond it was gone.

The door clicked and Patrick pushed it open. They all followed him through and he checked to make sure it was closed, thanking Collins for his helpful hint on false alarms.

They moved quickly now they were off the station and on the Endeavour. They paused at the end of the airlock as Patrick and Kirby checked the map and orientated the group.

"The Probe launching bay is next to the weapons bay on deck six. You'll need to take the lift at the end of the corridor to the right," Kirby said.

"I know the way," Angel said. "I've memorised the schematics."

"Great, we'll get to the bridge and wait for your word. I'll open a direct communications line with you once we are in position," Patrick said.

"Someone should stay with Angel. She'll need to concentrate and cannot waste time looking out for herself," said Ancient.

"I'll go," Costas said.

"Let's move," the old man said as the two groups formed.

Costas and Angel moved quickly down the corridor into the lift and onto level 6. Costas was impressed with Angel's sense of direction but kept an eye on where he was being led, covering himself should he need to return alone. They made it into the probe-launching bay more easily than Costas expected. Angel opened a storage unit and together they lifted the small probe onto a workstation. She opened her backpack, removed a few tools and one of Ancient's glowing balls.

"That thing really going to work?" Costas asked.

"We better hope it works."

Ancient sat in the Captain's chair and adjusted the touch screen controls to sit in front him. Moving steadily, he ran his finger down the screen and readied the controls for the probe launch.

"Just a few more little tweaks," his old digits tapping heavily the touch screen. "Done! As soon as Angel gives the word I can launch the probe from here. What are you doing Patrick? Do we have communication with Angel?"

Patrick, sitting at the communications station, was immediately annoyed by Ancient's Captain act.

"I'm running a diagnostic of the primary communications system. That was the cover, remember? I've patched into the secondary system to communicate with Angel. He shot a glance at Kirby and could see she was feeling a little nervous.

"Why don't you run a diagnostics of the data core on board. It wouldn't hurt to have a little legitimate cover for your presence here," Patrick suggested.

"Good idea," she replied and moved her fingers over the screen in front of her.

Patrick opened a channel to the probe launching bay.

"We are in position and waiting for your signal," Patrick said, in his best espionage voice. He was really beginning to enjoy the adrenaline rush.

"Probe is being prepped," Costas replied.

Angel removed the small power source of the probe and attached Ancient's glowing sphere. She replaced the probe casing and pulled up its schematics on the workstation's computer screen. She took her wireless drive from the back pack and began installing the shield code.

"I'm done," said Kirby

"Yeah, my diagnostic is finished too," said Patrick. "As soon as Angel is ready we need to get that thing launched, erase the logs and get the fuck out of here."

"How long is this going to take?" Kirby asked.

"I'm sure it won't be much longer," Ancient assured her. "It's very precise work she's doing."

"What exactly is she doing?" Patrick asked.

"Young Angel has developed a force field that can withstand the sun's heat. She is programming the protective field of the probe so that it can move into the sun. The field is on a timer so that once the probe is in the heart of the sun the force field will switch off. My little ball of light, as you like to call it, will then come in contact with hydrogen and helium atoms at the core of the sun and begin the molecular re-programming required to perpetually cycle the sun's hydrogen and helium conversion process. Even after all the energy in the universe has reached its predestined state of entropy our precious little star will still be shining."

"How does she know what she's doing?" Patrick asked.

"Call it a natural talent," Ancient replied.

"Do you think you could ever give a straight answer?" Patrick replied. Ancient turned and smiled. He longed to give Patrick the straight answer of 'no' but enjoyed annoying him too much.

"The probe is in the launch bay," Costas' voice said through the speaker on the communications station. "We're ready this end."

"Excellent, you might as well come and meet us up here," Patrick said.

"That's a good idea," the Station Commander said. "I'd like to meet everyone involved."

All eyes turned to the Station Commander and his security team standing at the entrance of the bridge with Professor Gardener, Virginia Fong and Eko standing behind him.

Ancient moved his hand towards the launch controls but was stopped by the Commander's voice.

"Move back from the screen, old man," the Commander said, a guard pushing the controls out of his reach.

"Now, who's going to tell me what the fuck is going on?"

SIXTY-SIX

Patrick opened his notebook. Much had transpired since that last entry. He read it now with a different sensibility, a sense of clarity not available to him at the time his pen had scratched its way across the paper that twilight in the office. He'd been exploring, playing with the idea of what life on this planet really was, not the insane construct that humans made believe was life, not all the pressing concerns built by the human brain, but the actual nuts and bolts of life – his little, random life, created by the violent chaos of chemical reactions, sustained in a bubble of oxygen, nitrogen and carbon dioxide, held together by the gravitational forces celestial bodies exerted upon each other.

The moments that followed his observation, the discovery of that wretched classified document, learning how completely disconnected his species had become from its origins, their actions so alarmingly self destructive, were just ideas now, memories. They had moved him from the complacency of his notebook, from the inertia of his desk and propelled him into action, literally shifted him to his feet and sent him into the unknown.

There he'd met the old man who was more than he could imagine, a man whose very existence drew all the elements of Patrick's discontent into a single focal point, into a moment complex in its construct but so very simple in what was required of it.

As they had all stood on the bridge of that PetroSynth spacecraft, some poised for action, others for reaction, Patrick had become frozen. The moment they'd all been working towards, all been heading to, some with awareness and others blindly, was there for him to exist in and to de-construct.

Patrick heard them all talking, he even threw a few lines in from time to time, yet he was also observing. As the moments unfolded he was both participant and examiner, seeing it as a memory at the same time as it transpired.

The old man, wanting to save the planet, wanting to right the wrongs of his past, by simply pressing a button. All he asked of the Station Commander was permission to send his probe, send it into the heart of the sun, let it do its thing with hydrogen and helium molecules. It sounded so simple but what lay between the two men was far more complex. As they spoke Patrick became aware of their similar features. Their words flowed into Patrick's ears but didn't register fully with his brain. His focus was drawn to their mouths as they moved, their eyes, the shape of their noses. Could they be brothers? Was that it? The Station Commander was much younger – no not brothers.

The resistance by the younger man suddenly became clear. They stood so close now, facing off. Their eyes engaged as they spoke. Neither looked away. Patrick was aware of his own fixation while somehow also knowing what everyone else in the room was doing, all frozen as the moment approached, all steadfast, as everything that had been held so tightly closed was now being prised open.

No not brothers. They were not brothers. They shared a fate but not camaraderie. They shared a name, they shared a past, more an empty space, a void brought into existence by each other's absence, everything between them the product of events that never were, a bond formed by separation as opposed to one created from shared experience.

The Commander stood his ground. He didn't falter when the old man began referring to him as Franklin. Who was Franklin? That wasn't his name, yet the commander responded to it without question. Ancient's tone was soft. His demeanour towards the Commander accepting and open. Patrick had seen Ancient act that way before, when they first met, in gentle moments, easing him from situation to situation. Behind that enigmatic veil Ancient had taken him from the outskirts of 'Neverville' to Angel's home, from the unknown to knowing, from lies to the truth, from denial to acceptance.. Patrick recognised it, he saw the paternal look in Ancient's eyes and realised finally who Franklin was. No, Franklin wasn't a brother, how could he be anything other than Ancient's son?

Was anyone in the room who they said they actually were? Patrick's memory blurred with the moment as it happened, what he'd learned later merging with what he didn't know at the time, or it felt that way. The old man and the commander locked in their moment, a point in time one had worked to avoid while the other had been tirelessly engaged in engineering it to occur. Even that idea seemed to oversimplify what lay between the two men.

Was it the old man's invasion into his mind that took Patrick from where he was and scattered him across Franklin's life? More than the proverbial fly on the wall, Patrick almost inhabited Franklin, as he had the PetroSynth Executive, in what he thought had been a dream. This was more than observing; he felt Franklin's consuming rage at being abandoned; he saw over the years how his mind had built a reality where the lack of his father's presence impacted as greatly as the solid grounding his mother gave him every day of his upbringing. The anger was overwhelming, crippling even, directed at Ancient and PetroSynth for taking his mother away from him prematurely. Patrick had the man's whole history in his head, his lies, his truths all poured into an obsessive need to expose his father, to bring him into the light. He'd poured over the cache of his father's papers left behind by his mother, he'd fabricated where needed, he'd shaped and formed, rewritten. He'd created a belief system that would appeal to the weak-minded, the spiritually vulnerable, the masses who desired ideas that gave them hope in the face of their fear of death, of destruction, of emptiness. He'd filled them with the longing to be with the man who gave their lives meaning, channelling their energies to his purposes, feeding his wild insecurities into thousands of followers, just that little bit more insecure than himself.

Patrick marvelled at the derangement, the tireless energy that Franklin had drawn on to build his empire, not for money or power, but only to understand why a father who helped give him life had also so profoundly rejected him.

Everything fell silent, with the two men looking eye to eye. Patrick continued to explore; the moment elongated, became pliable to his will. He discovered his power of insight was not restricted to Franklin. He could move into the consciousness of others in the room. Fleetingly at first into the guards, their minds racing to understand what was going on, but their will to do as directed by Franklin unquestionable. He had infiltrated their consciousness with his spiritual mis-appropriations. They saw Ancient in the light Franklin had painted him in and would act accordingly. Neither fit Patrick's assumptions about security professionals, and knowing they were Khartuist operatives made it clearer.

He moved into Virginia Fong's mind, saw her implicit deceit driven by self-preservation, her sense of superiority and entitlement. It sickened him and he felt full of judgment. Then Professor Gardener. He didn't want to stay there long, enough to see the most pitying self-loathing one could imagine, a vile creature trapped by his own perspective, aware of his repellent physical traits yet unable to control his afflictions. The man's obsession with Kirby was understandable, but it soon became a stream of unwanted images Patrick had no desire to have in his mind.

He needed clarity. He needed to be somewhere familiar. This knowing, this way of seeing into another so deeply was intoxicating. Kirby came to mind and Patrick shifted the moment to inhabit his wife. Her mind was like an unassailable wall; there was no means of entry. Whatever it was granting him this ability, it was now showing him the limits. Angel and the old man were off limits too. Try as he may they were impossible to penetrate.

Not wanting the power to fade Patrick moved through the mind of Costas. So unaware of how he was perceived by others, his intensity of feeling for Eko driving him beyond his own powers of reason. And Eko, a complicated young woman; Patrick saw her confusion, being driven by her unexpected feelings for this odd detective and her loyalty to the Khartuists. Her whole persona a lie, a story invented by Franklin to help expose The Founder. Her deployment created to uncover a suspected link between Wilfred Fong and Klondike. She shared a history with Franklin that was long and manipulative and she struggled now to understand what her true feelings were.

There was so much opinion flying around, so much pain. Patrick's own judgments becoming distasteful and pushing him into an unforeseen place of acceptance. He saw them all for who they really were, the personas they had created and what those personas masked, the being that underpinned each individual construct. The rejected child, the wounded lover, the insecure lonely and frightened beings, so afraid of the unknown that their minds created something that would pacify or at least distract them from the fear they felt.

Compassion flooded Patrick the more this moment revealed itself. These beings, these delicate precious beings, so caught in playing the central role of their own existence that they failed to see anything past the façade. He wanted to weep for them, he wanted to weep for himself. If this was what it was like in other people's minds, it was likely to be the same in his own.

And then Patrick understood; he finally understood why he'd been given this front row seat to everyone else's existence, why he was tapped into this moment so fundamentally that he saw it from almost every conceivable angle. He saw it with heartbreaking beauty. If they failed to see their own self-destructive traits this only made him feel more forgiving, more compassionate. He wanted beyond anything to give them the awareness he was experiencing. While they were still trapped playing their roles, he was now free, free to act with choice beyond the patterns of behaviour his life experience had taught him. Patterns that he now saw served only to create limits.

Patrick held the moment, held all the players in their spots, Franklin and Ancient's mouths frozen in mid-speech. He moved between the two men then pushed them closer, manipulated their arms, wrapping them about each other, placing Franklin's head on the old man's shoulder, Ancient's arms holding Franklin the way they should have held him when he was a child. Then before letting the moment go, before releasing his control, Patrick readied one hand at the launch controls and with the other he took hold of Kirby's, gently interlocking their fingers.

He closed his eyes, unsure how this moment had become his to control, but ready now to relinquish that control. Unsure even where he was or where he would be when he opened his eyes. Was he still in that moment or had it passed? Was he safe somewhere, recording everything in his notebook or about to live it? He had only to open his eyes to find out.

PART FIVE

KLONDIKE KHARTU

Age was not a concept he'd contemplated all that much before this incarnation, this strange and wonderful manifestation. This was an existence so entrenched in mortality, so rigidly locked into a fear and lack of understanding of its own end that its entire consciousness was often wasted on thoughts and fears that flowed from that end.

His younger lover, who now lay softly breathing next to him seemed oblivious to it, perhaps a sign of her age? The difference was not that great, only 10 years and Klondike certainly didn't feel all his 45 years. In fact he scarcely took note of the time he'd spent on the planet. It had been a whirlwind of ideas, science, work, a string of meaningless physical connections that his body and its chemical reactions had driven him to, regardless of his conscious mind's engagement in other pursuits.

The physical connections had brought him immediate pleasure, but his work, his mind's activities, that is what had borne the real fruits. His greatest achievement, a genetically engineered shrub he'd called the 'Power Plant'. A single pot -sized plant could sustain the energy needs of an average home for six months.

Klondike felt warm and snug tucked up in bed next to Maria. A feeling of satisfaction mingled and meshed, becoming indecipherable with the afterglow of love-making. Satisfaction for developing his miracle plant but also for creating the means to harness it. The technology to use its every cell, to capture and store the energy it created, to apply it to any existing power grid in the world. He moved a little closer towards Maria's warm body and her embrace tightened in response.

Looking down at the amazing creature beside him, he felt ready to hand his gift over to the people of the planet. Not only to protect her future but to sustain them all, to stop them destroying the only home they had, stop them from eating away at the source of their own existence, demolishing the very ground beneath them as if they were mice and the soil below some irresistible cheese.

Maria's warm breath against his chest entered the realm of his favourite sensations, along with eating chocolate, making love and thinking about the quite remarkable legacy he'd created. The precious little plant that he'd laboured over in the lab, his masterful genetic reprogramming allowing his creation to grow in any environment, including the most arid lands and even, with proper care, in some Arctic regions. Naturally enough it could be easily cared for indoors and its ability to reach full maturity in a month perfectly rounded out its makeup.

The process for harnessing its energy was relatively simple and didn't require burning or the production of any waste. The entire plant, when heated to the correct temperature, simply chemically altered. Its cell structure rearranged to a pure clean form of energy a million times more powerful than the heat required for creating it. Naturally it would flower and produce seedlings before it would be harvested and it was relatively easy to propagate. It used little water and had a nifty little side-effect of neutralising carbon emissions if any were in the vicinity.

Looking down again he wanted to kiss Maria. He wanted to rouse her gently from her sleep with caresses, soft delicate touches; to move her from unconsciousness to arousal and bring their bodies together again in that perfect blend of friction the likes of which he'd not quite felt before. She kept using terms like 'natural' and 'organic' to describe their connection, their lovemaking, and Klondike believed her. If he could just get them both in the lab long enough to run some tests he was sure he could work out exactly what the compound was that triggered them both into a state of mind that desired physical and emotional union with the other. He'd felt that lust before, that desire, but never had this other feeling crept into the equation. Never had he felt as if he belonged, and in Maria's arms he belonged.

He moved his hand across her back. Her flesh warmed his fingers and his mind shifted back to his work, her smooth silky complexion reminding him of the soft surface of his little genetically engineered creation. His mind flowed to the near perfect home-based system of his design, that would make each citizen of the planet responsible for their own power needs. Growing their own 'Power Plants', processing and storing their own energy and effectively removing the need for reliance on a centralised power grid, leaving governments and corporations to take care of their own needs at a local level. Schools, hospitals, offices and apartment buildings, all with their own local crop, on rooftops or in basements or even scattered throughout the internal décor, providing an immediately accessible power grid. Naturally public transport operators would require larger processing, but essentially, in Klondike's plan, it was simply a matter of scale. Of course it would revolutionise world economies, but it would serve to give governments scope to focus on true issues like hunger and poverty. With this one gift, Klondike realised how much he was actually giving.

Suddenly it was not so strange that this gorgeous person had appeared at this time in this incarnation, their connection almost like a gift for all his hard work, all those years of focus, testing and determination, and remarkably when it was all but done here was this divine creature who wanted to spend time with him, and more incredible to Klondike, was the realisation that he wanted to spend time with her, even post-coital. And now without complaint, worry or concern, without the need for discussion or plans or commitments or signing pieces of paper or making vows, Maria's rounding belly served to draw them even closer.

Having children was not something he'd considered. It wasn't that he'd always been alone or lonely. He'd enjoyed many liaisons. He particularly enjoyed the company of women, but he'd never considered his attachments binding or felt strongly enough about any one particular person to do anything much to hold on to them. That was until now. Things with Maria, were distinctive and while he pretended at some level to carry on as if there was nothing different he found himself excited by the end of the day, when it was time to go home and be with her. And now with her gorgeous round belly, she was there more often. She had shifted from the M4 Corridor Lab of Petro International, where they met, to working from the home they'd inadvertently made together, or perhaps she'd made it around him; he couldn't be certain quite how all that had happened. What he did know was that Maria was the first woman he'd actually cohabited with.

Klondike gently removed himself from her arms. He placed a pillow under Maria's large belly as he removed the thigh she'd been resting it on. She gently stirred, but didn't wake.

Today was going to be amazing. Everything was in place, within Klondike's mind at least. All the work done, all he needed to do was release it to the world. He kissed Maria gently on the check, whispered 'Today, my love,' in her ear and left her to her sleep.

Complete satisfaction and a sense of intense goodwill filled Klondike's movements as he made his way to work. Nothing had felt quite so wonderful, freeing or so completely right as his intention to release all his work to the world to do with it what they may. As long as, he hoped, they actually used it to save themselves. The excitement for his 11 am press conference was building and he didn't quite know what he'd do with himself between then and 8 am when he would unlock the doors to the lab.

He approached the door with his swipe card ready for action. Strange that when he moved it through the scanner the door failed to unlock. Another swipe, but still the door remained closed. A knock achieved nothing. A further louder knock also failed. A phone call to an assistant was met with voice mail. A call to security was met with the first truly alarming thoughts. His access revoked. No explanation. He'd have to wait for business hours, still 90 minutes away. He called Maria. No answer, she must still be sleeping. He went back to the parking lot, his car looking forlorn and lonely in the middle of an otherwise empty car park. The building was suddenly soulless. Where was the usual early morning movement? Where were all the drones who came to fill their days and get a pay cheque? Where were the dedicated scientific community who would turn up even if they didn't get a pay cheque? Where were the admin and support staff who needed their jobs to pay for their mortgage or rent, phone plans, internet connections, big screen TVs, alcohol and recreational drug-fuelled nights out, overseas holidays, expensive dinners, clothes, ornaments, games? How would they obtain all their objects of desire if they didn't turn up for work today?

Klondike moved himself to the coffee shop in the estate. It had a view of the entry to the lab's car park, if he sat at the end table and pushed himself tight against the window. There was plenty of regular traffic on the estate and people in and out of the coffee shop, but none of them Petro International.

"Are they having a holiday they didn't tell you about?' said the waitress as she brought Klondike his third coffee.

'Something like that,' he replied, the caffeine now ramping up his nervousness.

He watched intently for the next hour and a half and saw not a single car come or go. Petro International had apparently shut down, today of all days, and no one had managed to tell their star scientist about it. He called Maria again. Still no answer. Back to the car park and his revoked access now had him locked out. He couldn't even retrieve his car.

A panic began to grow as the cab made its way back through the morning traffic to his home, his brain cycling through all the possibilities of what could be occurring. He longed to be with Maria, to talk through what was happening, to see if together they could find the answer.

The first thing he noticed when he walked in was a coldness. The windows were open and the temperature was unusually cool. Maria always liked it warm and snug. Klondike placed his bag down and walked to the bedroom. The bed was made and cleared of Maria's imprint. He'd often asked her not to make the bed just so he could enjoy the feeling of her having been there.

Moving around, the sense of panic increased as every room he entered proved to be empty of her presence.

'Maria,' he called before entering the bathroom, the kitchen, even the spare room. He checked down in the garage. She was nowhere. She must be somewhere, he thought. She was just nowhere he could see.

Back inside something small caught his attention. Her desk was cleared, her computer gone. Back in the bedroom, all her clothes were missing. As he checked every room again for her all he found were more things missing. The kitchen no longer had her tea bags, her favourite cup and saucer, her teapot. All gone.

He sat back on the edge of the bed. His hand moved across the covers that earlier had held him and Maria together. His mind still racing through what was happening, he closed his eyes and retraced the morning. It appeared to him as photos, a series of images connected by his movement through them. As his mind made it through the final stages, images of his and Maria's home, now mysteriously void of her, he breathed deeply. He looked through his recent memory for any clue, any note or other communication that she may have left.

There was nothing to go by, until his phone vibrated in his picket.

'I've gone,' the text read. 'I was employed as a distraction. I was never meant to fall for you. They wanted everything you created and they have taken it before you can give it away. You are locked out of everything. I wanted to stay, but I didn't think you'd ever forgive me.'

The phone dropped to the floor, his plan to save the world in pieces, his companion and unborn child gone. So much taken forcibly from him just as he was ready to give so much away freely.

He kicked his shoes off, removed his tie and shirt, unbuckled his belt and let his trousers drop to the floor. He climbed into bed, pulled the pillow close and tried to detect any fragment of Maria's scent, but there was none left. She was gone. He held the pillow tighter and for the first time in his life he wept.

EPILOGUE

Patrick sat in a canvas outdoor chair and let the warmth of the earth move between his toes. The sun would soon be gone from the sky but the warm evening air would remain, and Patrick intended to keep his feet in contact with the dry red earth for as long as he possibly could. He turned his head from the setting sun and watched as three silhouetted figures walked towards him, their outlines familiar, their pairing strange. The shapes moved and blocked the sun as it finally disappeared from view, sinking noiselessly behind the horizon.

The shadows were upon him now and Patrick smiled warmly as one handed him a cool glass of water. His grin widened at the recognition of the familiar curve and shape of the shadow before him as it pulled up a chair next to him and took hold of his hand.

The cool water moved gently across his lips and Patrick allowed a few drops to run down his chin and onto his chest, exposed by an open, unbuttoned shirt. His toes continued to move in the soil and almost longed to take root as the water moved through his system. If only he could photosynthesis, he thought, he would gladly stay that way.

The other shadows sat opposite him and for a moment Patrick feared the worst, expecting the old man to reach forward, take hold of his shoulder and shake him awake. And where would he find himself if that were to happen? Flying though space, some unknown distance from his true home or just hovering around it on a chunk of man-made debris?

The old man settled into his chair and showed no sign of moving towards Patrick, sending a wave of relief through the younger man's body.

"When are you leaving?" the old man asked.

"A few weeks. They have to revive everyone first, give them the option to stay, thanks to you," Kirby replied.

"Are you sure it's what you want?" Angel asked, looking at Kirby but the question was clearly aimed at Patrick.

"I just want to be with Kirby," Patrick replied. "You two could still go you know?" Patrick added.

"Perhaps we will," Ancient replied.

"You know there's something I don't understand?" Patrick said. "Why?"

"Why what?" Angel asked.

"What caused the sun to prematurely begin to die?"

"Who knows, Patrick? Perhaps the plans to send humanity out into the great unknown were not well liked," Ancient replied.

"What do you mean 'not well liked', not well liked by whom?" Kirby asked.

"I don't know, but whoever it is may not have wanted all those little Earth beings out there causing trouble, making all that noise you make."

"You think it was deliberate, to stop us?" Kirby said.

"They'd be no better than us if they did something like that," Patrick added.

"Perhaps they are more similar than you think, not all good and not all bad. Maybe they just understand themselves better."

"Whatever the cause was Ancient, you and Angel stopped it. And knowing that this will always be here certainly makes it easier to leave. I can think about it and the picture in my mind will exist in reality," Patrick said.

Ancient and Angel got to their feet and Patrick braced himself for the old man to try and wake him up. He moved towards Patrick and placed one arm gently on his shoulder and then gave him a warm affectionate pat.

"You'll be alright up there, Patrick. Just don't pretend to be anything less than you are." Ancient stopped and turned to Angel, putting his hand out for her to take.

"Now, shall we go for a walk before dinner, young lady? See if we can't catch a glimpse of those Min Min lights that get the tourists so excited." Angel took the old man's hand.

Ancient and Angel passed Patrick without turning around, walking steadily towards the glowing crimson sky. The last remaining rays of twilight disappeared and the night sky began to fill with stars.

Patrick turned to Kirby, glad to have her with him and he looked into her soft brown eyes. There was something strange there, something small, something reflective, something moving.

Both Patrick and Kirby turned in the direction the old man and Angel had walked, their silhouettes barely visible as they moved beneath the undulating colours painted across the sky, deep greens, purples, blues, one colour flowing into the other as they raised their hands in joy.

The lights vanished as suddenly as they had appeared. Patrick and Kirby's eyes adjusted slowly to the dark. Their pupils, wide and fully dilated, strained to locate the old man and his young companion. Stars began to fill the deep, black sky but Angel and Ancient were nowhere to be seen.

AUTHOR NOTE

If you enjoyed *Road To Nowhere,* please consider writing a review and posting it on shop websites, Goodreads, or your own blog. As an independent author, I'm reliant on word-of-mouth recommendations and I would greatly appreciate your rating and/or review.

To subscribe for new release updates or to find other information please visit my website
www.evanshapiro.net

If you are part of a book club looking for an author to meet with you via Skype or in person I always enjoy the opportunity to converse about my writing and the publishing process.

Please feel free to contact me via
www.cilentopublishing.com Contact Page,
on Twitter @noexpertbut or on Facebook
www.facebook.com/evanshapiro.author

Find my Blog at
www.evanshapiro.net/blog
noexpertbut.wordpress.com
www.tumblr.com/blog/noexpertbut

For more titles from Cilento Publishing go to
www.cilentopublishing.com

ACKNOWLEDGEMENTS

Thank you to my wonderful friends and family. You waited so patiently. Well, you were probably doing other things like getting on with your own lives and technically not just sitting and waiting. That would have been really boring for you. Loyal, but really boring. Every now and then however, you may have stopped and thought 'I wonder if I'll ever get to read anything he writes?' You encouraged without knowing. You supported regardless of the outcome. You were sounding boards and inspirations. Duties you performed with effortless beauty, simply by being yourselves.

To Hector Marcel my quantum friend.

To Kerren Heilpern, Daz Chandler, Mike Jury, Simone Payne, Jacqui Owen, Jamie Scott, Lara Sperling, Paul Smitt, Richard Buckland, Nadine Hattom, Franziskus Nakajima, Kahli Hall, Dmitry Kuznichenko, James McGovern and Stuart Lokhee.

To Lili Shapiro, Joel Shapiro, Adam Shapiro, Simon Shapiro, Tamara Sperling, Priscilla McCorriston, Jacqueline Chu, Karen Hazel, Sandra Heilpern and David Heilpern.

To Sid Sperling, Essie Sperling, Paul Sharp, David Owens and Anne Collins – gone but not forgotten.

To Editor Katie Leach.

To Leone Sperling and Ron Shapiro, wonderful parents and proof readers (though not so good with Dettol or forks).

To Denis Fisk and GS Johnston for the excellent suggestions and edits.

To all the 108 lives project team in Australia and New York and my dear friends in Nepal.

Georgina King, thank you! Your love and support feel boundless.

AUTHOR BIOGRAPHY

Evan Shapiro is a child of the 60s, raised in the 70s, defined in the 80s, reproduced in the 90s, divorced in the 00s and reconstructed in the 10s.

The second of four children born to would-be bohemian parents, Evan grew up on a diet of independent cinema, junk TV and chocolate biscuits. As a toddler he drank Dettol and shampoo and stuck forks into power-points. He was often reminded by his family that he was lucky to have survived past the age of five. While his parents blamed him for being dangerously active and carelessly inquisitive, he lays the responsibility squarely at their feet for repeatedly leaving Dettol, shampoo and forks within his grasp. Realising his parents were little more than children themselves when they reproduced, he eventually came to forgive them. Becoming a fallible parent himself also added fresh perspective.

Now instead of power-points he likes to prod people, metaphorically.

He lives in Sydney, divides his time between co-parenting, fixing his father's TV settings, changing his mother's light bulbs, graphic design work, writing and meditation. He claims to have found the secret to perfect parenting, but as the answer is endless patiences he's not sure it's any use to anyone.